SHADOWS
FROM THE PAST

SHADOWS
FROM THE PAST

Ashley Dawn

Tate Publishing & *Enterprises*

Shadows from the Past
Copyright © 2007 by Ashley Dawn. All rights reserved.

This title is also available as a Tate Out Loud product. Visit www.tatepublishing.com for more information.

No part of this publication may be reproduced, stored in a retrieval system or transmitted in any way by any means, electronic, mechanical, photocopy, recording or otherwise without the prior permission of the author except as provided by USA copyright law.

Scripture quotations marked "NKJV" are taken from *The New King James Version* / Thomas Nelson Publishers, Nashville: Thomas Nelson Publishers. Copyright © 1982. Used by permission. All rights reserved.

This novel is a work of fiction. Names, descriptions, entities and incidents included in the story are products of the author's imagination. Any resemblance to actual persons, events and entities is entirely coincidental.

The opinions expressed by the author are not necessarily those of Tate Publishing, LLC.

Published by Tate Publishing & Enterprises, LLC
127 E. Trade Center Terrace | Mustang, Oklahoma 73064 USA
1.888.361.9473 | www.tatepublishing.com

Tate Publishing is committed to excellence in the publishing industry. The company reflects the philosophy established by the founders, based on Psalms 68:11,
"The Lord gave the word and great was the company of those who published it."

Book design copyright © 2007 by Tate Publishing, LLC. All rights reserved.
Cover design by Jennifer L. Redden
Interior design by Leah LeFlore
Published in the United States of America

ISBN: 978-1-6024725-1-8
07.06.04

To my grandparents, Charles and Ernestine Mauldin thank you so much for being there for me through everything. I love you and appreciate your support more than I can say.

'Likewise, ye younger, submit yourselves unto the elder...'
I Peter 5:5

CHAPTER 1

Aurora stood there—frozen in fear. A man had *her* gun pointed directly at her brother, Lance. Time stood still. "Please, just let us go." Her voice shook slightly. Not enough to convey how truly terrified she was. She was trying not to anger the man, but getting more worried as each moment passed. Aurora was praying with all her heart. He was just a crook, this was a random robbery, but she knew that wasn't the case. The attack was too well planned and executed. The man stood in the shadows... silently watching them. His silence was unnerving—terrifying!

"Who are you?" Lance's voice was tight with worry. The man had been silent the whole time. No demands. No requests. Nothing. Only silence.

Aurora's thoughts ran wild. *Who was this man? Did this have anything to do with her undercover operation? Why involve Lance? He should have made some kind of demands by now shouldn't he?* She felt frantic. She just had to know the answers to her questions. It could mean the difference between life and death... hers and her brother's.

This man obviously wanted something, and she silently prayed it wasn't their lives. She didn't want either of them to be killed, but if one of them died tonight, she hoped it was her. Aurora didn't think she could bear life without Lance. He was the only family she had left in the world... the only person who completely understood her.

"Please, let him go. He knows nothing." She decided to try the route that would answer some of her questions. Lance, obviously startled by her words looked at her strangely. She couldn't explain to him now, she had to try and save his life.

"You should have thought about your family before you became a cop, Miss Kavvan." The shadowy figure finally spoke, but his voice was only a frozen, harsh whisper. Even at a whisper, the voice sounded oddly familiar to Aurora's ears, yet she just couldn't place it. Her mind was reeling. Whoever this man was, he knew she was a cop! No one around here should know that. She was undercover.

The man had almost knocked her out when he'd hit her on the back of the head, and now the pain was beginning to make her lose focus. She couldn't think clearly. Couldn't concentrate. All Aurora could think, "This is all *my* fault!"

"What's this about?" Lance's voice sounded almost foreign to Aurora. It was a tone she'd seldom heard. In fact, it was a voice she'd only heard once before in her life... the night their parents were killed. Lance was scared. But Lance doesn't get scared! His work was more dangerous than hers. She was the one who worried if she would ever see her brother alive again whenever he got a page and went on another assignment! He couldn't be scared. He was Lance—her big brother—her protector.

Aurora knew Lance wasn't scared for himself; he was worried about her. He was terrified he couldn't protect her. He had always been able to protect her. She loved him for being so protective, and right now they were both still alive. That is the way it had to stay. She reached over and slid her hand into Lance's. He gave her trembling fingers a gentle, reassuring squeeze.

"Well, you are going to die, and your sister is going to watch. It's that simple." The words were said in such an evil and emotionless voice that Aurora's blood turned to ice in her veins. This man was serious. She was right he had planned this! He was using Lance, *her brother*, as an example for her. A warning, she thought bitterly. He couldn't kill Lance! He'd said this was because she was a cop. It had nothing to do with Lance. Aurora fought through her hysterical thoughts and concentrated on what the man was saying to her.

"Now, say goodbye to your brother, Aurora, and know that he was killed because of you and with your gun. It is the price you pay for choosing to be a cop. Your brother's life...," with that he raised the gun. She heard a shot and watched Lance crumple to the ground at her feet, his hand sliding from hers.

"No, Lance... No!!!"

"*Aurora*, wake up!" Joe hollered as loud as he dared, trying to get through to her. He had to get her out of this dream! She was drenched with sweat and sobbing uncontrollably. He'd been trying to wake her since she started saying Lance's name. When she screamed her brother's name in sheer terror, a chill ran up his spine. She started thrashing, wanting to kill someone. Her fiery red hair was flying everywhere and it wasn't easy for him to pin her so she wouldn't hurt either of them. She might be petite, but she packed quite a punch. It was difficult to avoid all the kicks and jabs she threw, but somehow he managed.

"It's a dream, Roar. Only a dream. Shhhh." Her emerald eyes flew open, but he could tell she wasn't seeing reality. All she saw were the horrifying images from that night at the lake. She was still in her dream. He knew she was fighting the demons of her dream and not him, but she was a lot stronger than she looked. She was trying to attack him. Luckily he was a lot bigger and had her pinned well.

"Aurora, it's Joe! Come on, honey, wake up. It's only a dream." Finally, he saw the realization in her eyes. She slowly focused her tear-swollen eyes on him... and crumbled in his arms.

"Joe... it's you," her choked whisper almost broke his heart.

Aurora sobbed as she looked up into her partner's kind baby blue eyes. "Oh, Joe, I was at the lake again... Lance. He's dead and it's all my fault..."

"Shhhh... you know better than that Rorie." Joe soothed. Shutting his eyes, he felt the tears prick the back of his eyelids. It tore him apart to see her like this. She was the strongest, most independent woman he knew, and she was falling apart right before his eyes. He had been her partner for a little over six years and this was the first time he had ever seen her break down. Even after Lance's death she hadn't crumbled like this... at least not in front of him. She'd always been strong. She handled everything that was thrown at her on her own. She took it all in stride, never asking anyone for help, even though there were many people that would willingly help her. And he was at the top of that list.

Aurora had been fresh out of the academy when he'd met her. He was her first and only partner. They had been partnered to go on an undercover assignment the first day they met. They'd been the perfect pair for the operation. No one in Los Angeles knew Joe was an officer because he'd just moved from Chicago, and Aurora had just gotten out of the academy. No one would ever suspect the two of them to be undercover. At least, that's what they thought.

The first eight months, they had gotten to know each other really well. It was hard not to when you were completely trusting each other to stay alive. It was easy to get to know and like Aurora then; they shared the same faith and when they discovered that, it made everything easier to talk about. They had talked about everything from their childhood memories, to family, to what their future dreams were. They thought their assignment was going great, and that they would finally be able to bring charges on Charles Deveraux to put him away for life. All they needed was the hard evidence to back up the rumors they knew were true. They were close to finding what they needed when the whole operation had blown up in their faces. He would neither forget the day nor what had happened to his partner on that awful night.

Aurora had gotten a call from her brother, Lance, and gone to meet him at the lake. What neither of them had known was that Aurora and Joe's cover had already been blown, and there was someone waiting at the lake for her and Lance. Lance was murdered in cold blood right in front of his baby sister. He had raised her since their parents had been killed in a car accident when she was twelve and he was a senior in high school. Aurora and Lance had been closer than normal siblings, and Joe knew that Lance's death tore at her heart and made her the person she was today. He had been her only family and her best friend.

That night was when she stopped believing that God was good, just, sovereign, and that He knew what was best for everyone. In her mind, God had taken her brother away from her when she had needed him here on earth. She buried herself in work to get rid of the pain, and Joe had thought she was finding her own way of coping with it. He prayed for her every day. He had hoped everything would work itself out in time. But he now knew the truth; she was hurting worse every day because she was torturing herself with guilt about something she had no control over. The whole time she wore a mask of false bravado to hide the fact she was torturing herself with grief. He should have known. He was with her more than anyone. She felt like family to him, and yet he hadn't realized the pain she was putting herself through.

Now, Joe prayed for her like he had never prayed before. She couldn't handle this on her own, and she knew this even if she wouldn't admit it. She needed to let God help her through her pain and she was pushing Him away as well as everyone else.

***

Aurora concentrated on breathing deeply and controlling her sobs. Her head was starting to clear now. The dream was over. She was on a stake out with Joe, in an apartment building across from Charles' main drug lab... not at that awful lake. She never wanted to go back to that place again, she thought as a shiver shook her body. It was just the dream, actually nightmare, but it wasn't really happening. It was only her memory of what had happened—such a horrible, vivid memory. She still felt helpless because she couldn't change the past. She was alive, and Lance was dead. That was the fact she couldn't change no matter how much she wanted. It was this fact that she had wanted to change for the past five years. She momentarily shut her eyes only to reopen them immediately. It was Lance's face, pale and lifeless staring up at her.

"Thanks for waking me Joe." She sighed and tried to get up,

only to realize Joe was still pinning her. She looked up into his kind face and saw the friend she loved like family staring down at her... worried. "Don't worry. I'm completely awake now. I won't hit you if you let go."

"Promise?" Joe was smiling, but his baby blue eyes still held concern. He was trying to lighten the mood and she appreciated it, but her mind was still at the lake. She was somewhat embarrassed that Joe was seeing her fall apart like this, but knew she could trust him to keep it to himself. Now she needed to stop his questions before he got really worried. He was a great friend... the best friend she could possibly ask for but Aurora didn't know if she could handle that kind of discussion right now. She was too close to breaking down and telling him everything. That was something she just couldn't do.

"You'll just have to take your chances." Aurora forced a smile that she knew looked strained, but it was the best she could do. Joe let go, then grinned when she pushed him and he toppled to the floor. He stood and dusted himself off. "I guess I should be grateful you only pushed and didn't hit me."

Aurora's effort at a smile was half hearted at best. She needed to get some space and regain her composure. Right now, she was still more shaken than she was willing to admit. The dreams were coming more often and were so vivid. It was like reliving that horrible night over and over—like loosing her brother again and again. She remembered everything as if it were yesterday, the clothes, the pain, and the blood. She swallowed convulsively, trying to stop the vision from invading her thoughts. Her head hurt like crazy, but her heart hurt even more. Every time she had the dream, she was paralyzed, telling Lance to run in her mind, but never able to open her mouth. She knew telling him in her dream wouldn't change reality, but she didn't like the feelings and memories the dream always brought back. It was her fault that Lance was dead. Her fault! She felt like hitting something in frustration, but was too exhausted to move. Her brother was dead because of her recklessness.

She couldn't get over that fact. Never would. If only she hadn't let her guard down, her brother would still be alive and she wouldn't be living in torment every day of her life. She had known better. It was her job to prevent horrible things like what happened at the lake that night, not to walk blindly into them!

"Is it because it is near the anniversary of Lance's death that the dreams are back?" Joe's quiet question snapped her back to the present, and for that she was grateful. No matter how many people tried to convince her that it wasn't her fault, no matter how many different ways she looked at the facts in the case, she always came to the same conclusion. It *was* her fault. When she closed her eyes all she could see was Lance's lifeless body lying on the ground in a pool of blood, and she could still hear the shadow's evil laugh. She hated that laugh! And she still felt the total helplessness and rage she had always felt. She hated feeling helpless. It made her vulnerable. She'd tried to catch Lance as he fell, but couldn't support his weight and had fallen with him. When she looked up, the man was gone and the investigators hadn't been able to find a trace of where he'd gone. He'd left her gun in the shadows where he stood and disappeared into the night.

"Yes." She lied.

In all reality the nightmares had been coming almost every night for a month and getting more intense. Exactly the time she had been on this stake out. Only three days left she thought with relief. She'd been mentally ticking off the days until this was over, hoping her dreams would end with the stakeout. It was getting unbearable and impossible to hide the effects from Joe. No other stakeout had bothered her so much. It didn't make any sense! This was a routine she had done a hundred times before. Why this one? What made it so different from any of the others?

"I think I'm gonna call J.D. and Daniel and have them come a little early to relieve us." Joe motioned towards the phone. He was still worried and she wasn't helping that fact by reliving the past in front of him!

"No, I can handle my job, Joe," Aurora snapped. Annoyed that he was trying to protect her like the big brother she'd lost. Seeing the worry in Joe's eyes reminded her of how often she'd seen the same look in Lance's eyes when he had worried about her. She still missed him terribly. "When I can't handle it, I'll let you know. Okay?" She stormed to the door before realizing she had nowhere to go. She was stuck! She was on the job, and couldn't leave just because she didn't like what her partner had said. Still, she kept her back to him as she fumed.

She knew she was acting childish, but at the moment Aurora didn't care. She stood trying to stop the tears that threatened to fall, shaking with pain and anger.

"Do you want to talk about it, Rorie?" Joe's always-too-kind voice enfolded her, making her feel like a heel.

She hated the fact he could make her feel two inches tall after she'd lost her temper. He wouldn't say a word about her outburst, but the way he immediately forgave her made Aurora feel terrible. It never mattered what she did, Joe would always forgive her. She wanted to be mad! She turned and looked at Joe and knew it was a mistake. She couldn't stay mad at him. His concern for her was too evident in the expression on his face. Still, she could avoid his questions. He couldn't invade her privacy if she didn't let him. And she'd made up her mind, she wouldn't let him!

"I'm sorry, I didn't mean to snap at you but these dreams are making me edgy." She sat down on the couch and stared out the window toward the drug lab. *Nothing's going on over there!* she thought angrily. They'd been watching and listening for weeks and had absolutely nothing! It was as if Charles knew they were here and he was waiting until they left to conduct his business. None of the known men from his organization had shown their faces at the lab. Not even any of his thugs. She had hoped they would get lucky and nab either Charles's son, Chris, or his second in command, Jim. No such luck. She hadn't even thought of catching Charles himself over there. He always managed to keep the appearance of being a clean businessman. They had cameras and listening devices hidden all over the lab and it was as if all illegal activity had been stopped for the past few weeks. It was very suspicious.

She wished they could hurry and catch Charles in the act of making or selling drugs and put him away for good. It had been so long since they had last been this close to catching him. Almost five years. She didn't have to calculate anything. It was the same day her brother had been killed that they had lost their evidence against Charles Deveraux. It had just disappeared into thin air. No one knew where it had gone and there was no possible way they could win a case without it. That fact was not lost to her. She knew in her heart that somehow those two events were connected. She just needed to find the evidence to prove it.

She looked over at Joe and he was staring at her as if he'd like to throttle her. What had she said to upset him now? Her anger was draining and she felt extremely exhausted. She rubbed her eyes trying to clear her mind.

Trying to concentrate on anything but her partner's angry face, Aurora surveyed the apartment where they were staying. The L.A.P.D. had really outdone themselves on this place. The apartment was nicer than any of the others she had stayed in while on stake out. Why hadn't she noticed that before?

Joe finally voiced what was on his mind. "Dreams? You didn't tell me that they were recurring. How long has this been going on?" Oops. Had she really just admitted to having *dreams*? Leave it to Joe to pick up on the one word she'd let slip. She must be more tired than she thought. She mentally kicked herself. *Remember to watch the words you use, your partner is no dunce.*

"Not too long." She lied and hoped Joe bought it. But he was a pit bull with a piece of meat when he latched onto a piece of information and wanted answers. He wouldn't give up until he found out what he wanted. He didn't believe her lie, but she had known that he wouldn't. He read her too easily. Sometimes that was a good thing, but right now Aurora wished he didn't know her quite so well. He gave new meaning to the word stubborn.

"And exactly how long would that be? Don't lie to me Roar. I know you better than you're willing to admit anyone knows you." Aurora knew that was true but still didn't want to talk about it. Talking just made her remember that it was her fault that Lance was dead. But then, everything made her remember that. Her headache was getting worse, and it was really close to unbearable. She needed to take something before she became completely useless.

Aurora really didn't feel like this discussion and wished Joe would drop the subject. She knew he wouldn't, but maybe she could avoid it for a while.

"Between you and Alex, you two know me better than I know myself." She tried to divert his attention to his beautiful blonde wife... her best friend.

Alex had been Aurora's best friend in high school and college. In fact, Aurora was the one who set Alex and Joe up on their first date. That was one thing she was proud of. She had known from the minute she met her partner that he and Alex were made for each other. In the first two months of their first undercover assignment Aurora had shown him pictures and talked a lot about Alex. Telling him all her good points and making sure he noticed how pretty she was. Not that he could miss that. Even in her worst pictures, Alex could have passed for a model. Even though, to her dismay she was way too short to be a model in reality.

Aurora fondly remembered the discussions she and Joe had then. Their assignment was to infiltrate Charles' "gang" and get enough information to arrest him for drug dealing. They had posed as accountants, business associates, which had been perfect. They could still live in their own apartments and date anyone they'd wanted because their cover had been complete. Or at least that's what they'd thought! Joe had even allowed Aurora to set him up with Alex six months into the assignment. Aurora had been so pleased with herself because she knew that she'd just set up a couple who would be together for life.

She glanced over at Joe. His jaw was set in that determined line she had grown to know only too well. Apparently Joe wasn't in a mood to talk about anything but her dreams, even though his eyes took on a special shine when he heard Alex's name. Aurora knew that Joe missed Alex and was ready to see her. A month was a long time to be away from home, especially when there was someone waiting for you... someone you were missing and love very much.

Seeing that look in his eyes made Aurora's heart ache. She yearned for someone to get that look in their eyes when her name was spoken. She wanted to be in love and be loved. That was an impossibility! She had a chance at love and it hadn't worked out.

Just water under the bridge, she reminded herself tersely. Besides she was too busy to date anyway. At least that was what she would tell herself and everyone else. There was no way she would admit that maybe she still hadn't gotten over her first and only love. Her mind drifted to a man with dark brown hair, ocean blue eyes...

"The dreams?" Joe insisted. He was awfully stubborn when he set his mind to something. Aurora guessed that was one of those traits you have to over look in the people you love. Even though Joe infuriated her by intruding in her life, she loved him very much. They had a strong bond, formed over many years. They completely trusted each other with their lives, and were extremely close friends. He and Alex were people Aurora considered her family. Even if she didn't totally open up to them. Some things were just too personal, even for family.

Aurora finally gave in with a frustrated sigh after a few minutes of silence and gave Joe a look that said she wasn't happy about this. He really didn't seem to care.

"The dreams began the night we started this stake out." She admitted grudgingly, putting her head in her hands and beginning to massage her temples. If her headache got any worse she was just going to scream and get it over with.

"Why in the world didn't you tell me?" Joe looked really close to being mad, if he wasn't there already. If she wasn't the one he was mad at, Aurora would have thought it amusing to watch his reaction, but as it was, she was inwardly cringing. First his face turned red, then his baby blue eyes grew comically wide and you could practically see sparks flying out of them. The only problem was that the sparks were flying in her direction at the moment. "I knew you looked tired but I thought it was just the stress of being here." Joe stood up and started pacing. "Do you really not trust me, Roar?" He stopped and stared at her, waiting for her to answer.

"I trust you more than I trust anyone." She avoided directly answering the question, and looking into his eyes. She chose to look at a spot on the wall behind him, and Joe noticed. In truth, she trusted him completely, but there were some things she didn't want to worry him with. She wasn't sure how to fix the problem she'd just created. She wanted to tell him she was sorry and just hurting, but her throat closed and the words stuck there.

His eyes narrowed and he studied her in silence for a moment. "You don't trust anyone anymore do you? You're afraid if you trust someone and admit you need their help that you can't hold on to your anger over Lance's death. Or is it that if you trust someone else you might lose them too?" When she just looked away he plunged ahead. "I'm right aren't I? You know it wasn't your fault that Lance died. He was the one who wanted to meet you. He called and set up the meeting at the park. Come on Aurora think! Be reasonable for heaven's sake!"

All thoughts of apologizing flew out of her mind at his words. "Be reasonable? My brother was killed with *my* gun, Joe! I'm a police officer, it should never have happened."

Joe didn't even flinch at her harsh tone. "How long are you going to torture yourself?" He shot back. "It's been five years, Roar. You stopped going to church. You work yourself ragged on your regular job, and your off time is spent looking for the man that killed your brother." She started to interrupt but he wouldn't let her. "I don't blame you for wanting this guy caught, but you could ask for help instead of relying only on yourself. You take too many chances following leads in Lance's murder case. Take a little time for yourself. I know Lance wanted you to get married and be happy. You don't even date anymore."

"My brother is lying in a grave because of my carelessness and the man who killed him is loose somewhere probably happy and carefree and all you can think about is my social life?" Aurora bit out, but felt terrible saying those things to Joe when she had been thinking along the same lines just minutes before. She went on never the less. "When I figure out who killed Lance, I'll try to get the social life you seem to think I need. Does that work for you, Joe? Because that's all I'm gonna promise. That's all I can promise. It's my fault that Lance is dead! And as for church, I'm not really sure I want to serve a God who took my brother away." She really hadn't meant to be so sarcastic. She knew that she'd just made Joe think that she thought of him as completely insensitive. Which wasn't the case. She just wanted him to leave her alone. Plus she was getting mad. Any intelligent human being knew to leave her alone when she got mad, but then again who had ever called Joe intelligent?

"Rorie, listen to me." He'd used the nickname that he'd given her the first time they met. She liked that nickname and it always made her remember that he was her friend as well as her partner. He knew it and used that to his advantage. He knelt in front of her, putting him at eye level. "I know you feel responsible for Lance's death, but it really wasn't your fault." He waited until she looked him in the eye to continue. "Lance was an FBI agent. He knew that you were a cop and that both your jobs were dangerous."

Aurora knew if she listened to anymore she would break down and start crying again. She stood abruptly, "Just drop the subject. All Right? I'm tired."

"Let me just say one more thing. God still loves you. He wants you to come back to Him. It's the only way you will ever find real peace. Alex and I still love you and only push you to date because we want to see you with the glow in your eyes that we've seen once before." He stopped for a minute squinting at her, unsure of her reaction to what he had just said. Then he went on softly. "We only want you happy. And please, the next time you have a lead on Lance's case, ask for my help, ok?"

"I'll think about it." That was all she could say. She didn't want to bother Joe, he'd done so much for her, and besides he was a busy man. He had a family, church, friends, and a job. She just had the job. It was her life. Joe didn't like the answer and started to say something else, but she cut him off. "I'm gonna see if I can get a little more sleep now."

"Fine, but this conversation isn't over." From the look on his face Aurora knew Joe was extremely serious. She impulsively hugged him, "Don't worry so much about me Joe. I'll be fine, really."

"That's what I'm praying for." His comforting words followed her down the hall. She paused at his words but didn't turn around.

Then she determinedly walked to the bedroom and shut the door. She really needed to take a nap.

She was still thinking about what he'd said about the glow in her eyes when she took some medicine for her headache and laid down. She smiled just thinking about the man that had put it there. She really missed him, but wouldn't admit that to anyone else. Besides it didn't matter. He had loved her a long time ago, it seemed like an eternity to her. Too exhausted to think anymore, she dropped off to sleep.

CHAPTER 2

Aurora woke with a start. *What woke me?* She was completely confused. One minute she'd been having the most wonderful dream and then suddenly she was wide-awake. She lay quietly and listened to the sounds of the apartment. Nothing unusual. Joe was walking around, it sounded like he was getting another cup of coffee. The man didn't really need any more caffeine. He had been plenty worked up the last time she'd seen him and he didn't need to add more fuel to that fire. If he did she hoped his extra energy wasn't aimed towards her. The heater kicked on, fans were going, and there was no noise from the police scanner. Nothing unusual that should have awakened her. Still she couldn't shake the feeling that something was seriously wrong. She lay still for a moment longer, listening.

Then she heard it. A metallic clink. It sounded like someone was trying to pick the lock! That was impossible.... wasn't it? That would mean that someone had found out about the stakeout and that couldn't happen! Not again.

Aurora sprang out of bed with a million different thoughts running through her head. Her gun was already in her hand and she was poised for action. She didn't even remember unfastening her shoulder holster. She hoped that Joe heard the sounds from the front door too, but from the sounds he was making, she guessed he was walking back from the kitchen. From there she was sure that he couldn't have heard the noise. It was too soft, she probably wouldn't have heard it if she hadn't lain and specifically listened for it.

She ran to the bedroom door and opened it, as she did she saw the front door opening quickly. She couldn't get out there fast enough to help Joe!

A man came in and shot once. She couldn't see Joe, but she knew that he'd just been shot. She must have made some kind of noise because the man's gaze swung to her. He was turning his gun on her when she fired. His shot missed completely and splintered the wood on the other side of the hall, but hers hit home. The man crumpled to the floor.

Aurora carefully walked up to the man and kicked his gun away. Checked the hall to make sure he was alone. Aurora checked the man for a pulse even though she knew she wouldn't find one. She had to be sure he wouldn't pull a gun the moment she turned her back to help Joe and shoot them both. She'd already been careless enough without adding anything else to that long list. There was no reason for her to worry. He was dead.

She turned to look for Joe. He had to be alive! She saw him immediately. He was right in front of her, lying on the floor with his gun in his hand.

"Joe!" She cried as she ran toward him. It only took her three steps to get to him, but it seemed like a hundred. All she could think when she saw him was, there was too much blood. This couldn't be happening. Not again. This man wasn't her brother but seeing him like this felt like déjà vu. She'd lost Lance. She couldn't lose Joe too.

"Looks like we are going to go home early after all." He tried to smile but it turned out more like a snarl. Then he passed out. Aurora's training took over. She bent over to make sure he still had a pulse while she called in that an officer was down and a suspect dead. The operator she was talking to tried to keep her on the line, but that was a trick they were to use on civilians, not cops. She hung up and started to examine the wound. Left shoulder. "Oh Lord, please no. Not Joe. He's one of Yours!"

She pressed a cloth to the wound trying to stop the bleeding, not even realizing she had spoken those words. He was still breathing. Shallow breaths but he was alive!

The wound she was pressing looked more like an exit wound than an entry wound. *That's strange.* She bent closer to inspect the wound. It was an exit wound! Joe had been shot in the back. Which meant Joe hadn't had time to draw his gun before he was shot. Her mind was reeling and she sat down beside him with a thud. Then she realized Joe had been going to try to keep the man from getting to her! That was the only logical explanation! That was the only way he would have been able to stay alert that long. He was going to protect her. *The idiot!* She thought affectionately. She didn't want someone she loved to get hurt trying to protect her. She felt tears stinging her eyes. She should have been out here with him. If it hadn't been for her losing her temper, she would have been out here to help him! She mentally berated herself. She should have been quicker. Called to him. Anything.

Looking at all the blood she wondered how he could have possibly been coherent enough to talk when she found him, much less crack a joke. A really bad joke.

What in the world was taking the ambulance so long? She started praying the bullet had completely missed his heart.

Praying... something she hadn't done in almost five years. She would try anything if it might save Joe's life. Finally, she heard the ambulance. He had to make it. As the paramedics came into the room and took over, Aurora studied their faces. Grim. Did they think Joe wouldn't make it?

She squeezed Joe's hand and whispered, "Hold on partner, you're gonna be fine. Help is here."

It seemed to take them forever to get Joe ready to transport. They put him on the stretcher. Hooked him up to all kinds of different machines and gave him an IV. He looked pale as a sheet and Aurora was terrified he wouldn't make it to the hospital. She hadn't asked any question because she feared the answers. Finally they had him ready to go.

One of the cops on the scene insisted on taking Aurora's statement. She told him what she could as they were getting Joe ready and then hopped into the ambulance with Joe for the ride to the hospital. If the cop really wanted her statement he could get the rest of it there. She had to make sure Joe lived. There was nothing she could do but sit and hold his hand, but she felt like if she left his side right now he might die. She didn't want Joe to die, much less die alone. Aurora had only felt this helpless once before in her life, and she never wanted to feel this way again.

***

"Six months of undercover work down the drain!" Jordan knew he sounded frustrated, but who wouldn't be. He threw the file he was carrying down on his desk with a little more force than he'd meant to. Papers flew off his desk and fluttered to the floor. He looked down at them disgusted. He would have to pick them up and sort through them again. They had all been sorted and stacked nice and neat on his desk until he'd done that. With a sigh he bent to pick them up. He rubbed his chin and felt the rough whiskers of two days growth. He should have taken time to shave before he came into the office.

"Hey, we'll find who sold us out. Don't worry about that." His new partner, Kami, patted his shoulder sympathetically as she walked by.

New partner! They'd been working together for over two years. Closer to three, but he still thought of her as his new partner.

He looked at Kami and thought about his partner that had died almost five years ago. Lance Kavvan, his best friend. After losing Lance, Jordan had refused to work with anyone else for a long time. They'd called him a rogue but he didn't care. It had hurt too much to lose Lance. They'd been closer than partners and he couldn't see anyone ever taking Lance's place as his partner. Finally, the agency hadn't given him a choice. He'd been paired up with Kami, and he had to admit it wasn't so bad. Kami was a great partner. She hadn't taken Lance's place. She'd made one of her own. She was a good friend and Jordan would do anything for her, but she definitely wasn't Lance.

As always, with the thoughts of Lance came the thoughts of Aurora. She was the woman who had stolen his heart almost six years ago, with her beautiful red hair, green eyes, and peaches and cream skin, Her eyes could sparkle with anger or laughter, depending on her mood. She was an absolutely beautiful woman, on the inside as well as the outside. Her always ready smile made her breathtakingly gorgeous. She could charm an Eskimo into buying snow from her, and make him think he needed it. He smiled as he thought of her. After not talking to her or seeing her, at least face-to-face he amended, in about four years he could still picture her smiling face. He missed her. Oh sure he had *seen* her, but he'd made sure that she hadn't seen him. He still knew a lot about her life, and Joe made sure he mentioned her from time to time. He kept tabs on her and knew what was going on. He knew about how hard she was digging to find Lance's murderer. He'd even sent some evidence her way a couple of times; knowing he'd gone through it too many times and hoping she could see something he'd missed. Of course, she never knew it was him that sent the information. He'd officially been told the case wasn't his to work on and to leave it alone. He hadn't, but the inquires that he made about it had been quieter and Aurora had been able to actively delve into the leads. He'd sat in a car watching a house as she questioned people numerous times, making sure she was going to be all right, but never letting her see him. It annoyed him that she never took anyone with her as back up when some of the people she was questioning could be dangerous. He knew she wanted to do this on her own without asking for help, but he didn't have to like it. It was a bittersweet torture watching her and knowing he couldn't approach her.

He still couldn't believe she wouldn't speak to him.

The last time they'd spoken was a little over four years ago. She had given him her engagement ring and told him that she never wanted to see him or the ring again. Then, she had walked out. No explanations or reasons, she just left. He knew the reason. It was Lance. His death would always stand between them and Jordan didn't know how to fix it. He didn't know how to help her get past her feelings of guilt over his death.

He did know that for about a year after the day she'd broken off their engagement that she had kept tabs on him. Then all of a sudden she'd stopped. That hurt him worse than anything, to think she completely stopped caring.

He hoped the real reason she stopped checking up on him was she found out he knew what she was doing. He still loved her. There was no doubt in his mind that she was his soul mate. He just had to convince her of that. The problem with that was she didn't want to talk to him.

But for the past month he had been worried about her. For some reason he couldn't quit thinking or dreaming about her. What worried him was it wasn't good dreams that he was dreaming. In the dreams he was walking around in a thick fog. Aurora was in trouble and calling to him for help, but he couldn't get to her. Everywhere he turned all he saw was fog. Her voice was tortured and she was in pain, but he couldn't help her. It was extremely frustrating.

He had to know if something had happened to her. He decided to call her best friend, Alex. He'd stayed close to Joe and Alex over the years. In fact, it was Joe who kept him up to date on Aurora. He needed some reassurance right now. Picking up the phone, he dialed the familiar number. On the fourth ring, their neighbor, Mrs. Matilda, answered the phone.

"Hello Mrs. Matilda. This is Jordan Reiley. Are Alex or Joe home?"

"No, Alex is at the hospital with Joe."

Jordan's stomach tightened with apprehension. Aurora. Why else would they both be at the hospital?

"What happened?" He was so tense right now that you could probably surf on him. He should have checked on Aurora sooner.

"Oh, haven't you heard? Joe was shot this morning while on duty." She stated matter-of-factly.

Jordan finally remembered to breath again.

"Thank you very much, ma'am." He hung up the phone and stared at it for a minute, completely stunned. Joe was shot? It didn't seem possible. His heart stopped beating for a full two beats. Aurora! She must have been there with him. Was she hurt too? No. Surely Mrs. Matilda would have said something about it if she had been.

Right?

Right.

This was the last thing Aurora needed. If she wasn't hurt, she would somehow convince herself this was her fault too. *Lord, I need your help here.* He silently prayed as he grabbed his coat and headed for his truck. Without a backward glance he drove to the hospital. She might not want to see him, but he *had* to see her; to make sure she wasn't hurt. He needed to be there for her, whatever she was going through, for his sake as well as hers.

CHAPTER 3

Aurora paced the hospital waiting room still in shock. She couldn't believe that man had shot Joe! He'd just opened the door and shot him. On top of that, she'd killed the man. There was a terrible ache inside her as she thought about taking another human's life. If she were in the same situation again, she wouldn't think twice about killing the man. If she hadn't killed him then he would have killed Joe. He probably would have killed her too if he'd had the chance. She tried to reassure herself with that fact, but this was the first time she had ever had to take a human life. It was a strange feeling to know that you killed someone. She knew if she looked down she would see blood on her hands. The blood was Joe's, but she couldn't help but think of the man that she had killed when she saw it. She had been trained to do exactly what she had done. She hoped she never had to use that training again. The feeling she had over killing this man was a feeling she never wanted to feel again.

She thought about her partner as she paced and a smile curved her lips. Joe was a hunk to put it mildly. Blonde hair, baby blue eyes, and he had a magnificent build. Exactly six feet tall, and one of the best men she knew. He was compassionate, caring, loving, everything that a woman could ever want in a man. Alex was lucky to have fallen in love with such a great guy. They really were a strange pair, those two. Alex was barely five foot one next to Joe she looked smaller than she really was. Aurora smiled as she thought of them. Alex was petite, but not too thin. Her eyes were a gray blue, and her hair was blonde.

Add to that she was completely in love with Joe. Anyone who saw the two of them could tell they were in love. They were both extremely close to God, Aurora thought with a twinge of envy. She wished she still had that close of a relationship with God, but He hadn't been there for her when she really needed him. He hadn't been there for her when she'd prayed for Lance, why would he be there for her now? She'd prayed for Joe on the way to the hospital but she didn't really expect any good to come of it. Whatever happened was supposed to happen whether she prayed or not. She knew that was the wrong attitude to have, but she was hurt. She had a right to be mad at God.

Right?

He had let her brother die! Add to that, He let Joe get shot, and she'd had to kill a man. What kind of God would let something like this happen? Enough of that kind of thinking, she thought with an unladylike snort. It wasn't doing anyone any good, especially her.

Aurora started thinking about Joe and Alex again. They were the two most important people in her life now, and she didn't remember ever telling them that. They were the best friends that anyone could ask for. They would do anything for her. She needed to tell them how much she appreciated and loved them, and made a promise to herself to do it soon. Joe would have given his life today to save her and Aurora knew it.

Alex was definitely a lucky woman to have a man like Joe. When Aurora thought about it, Joe was lucky too. Alex was a jewel and any man would be lucky to have her. She didn't deserve the agony of knowing her husband was shot, or, having to wait to see if he would live or die. She felt her anger rise thinking about the man that shot her partner. Joe shouldn't have been shot. He was one of the good guys, dang it! One of the few left in the world.

She stopped mid-step with that thought as a picture of Jordan Reiley flashed through her mind. He was one of the good guys too, and she hadn't hung on to him. She wanted to. Oh how she had wanted to! But he had been her brother's partner and it was her fault that her brother was dead. She was sure that Jordan resented her for Lance's death, even if he would never admit it. He and Lance had been closer than brothers. In fact, Jordan had been the one with Lance when he finally came to Christ. She smiled softly as she remembered Jordan telling the story.

He would joke that getting shot was the only thing that saved Lance's life, but it was true. He'd been such an animated storyteller that she could actually see what was happening to them as he told the story. They'd been helping the local cops on a routine drug bust, and according to both Lance and Jordan, something hadn't felt right. They'd come in through the back and looked around, but there was no one in sight. From the front, came shouting and gunfire. Before either could react, a man came around the corner, firing wildly. Jordan and Lance dove for cover but Lance had been hit in the shoulder. He'd said it was a fluke because he was sure that the man never saw them until Jordan shot him in the knee. Then he had waited until the cops came to take over before he could check on Lance. He said that Lance was just sitting there as if he was in a trance. Later, Lance had said that his life flashed before his eyes and he hadn't liked what he had seen. Right then he decided to change, and he did. He had always been a good man, but having Christ in his life had made him a great man. She knew that Jordan had been as proud of Lance that day as she'd been and that only made her love him more.

He'd been so good to her after Lance's death and stood by her no matter how badly she had treated him, or how hard she tried to push him away he had stayed. She had finally succeeded in ruining her life by pushing God out and then pushing Jordan out. Jordan had to blame her for Lance's death, didn't he? She definitely blamed herself.

When she turned back around to continue her pacing, she could swear she saw Jordan coming towards her. She laughed out loud at the absurdity of her imagination and continued to pace. She must be going crazy. Maybe she needed a vacation. She was starting to hallucinate. But when she looked up again he was still there. Over six foot three with a body that would make any body builder jealous, and he was watching her carefully as he approached. What was he doing here? Was everything Okay with his family? Terrible possibilities were running through her head, and she was extremely worried by the time he reached her.

***

Jordan stood at the end of the hall watching her pace. She looked like she hadn't slept for a while and she had blood all over her shirt; however, he had never seen a more beautiful sight in his life. She was alive and unhurt, at least on the outside. There was no telling what inner scars this had left on her.

He started walking slowly toward her, afraid that she would see him and immediately send him packing. Then she looked up and saw him, he held his breath. Would she demand he leave? She laughed and looked away. He was extremely puzzled by her reaction to him. It didn't make sense, did it? He expected anger, not laughter. She had looked away and started pacing again. Then she looked up again and the look on her face was one of bewilderment. Then it turned to worry. By the time he reached her she looked downright panicked. He hated that he caused that reaction in her. Maybe he should just leave, but he couldn't. Not yet. He had to at least talk to her and convince himself that she was really going to be fine.

"Jordan, is everything okay? Your mom and dad?" She sounded truly concerned and that made him feel better. She thought that he had come to give her some bad news about his family. He was relieved it wasn't his presence that made her panic, and visibly relaxed. She had gotten extremely close to his family when they were together. It was obvious from the worry in her voice that she still cared deeply about them. That had to be a good thing.

"No, my family is fine. Don't worry." He assured her and she took on a bewildered and untrusting look that he didn't like. He wanted her to trust him. "I came to check on you, see how you were doing and how Joe is."

"I'm absolutely fine." She snapped, and as he watched, her eyes turned cold and distant. A complete change from the worried woman that had been talking to him seconds before. "I don't need you to check up on me and make sure I've not gone crazy yet."

She'd snapped at him! She never snapped at people. It was only because his concern for her confused her. His voice was the same as she remembered. Soothing and kind. Shouldn't he still be mad at her? Not worrying about her? This man was a paradox. He must already know that this was her fault too.

"I didn't think that you'd gone crazy Rorie." His voice was so soothing that she could almost feel the warmth in his tone. "I thought maybe you needed a friend. Someone to talk to and lean on."

Her gaze flew to his. Was he joking? She searched his face for any sign of scorn or mockery, but all she could see was concern. Now she was more confused than ever. He wanted to be there for her? Wanted her to lean on him? This sounded too good to be true, that meant it had to be.

"Look Jordan, I don't know why you're really here or what game you are playing, but I don't feel like arguing with you right now so can we postpone this little discussion?"

Jordan flinched, either at the tone of her voice or the words she had used, Aurora wasn't sure which.

"I already told you why I'm here. You just choose not to believe me." He sounded hurt by her accusations and a little bit irritated. "How is Joe?"

She softened. Joe and Jordan still kept in touch. We're still friends. Not near as close as Jordan and Lance had been, but they were still close friends. They shared a profession, were protectors. When she thought about it they really weren't that different. He was here to check on a friend, and not to see her after all. The thought stung her pride a little, but she wouldn't let him know.

"He's still in surgery." She told him quietly. Not wanting to really talk about it. Afraid she would start crying, and that was the last thing she wanted Jordan Reiley to see. "The bullet missed his heart by less than a quarter of an inch, but it did a lot of damage to everything around his heart. A quarter of an inch lower and he would have been dead."

Her voice sounded dull and her eyes were haunted.

Oh, Lord please, not this again. Jordan could tell by the sound of her voice and the look in her eyes that she blamed herself. Plus, she had killed a man to save her partner. Jordan inwardly groaned. He didn't think he could take this again. He'd tried helping her through her grief once and failed miserably. To put it bluntly, he had fallen flat on his face. He hadn't helped her one bit back then, but he was going to try to help her again. It hadn't been her fault then and it wasn't her fault now. She had done her job, and that was all anyone could ask of her. He knew that and so did everyone else. She was the only one left unconvinced.

He sighed and reached out to take her hand. She let him take it, surprising them both. He intertwined his fingers with hers and then he studied their linked hands as if he had never seen them before. After a minute, he looked up at her, but he didn't let go of her hand. In fact, he started rubbing his thumb back and forth across the back of it, it was very reassuring to have that contact with him. But it was making it a little hard for her to think clearly about what had happened. She was remembering how it was when they were together. He had been great at just being there for her. He would listen to her problems and never criticize her, and she would do the same for him. Could they get that back? The friendship? The love? That last thought startled her a little, but she couldn't help but wonder.

"Do you want to talk about what happened?" That question snapped her thoughts away from love or anything else along those lines. His voice was soft and persuasive. She immediately bristled. Oh, now she knew what he wanted. She was angry more at herself than Jordan. She'd almost believed that he really wanted to be there for her, he wanted to be her friend. But he was just like everyone else. He only wanted someone to blame and she was the obvious and easiest choice. She couldn't blame them though. It *was* her fault.

"If you want to know whose fault it is Jordan, it's mine. I wasn't doing my job right, okay? You can go check out the report on file at the police station to verify that." She snapped at him again. That irritated her. She let him get to her, she didn't usually snap at people, but she had already snapped at Jordan several times. Normally she kept her cool around people but somehow Jordan had gotten under her skin. She was really tired of this conversation.

The police officer that had started taking her statement at the scene had followed her to the hospital and she had distractedly finished her statement. He had annoyed her but she knew that it was just part of his job and he wouldn't have been bothering her if he hadn't needed to for the report. Still she was taking out that frustration as well as everything else on Jordan and it really wasn't his fault that she'd had a really, really bad day. Still, he didn't have to add to it by coming here and asking her questions.

He looked a little startled at her outburst, but didn't let it stop him. "Sweetheart, I know you would have never done anything to hurt Joe, so I don't quite think it is your fault that he was shot. Secondly, I've already talked to a friend at the station and he told me what was in the report. I don't care about the facts. I care about you and the fact that you blame yourself for this." He finished softly hoping to convince her that he was telling the truth. He avoided mentioning the man she had killed because he didn't think she was ready to deal with that problem just now.

Her anger at him disappeared at the sincerity of his words. She knew this man, and he didn't fit into the category she'd been trying to place him in. He was an honest to goodness, good man. They didn't come any better than Jordan Reiley. All he really wanted right now was to be there for her, she could see it in his eyes. But she didn't deserve someone to be there for her because she'd let her partner down. She hadn't been there for him when he'd needed her. "Jordan, you're a good guy. You don't want to think badly of anyone, but this really was my fault just like five years ago."

She sounded so tortured about it that his heart melted. It hurt him to know that she felt responsible. Right now all he wanted to do was wrap his arms around her, tell her everything was going to be all right, and take all her pain away. He knew he couldn't do that and didn't think she would even accept his hug. Even though she no longer seemed to be mad at him, he didn't think she trusted him either. He didn't know how he was going to help her, but he was going to try. He prayed for God to guide him and give him the right words.

"Aurora, I know you think that, but I don't believe it for one instant. You would never do anything to hurt anyone. That I know for a fact." He saw Alex coming towards them. "Let's finish this discussion later okay? I don't want to upset Alex anymore than she already is."

"Oh, heavens yes." Aurora agreed quickly. She never wanted to upset Alex. She'd been the one to call Alex and tell her that Joe had been shot. That had nearly undone Aurora, but Alex had been strong. Stronger than Aurora thought she could ever be if this had happened to her. Alex had met the ambulance at the hospital and gotten a glimpse of Joe before he went into surgery, and he hadn't looked so good. The whole way to the hospital Aurora was so afraid that the paramedics would stop working on Joe and tell her they were sorry but he was gone. She was so relieved when they finally made it to the hospital. She saw the worry and pain in Alex's face when she realized Joe's wound was serious.

Aurora could still feel the fear that had gripped her when Alex had asked her to pray with her. She was really rusty praying, but couldn't have told Alex no for the world. She had said a heartfelt prayer that she was sure sounded terrible, but Alex had smiled through her tears and said "Thank you, that was the most beautiful thing I've heard in years." Alex had been completely sincere. Aurora could still see her smile and hear the assurance in her words. It was strange that something so simple could make her friend so happy.

Now she turned to see Alex walking towards them. Only when she saw Alex's knowing smile did she remember that Jordan was holding her hand. Aurora hurriedly removed her hand and walked toward Alex, but she knew Alex would mention it later. And she wouldn't believe that it had only been a friendly gesture, which was the truth.

Alex had been in a conference with one of the doctors and should have some news about Joe's condition.

"He's going to be okay!" Alex nearly shouted when she got

within hearing distance. Even from where she was Aurora could see the relief in the huge smile on her best friend's face. She was beaming with pleasure. The only sign that anything was wrong was that Alex's eyes were still a little red and puffy.

Aurora hurried to meet her friend and hugged her tight. "I'm so glad Al. And I'm so sorry that he got shot in the first place." She whispered.

Alex pulled back, looked at her. "Roar, I know that you're going to blame yourself for this, but I want you to know one thing. I don't blame you for Joe getting shot; it's a part of his job. What I *am* thankful for is that you didn't get shot too."

"I completely agree with that statement." Jordan's soft voice came from behind her. "Hi Alex. I'm really glad that Joe is gonna be okay." He bent down and gave Alex a hug. While they were hugging, Aurora took the time to study Jordan. He was still the best looking man she had ever seen. Dark brown short-cut hair, ocean blue eyes, taller and better built than any man had a right to be, and he was still the nicest man on earth. She really missed having him in her life.

"Me too, Stranger. It's been a while since I've heard from you. Been busy?"

"I've been on a case for the past six months. It's been really hectic. Sorry that it's been so long."

Aurora read between the lines and the tone of his voice. He'd been undercover, and things hadn't gone the way he had wanted them too. She looked up at him as he looked down at her and could swear that he could read her mind because she thought she saw a slight nod. They use to connect like that. Almost read each other's mind. She really missed that. Another one of the million things she missed about this man. His gaze trapped her and she knew that he saw that longing in her eyes and he knew why it was there.

"Dr. SueSue said that she would be out soon to tell me more about how he is doing, and when I can go back and see him." Alex continued talking, unaware of the silent conversation they were having.

Finally Aurora broke the eye contact and the magical connection they shared. "I'm sure that he'll be back on his feet in no time Al. He is still one of the most stubborn men I know." She thought about Joe being shot, but going to try to protect her regardless of that fact. She'd told Alex about that and knew Alex was thinking the same thing because Alex moved towards her and put an arm around her shoulders in a friendly and reassuring hug. "Roar, he loves you as much as you love him, and you would have done the same for him if you could."

That was all she said and Jordan looked at them with a puzzled expression, but didn't ask any questions. Just then Dr. SueSue came out to give them a report on how Joe was doing and when Alex could see him. "He'll be in the hospital for at least two weeks, but it looks like he'll make a full recovery. He was lucky. Since he's in such good shape it won't take him as long to recover but he'll still have to take it easy. He will be in the recovery unit by now. Give them fifteen minutes to get him situated and then you can go back and see him, Alex. He's knocked out and probably won't wake up for a few hours but you can go back and see him for yourself."

Aurora heard this and felt Jordan squeeze her shoulder. She appreciated his silent gesture of support and smiled up at him. Big mistake, when their eyes met, it hit her like a hammer that she was still totally in love with him. It wasn't the fact that she hadn't gotten over him, yet, that kept her from dating; it was the fact that she would never get over him. She'd known it in her heart for a long time but when she looked up into his ocean blue eyes, she was forced to admit it, if only to herself. She needed to get away from him, fast. She didn't think she could stand it if he figured out that she was still in love with him, especially since she knew there was no possibility that he could still be in love with her.

As soon as Dr. SueSue left Aurora made her excuses. "Al, I think that if you'll be okay I'll go back to my apartment for a while and try to get a shower and a nap. I'll be back later tonight."

"Don't worry about coming back tonight Roar. I think that I can handle staying by my husband's side alone for one night." Alex said with a twinkle in her eye. "Besides you look like you could use a good night's sleep."

"Is that your way of telling me I look terrible?" Aurora asked, acting hurt by the suggestion.

Alex smiled, but Jordan was the one who answered. "Honey, you could never look terrible, just tired." His voice was as sweet as his smile when he looked down at her. Then he turned her around and gave her a gentle push towards the door. "You go home and get some sleep and I'll stop by and check on you later."

"You don't have to check on me Jord. I can handle myself." She told him defensively, as she whirled around to glare at him. She didn't want him to think of her as incompetent. She could take care of herself.

"I know you *can*, but *I* want to make sure you're okay." From the sound of his voice he was serious. He did think she could take care of herself. That made his offer sound a whole lot more appealing, than if he had offered because he thought of her as an idiot that couldn't take care of herself. He sounded genuinely concerned.

"Oh, well...." She was at a loss for words. She hadn't expected him to still want to protect her. It made her feel special, even though she knew she shouldn't. Nothing could ever be like the way it had been between them, and it would be good for her if she would remember that.

"Come on, I'll bring supper." He coaxed and treated her to one of his killer smiles. There was no way she could resist!

"Well, if you put it that way, how can I resist?" Aurora didn't know when exactly she'd let her guard down around Jordan, but apparently she had. She had to remedy that.

"Then, I'll see both of you later." She looked over at Alex one last time to make sure that she was going to be okay and then walked off.

***

Alex waited until the door closed behind Aurora before she said in an awed whisper, "I can't believe that she actually talked to you." Alex sounded as shocked as he felt. Jordan finally started to breath again. He'd been holding his breath since he told Aurora that he'd come by her place, hoping she'd agree, but almost positive that she wouldn't. It had shocked him that she had agreed with so little protest. Maybe that meant she really wanted to see him. It had shocked him that she hadn't decked him on sight. He had to smile at that idea. She definitely had a temper to match her red hair. The red hair had come from her Irish father, that's also where she got her hot temper. But not many people knew about her temper. She kept all her feelings to herself, hidden, but if you knew her, really knew her, you could read her feelings in her eyes, and he could swear that he'd seen love in the look she had given him earlier. It had quickly been hidden but he was almost positive that it was there. That look gave him hope that there would be a future for them.

"I think she was even glad to see you."

"You didn't see the greeting I got." He told her warily, leaning back against the wall.

"Oh, tell me she didn't lose her temper on you." Alex groaned.

After what he had just been thinking, he found that funny and laughed. Alex looked at him as if he had lost his mind. "Are you sure you're remembering the same temper as I am? Because the one I remember is no laughing matter." That only made Jordan laugh harder. An older couple walked by and looked at him curiously. Jordan knew if he didn't stop people were going to think he needed to be put in a straight jacket and taken to the nut house, but he just couldn't seem to stop laughing.

After a few more minutes he had himself under control, but Alex was still looking at him as if he'd lost his mind. "Yes, I definitely remember Aurora's temper and it is most definitely not a laughing matter." He chuckled again. "And no she didn't lose her temper with me." He sobered as he remembered the look in her eyes and the agony in her voice when she admitted that she blamed herself for all of this. "She thinks that I'll blame her for all of this. She still thinks that I blame her for Lance's death."

"She told you all of this?" Alex asked incredulously.

"No, I could tell by the way she talked to me and looked at me. She doesn't trust me. Maybe she is beginning to... she did say I can come over, but you know me. I'm extremely impatient. I want her to completely trust me now. I want her to tell me everything that's bothering her and ask me for help."

"You'll just have to be patient, and convince her that you don't blame her. I think she still trusts you, but doesn't want to admit it. So what did you say that changed her mind about you?"

"Alex, I honestly don't know but I really wish that I did. And convincing Aurora of something she has her mind set against is easier said than done." He was starting to get excited about the fact that he was going to see Aurora again. Twice in one day. After four years of having to see her from far off and not being able to talk to her, he couldn't believe his luck. He still wasn't sure that he wouldn't wake up any second and find out this was all a dream.

He was really going to go to Aurora's house tonight to talk to her. He didn't think he could get much happier. Well... actually if he could talk her into completely trusting him again, maybe even loving him he'd be as close to heaven as he could get while still on earth.

"Al, I hate to leave you alone, but I've got a mountain of paperwork lying on my desk. I left in a slight hurry when I found out what happened. I'll check on Rorie and come by to see you later. Okay?"

"Don't worry about me tonight. I'm a big girl and I can handle the *scary* hospital all by myself. You try to work things out with Aurora. She still loves you, you know, and I'm just guessing that you feel the same about her."

Jordan didn't say a word. He just smiled, bent down to kiss her cheek, and left. Alex watched him leave and had to smile. Those two were meant for each other, and she knew it. Neither one of them ever answered her direct questions about their feelings. That in itself gave her all the answers she needed to know that they still loved each other. Now she hoped that they would figure it out before it was too late. But right now there was the more important matter of going to see how her husband was doing she thought as she turned towards the recovery room. Doctors could say what they wanted, but she wouldn't know the truth about how Joe was doing until she saw him for herself.

***

"Kill her. I don't care how, and I don't care where, but I want her dead now!" Charles was getting mad at his hired killer. He questioned everything, and he didn't follow orders. Hired help were supposed to follow orders, get paid, and be on their way, not question every order given. This man was just being difficult.

"But won't it look suspicious if there is an attempt made on her life so soon after the stakeout was taken out? If you had waited on me to handle it instead of sending some thug in, you wouldn't have a problem right now." Garland Jones was a hired mercenary, and he was one of the best. He knew it. He'd been brought in especially for this assignment, and couldn't resist a jab at his current employer's lack of wisdom.

"You took too long. She knows too much... even if she doesn't realize what she knows yet, she can put two and two together anytime. I don't want that possibility lurking around every corner! I have a business to run."

"That is fine with me. My fee will be the same either way. I just thought you didn't want any attention drawn to her specifically."

"I'm past the point of caring. She is always involved in the investigations into my dealings. That can't be a coincidence. Five years ago I warned her. I found out about the meeting she was having with her brother. When they showed up, I killed him because she was getting too close. Now the case of her brother's death is cold, but she won't leave it alone. My police source has blocked all of her leads and made them turn into dead ends. He warns me if she is getting close to finding out the truth, and some how the lead she has always hits a brick wall. If she figures out who my police source is then my whole operation is gone. I've worked too hard to let some female Dirty Harry take it away."

"I agree with everything you said, except, she don't look like no Dirty Harry that I've ever seen." An evil smile flitted across Garland's face. "It'll be done tonight."

CHAPTER 4

Slowly, Aurora opened the front door of her apartment, set the security system, and went directly to the shower. She was exhausted but didn't think she could stand another minute in these blood soaked clothes. Not to mention the blood on her hands and arms. Aurora shuddered as she thought about all the blood her partner had lost. She threw the clothes in a trashcan. They were her favorite jeans and t-shirt but she couldn't ever wear them again. Not after all the blood that had soaked them. If she wore them it would just remind her of this horrible day, and she didn't need the extra reminders. The nightmares would be enough.

She'd gone by the cemetery after leaving the hospital. She wasn't sure what had drawn her there, but she'd needed an older brother to talk to. She needed him back to be the one to understand her. No one else in the world ever had. She missed him. When she'd gotten there, she'd been surprised to find fresh flowers with Jordan's signature on the card. She knew he came to Lance's grave often, but that had just added to the emotions of the day and she'd sat down beside the grave and talked to Lance and cried. She hadn't taken time to sit and talk with him or even cry in way too long. She felt refreshed, cleansed.

When she got out of the shower she dressed in a comfortable pair of jeans and sweatshirt. She knew Jordan was coming and normally would have dressed up a little more for company. She would have at least put on a little makeup and fixed her hair. But today had definitely not been a normal day. Even knowing Jordan would be by later she didn't have the energy to do any of that right now. Maybe later. She still had a few hours before she expected him here. Take a short nap and then get up and get ready. Too exhausted to do anything else, Aurora fell asleep on the couch.

She didn't have the nightmare she'd been expecting. This time she didn't dream about Lance or even Joe, she dreamed about Jordan. How close they had been. All the wedding plans that they had made. The picnics they use to go on just to get away from work for a day. The way he would make her feel like the smartest, most beautiful woman in the world. She could even feel his hand brushing the hair away from her face... it felt so real.

All of a sudden Aurora couldn't breath. Her eyes flew open and met a strange pair of hazel eyes. Someone was suffocating her. All she could see were eyes, and they were pure evil. This man's eyes were void of all emotion except hate. The rest of his face was hidden by a black ski mask. Whoever this man was, he definitely wasn't Jordan or anyone else she knew. Thoughts raced through her head. How had he gotten into her apartment? There was a security system. Aurora kicked and scratched. Putting all five feet and three inches into making this guy wish he'd never laid a hand on her. She finally got in a lucky blow and hit him in the nose. He loosened his grip enough for her to get a breath, and that gave her the strength to kick him in the stomach. He let go of her completely then. She struggled to stand up and did, but it was a short-lived victory.

The man had her by the time her feet hit the floor, but he hadn't started strangling her again. He just made sure that she knew he could kill her anytime he felt like it. She felt like a twig in his hands, anytime he wanted, he could snap her in two.

"Who are you?" She gasped out. Her air supply was short at the moment to say the least. Aurora wasn't sure if her problems with breathing all came from the lack of air when the man had been strangling her or from her fear at being so helpless.

She tried to mask her fear, trying not to let him see how terrified she was. She glanced over at the front door frantically hoping that her security system had alerted the police only to find the door standing open and the red light that had been blinking when she'd set the security system was no longer blinking. Somehow he had disabled her state-of-the-art security system!

She looked up at the man. He was at least seven inches taller than she was. Jordan would still tower over him. She was going to be killed and all she could think about was Jordan!

"Oh, don't worry, baby. I'm just gonna kill you. That's my orders. If it were up to me personally, I'd have some fun with you first and then kill you, but orders are orders." He ran his finger down her cheek in a provocative manner that almost made Aurora sick. The words were all said in a hateful whisper. She couldn't tell a thing about his voice, and she hated the way he was looking at her. It made her sick to her stomach. The leer in his eyes was absolutely revolting.

"Who ordered you to kill me?" She gasped out, now sure that it was only fear making it hard for her to breath. Keep him talking and maybe help would come, she could always dream! Aurora knew the truth; in real life fairy tales don't come true. No knight in shining armor would come bursting through the door to rescue her. She was going to die... tonight... in the next few minutes.

She wished she could tell Jordan the truth, that she loved him. She wished that she hadn't stopped going to church, but she couldn't change what had already happened. She prayed.

"Now if I told you something like that, what good would it do you?"

"Let's just say I could die a happy woman. Does that work for you?" How she managed sarcasm was beyond her understanding at the moment, but she was glad that she at least sounded normal. On the outside she might look normal, but on the inside she was shaking like a leaf.

"Sure," he agreed as he moved behind her. "I'll tell you who hired me... it was..."

But Aurora never heard the name. Pain exploded from the back of her skull and her world went suddenly black.

***

Jordan was running later than he meant to be. It was almost nine thirty. How had he let the time get away from him like this? He shouldn't have stayed so long in Cassie's office demanding answers on Aurora's case. But if he hadn't stayed and annoyed her, he never would have known what he knew now. They were closer to catching Charles than ever before. It was strange that every time they got close to catching him, something happened and they lost the evidence that could convict him.

Jordan was going to do some investigating of his own into all of the coincidences in the Charles investigation. All the pieces didn't fit. He had a feeling that there was something in the files that would point out a traitor, but he wouldn't worry about it tonight.

Right now he just hoped that getting Aurora's favorite take out meal, chicken fajitas from El Mexicano with white cheese dip on the side would earn him forgiveness for being so late. He pushed the accelerator of his truck down a little harder and took a shortcut across town. It wouldn't save a whole lot of time but every second counted when he was spending time with Aurora.

When he got to her apartment complex he took the stairs two at a time hoping that he could make up for the time he lost in traffic. Some shortcut! There had been more traffic on those side streets than there could have possibly been on the regular roads.

His mind was on what he would say to her when all of a sudden he got a feeling that something was wrong, very wrong. The hair on the back of his neck stood up and a chill went down his spine. He looked up towards Aurora's apartment and saw her front door was standing wide open. She never left her door open. She was too safety conscious to do something like that. Joe had told him that they'd just installed a new security system at her house. There was definitely something wrong.

He sat down all the food he was carrying and took out his Glock. Slowly he walked up to the door and looked inside. The living room was completely dark inside, but there was a street light on behind him. He waited impatiently for his eyes to adjust. It seemed to take forever but finally he made out the shape of Aurora on the couch. She looked like she was asleep. *What in the world was going on?*

"Aurora, honey? Are you ok?" He called quietly, but got no answer. She didn't move a muscle. *That's odd.* Slowly he walked into the apartment with his gun ready. He scanned the room. Nothing looked out of place. In fact, it looked the same as it had five years ago. When he reached the couch he bent down to wake her up. As he bent he caught a glimpse of something moving out of the corner of his eye. He turned just in time to see a gleam off the blade of a knife. He tried to stop the man, but wasn't fast enough.

His attacker kicked the gun out of Jordan's hand at what seemed like the same instant Jordan felt the slice of the knife across his ribs. Jordan threw a left hook and caught the man in the chin. The man jumped back and started circling with his knife. Jordan now knew how a trapped rabbit felt, and he hated it. Jordan wished he had brought his back-up weapon, but it was in the glove box of his truck. Still he had to win this fight. Aurora was lying unconscious on the couch behind him, and he didn't know what this man had done to her. He couldn't change whatever had already happened, but he wouldn't let anything else happen to her.

Finally, the man seemed to tire of the game he was playing and lunged towards Jordan. Just as he did, Jordan heard a shot that was so close it made his ears ring. The man lurched backwards, his eyes widened in shock, and then he turned and ran out the still open front door.

Jordan turned stunned. "Aurora!" She was standing beside the couch right where his gun had landed, but she didn't look very steady on her feet. Her face was pale and she was swaying. He rushed to her and caught her right before she hit the ground. "Oh, honey. I thought he had... I couldn't stand it if he'd... I'm so glad that you're all right." He pulled her tight against him.

Aurora smiled weakly at her knight in shining armor. "Has anyone ever told you that you babble when you're worried?"

Relief coursed through his body and Jordan laughed at her observation. He had been scared, more scared than he had ever been in his life. More scared than he thought was possible. "What happened?"

Aurora's brow wrinkled in concentration, "I'm not really sure. Maybe you need to call the police and tell them everything is under control before they come in here thinking that it's a hostage situation or murder scene or something else that might get us shot. I'd hate to get shot by one of the good guys." She sounded a little groggy.

Jordan nodded his agreement. "Ok. I'm gonna sit you on the couch now. Are you hurt anywhere? Cut?" He sat her down gently and looked her over from head to foot, assuring himself that she was really alive and breathing. He still couldn't believe how close he had come to losing her. The thought made him weak. He never wanted to come that close again. He wanted her safe. Away from all of the danger, but he knew if he said anything right now he would lose what little trust there still was between them.

"No, I'm fine. Just another bump on the head." She indicated the back of her head that had a huge goose egg forming. Jordan went and got an ice pack from her freezer and insisted she it put on her head to make the swelling go down. She eventually complied even though she protested loudly. Hopefully her injury wasn't nearly as bad as it looked, but you could never tell with head wounds. She needed to be checked out by a doctor.

While Jordan called the police, Aurora leaned her head against the back of the couch and closed her eyes. Jordan paced as he relayed the information to the dispatcher. As he turned back towards the couch he glanced up at Aurora. *Oh, please no!* "Roar?"

"Mmm?"

He sighed with relief, *she hadn't passed out*. He covered the mouthpiece of the phone, "Honey you need to open your eyes. I don't want you going to sleep and not be able to wake you up."

"Huh?"

"You have a concussion."

Aurora opened her eyes a crack, "Can we discuss this?"

"No." He turned back to his phone call as if he expected her to immediately comply instead of argue.

She made a face at him for his immediate denial of her request but decided if she had to stay awake she might as well enjoy the scenery. She studied Jordan's back as he paced. He glanced over at her again and gave her a distracted smile. She knew he was just trying to make sure that she was still awake, and she appreciated his concern. It was kind of nice to have someone worrying over her, even though she would never voluntarily admit it.

Something's not quite right about the way he was walking. He acted as if he was hurt. She sat up straighter and started inspecting his clothing for any sign of blood. There was nothing on his back to make him walk that way. It was as if he was having problems breathing or maybe it just hurt to breath. She couldn't see any sign of a problem but she couldn't see the front of him to see whether he was hurt.

Jordan ended his conversation and sat down beside Aurora. He was watching her intently to see if she was going to pass out when she finally spotted what she had been looking for and gasped. *There was blood all over the front of his shirt!* Her face paled. "You're bleeding!"

He had forgotten, and now he was sorry that she had seen it. "I wish you hadn't reminded me. I'd forgotten about it." All of a sudden, he felt really weak and sank back into the couch.

"Take your shirt off. I've gotta stop the bleeding." Aurora tried to hide the fear she felt with her order. But as always Jordan saw through her bravado.

"You're awful bossy when you're worried. Has anyone ever told you that?" He tried to make her smile by using the same tone she had used when he had been so worried about her. It didn't work. She looked extremely worried, so he complied and took his shirt off. That hurt worse than he'd ever imagined possible.

His shirt was bloodier than the cut, so he laid it beside him. Aurora had seen enough blood today to last a lifetime. He wished she didn't have to see his blood too. It could only bring back bad memories, but there wasn't anything he could do about it now.

"Don't worry Roar, it's just a scratch. It'll be healed in a few days." He tried to soothe her worry. Even if it wasn't the whole truth, his ribs really did burn like crazy. He turned away from her where she couldn't see the worst of the cut. It didn't work she just got up and gently put her hands on his shoulders and turned him back to where she could see. Stubborn woman.

He tried to bite back a moan when she balled his shirt up and applied pressure to his cut, but didn't quite make it.

"I don't know what you consider a scratch, but I would classify this more as a cut. I know that it will need stitches. And it's all the way across your chest." She fretted.

"Don't worry. It only hurts when I breathe. If I stop breathing I'll have nothing to worry about."

Aurora glared at him not amused. "Don't you dare stop breathing," she warned, an impish grin curving her lips. "I don't want to have to explain this all by myself." She may have been knocked out and scared to death, but her spirit was still strong. It made him smile to know she still cared even if she wouldn't say it out loud. She would eventually. He just had to be patient.

"Oh, there for a minute I thought you might say you cared if I was still alive." He was hoping to get her to admit he did matter to her. No such luck. She just looked at him and completely avoided his baiting, "Lay back. I'm gonna try to stop the breathing, I mean bleeding now." She smiled sweetly and he couldn't help but smile back at her. He knew she was kidding. From the look on her face she was really worried and obviously did care that he was hurt. He liked the idea that he still mattered to her. He settled back and watched her work on his cut. He noticed it hurt less if he was concentrating on the intriguing woman and not what she was doing.

"How long before you think the police will get here?" He asked starting to feel a little light headed. His chest was really starting to hurt. Maybe if he could get her to talking he could forget about the pain.

"Soon I hope. You don't look your best right now."

"Flattery, now I like that, honey. That's the best way to make a man feel good about himself... tell him he looks terrible when he is already feeling bad. Kick him while he's down." He lied down and closed his eyes. He loved verbal sparing with Aurora. She was definitely a worthy opponent, but he still won most of the time. Okay maybe half the time. At most!

"I didn't say you looked terrible." Her sweet voice swirled over him. A little too sweet. He opened his eyes and looked at her. Her eyes were gleaming mischievously. "You said that yourself. I only said that you didn't look your best. But just for the record, I don't think you *could* look terrible."

Had she just said what he thought she did? He smiled to himself. She even blushed a little after she thought about what she'd just admitted to. So he wasn't hearing things after all. Maybe if he kept her off balance he could learn more about what she really felt about him. Right now all he knew was that she still thought he looked good. That was a start; a really big boost to his ego, but it wasn't enough. He wanted more... a lot more. He wanted forever.

"So you're saying that even all cut up, I look good with my shirt off." Now her blush was darker and completely covered her face, but she looked him square in the eyes and said, "I didn't say that, but I don't disagree with the statement. I just didn't want your ego to get too big. I mean being around a man who is so full of himself that he can't see what else is going on in the world is terrible. Don't you agree?" She cocked her head and smiled down at him inquisitively.

Ouch!

"I agree. Are you saying that you think I've got a big ego?" He quizzed, smiling at the fact that she had just implied that she was going to be around him more. He didn't think she realized what she said yet, and he wasn't about to point it out.

"Oh, not at all I just..." The sound of police sirens below them in the parking lot saved her from having to come up with an appropriate reply. Soon the room was filled with police and Aurora's friends and coworkers.

"Oh sure, Aurora. Life got a little boring for a while and you decided to liven it up huh? I was hoping to have a peaceful shift tonight, but you couldn't let me do that could you? I haven't even gotten coffee and my donut yet." Daniel was always giving everyone a hard time. Aurora knew he did it just to cover up the fact that he really cared. He was a tough guy with a reputation to protect. But more often than not, his lightheartedness made life more bearable for her and a lot of other people.

J.D. came over and knelt beside her, concern showing in his eyes. "Are you okay?"

"I am, but I think maybe Jordan here needs some assistance."

Jordan watched in wonder as Aurora visibly relaxed and joked around with her coworkers. Having people around that she trusted to take care of things seemed to take the stress off of Aurora's shoulders, and for that Jordan was thankful. He was also jealous. He wanted her to trust him like that, but at least she had people to lean on and trust. Maybe one day soon he would fit into that category.

"What happened?" Sergeant Corey Nickels bellowed as he stormed into the room. He looked madder than a hornet. Then again, he looked that way most of the time. Aurora smiled at her own mental joke and decided to press her luck a little bit.

"Oh, I decided to have a party and an uninvited guest showed up and crashed it, nothing major Sarge." Aurora loved seeing his eyes bulge out like that. She really shouldn't antagonize him, but it was so much fun. He wouldn't be so mad if he wasn't worried about her. He scowled at her. "Would you like to tell me why there is a "party" going on in your apartment that involves knives, guns, and two men trying to kill each other?"

"Well, let's see... first the bad guy tried to kill me. It would have worked, but Jordan showed up, and the bad guy decided he didn't like Jordan intruding and wanted to kill him. I got tired of the macho show going on and decided that enough was enough and shot... luckily, I hit the bad guy and not Jordan. I think that about sums it up." She was starting to babble and she knew it, but couldn't seem to stop. She knew she probably sounded like an idiot, but couldn't suppress a nervous giggle when Sergeant Nickels glared at her.

"So, do you wanna tell me what this "bad guy" looked like?"

"Oh, I'd love to, but I couldn't see his face..."

"Pardon me, I hate to interrupt such an important conversation, but if you will excuse me I think that I'll run to the hospital and see if they can stitch me up right quick." Jordan sat up and slid off the couch, trying not to show the pain that he was really feeling. He swayed slightly but righted himself as Aurora grabbed his arm.

"You are not gonna drive yourself!" She practically yelled at him. She looked mad about the very thought so he decided to goad her a little bit.

"Well, I hated to interrupt such an interesting conversation to ask for help. You stay here and finish your chat and I'll come back later and you can fill me in on all the high points." He said it trying to make her laugh. She didn't. In fact, she looked as if he'd just slapped her.

"I'm sorry. I forgot that you were hurt." Her voice softened. "I'll drive you to the hospital right now. I don't guess you guys brought an ambulance did you?" She turned her attention to her friends, trying to hide the way his words had hurt her, but not completely succeeding. Jordan saw the hurt he had unintentionally caused her and felt horrible. He hadn't meant to hurt her feelings. He'd meant to make her smile. This was getting frustrating. He looked around at her friends and saw that they were watching him closely. These men really cared about Aurora.

"No," J.D.'s voice was full of apology. "When we were told that it was your house and everything was fine we told the ambulance not to worry about it. We would handle everything. I'm sorry, Aurora."

J.D. felt everyone else's pain so much that it well could have been his own. "Don't worry about it... I need to get out of here anyway." She patted his arm reassuringly. She treated J.D. and Daniel like little brothers. But then again the whole police force acted like a family. After that thought, she helped Jordan start walking slowly to her car. "Oh, guys help yourselves to coffee, but try to clean up after yourselves, okay? And don't put fingerprint dust in my apartment, the guy was wearing gloves!" She called over her shoulder.

When they got to the car she looked at Jordan with concern and apology. "I'm so sorry. I completely forgot about you being hurt. I just started rambling and well... I'm sorry."

"Aurora, someone had just tried to kill you, and you shot him. There is absolutely nothing for you to be sorry for." He took her hand. "Honey, your reaction was natural. You just had an adrenalin rush and it was fading. When your friends got there you felt safe, and well you started babbling. I didn't mean to hurt your feelings in there. I was trying to tease you into smiling. I'm sorry."

"I know the adrenaline let down was natural, but I still feel terrible. What if he had killed you? I mean, first Lance, then Joe, and now you. I swear I'm just a dangerous person to be around." She was rambling again and had to force herself to stop and take a deep breath.

"Only dangerous when it comes to my heart." Seeing the look of hurt on her face he hurried to explain his statement. "It seems that you stole it a long time ago and never gave it back." He was going to have to think before he spoke. Everything seemed to be coming out wrong when he was around Aurora.

"Be serious Jordan! I feel really bad about you being hurt." She sounded a little testy.

"Aurora, I've never been more serious in my life." He told her honestly

"Oh..." She was speechless. What was she supposed to say to that? Had he just said that he still loved her? Impossible! She must be delusional. It had been almost four years since they broke up. There was no possible way that he was still in love with her! But aren't you still in love with him? A tiny voice argued in her head.

Jordan squeezed her hand, "Just something for you to think about. We'll discuss it more later. Now come on and get in the car so you can drive me to the hospital." She was still staring at him like a deer in the headlights so he smiled up at her. "Please?"

That seemed to snap her back from whatever she'd been thinking. She practically ran around the car. He wasn't sure if she was trying to get farther away from him or just in a hurry to get him some help. Hopefully she was just in a hurry to get him some help. She drove as fast as the speed limit would allow, and maybe a little faster, getting to the hospital.

Jordan couldn't figure out what her reaction to his statement meant, and didn't think he was in any condition at the moment to really try. She seemed shocked that he'd said that, well actually so was he. He hadn't meant to admit that to her yet. In fact he wasn't sure that he was planning to ever admit it to her. He'd wanted to know what her feelings were before he took that leap and told her that he was still in love with her. Once again his mouth had worked before his brain. She'd left him once and it had torn him up inside. He didn't think he could handle losing her again. He just hoped that he hadn't scared her off. He sighed at that thought and leaned his head back against the back of the seat, but turned to where he could study her profile as she drove. Only time will tell.

***

"Eight stitches! Oh Jordan, I'm so sorry. This is all my fault." Aurora had been pacing the waiting room while Jordan got his stitches. She'd hoped cleaned up the cut wouldn't look so bad and maybe Jordan wouldn't have to have any stitches. It wasn't many but she still felt so guilty. Jordan never should have been hurt. She didn't realize that she'd started to pace again until Jordan reached out and stopped her.

"What did the doctor say about your head?"

"He said that I was fine, just a concussion. Come back if I have any blurry vision or pass out." She told him, but couldn't seem to take her eyes off his stitches.

"Aurora, don't worry. They said I'll be fine. They gave me some painkiller and said I could go home. I've been hurt before, it's not like this is the first time." He grabbed a shirt that one of the officers had brought for him and began to button it up so she would no longer have the visual reminder.

"But it is the first time that it's my fault. Don't you understand that?" She sounded so pathetic that Jordan didn't know what to do.

"I understand that you blame yourself, but I don't. Besides if it meant saving your life, I'd gladly do it again." Aurora didn't seem to know how to handle this right now, so he decided to switch gears. He was sure that her mind was on overload after everything she had been through in the past twenty-four hours, and he hadn't picked the best time in the world to confess his love.

"Do you think this was related to the shooting this morning?" He looked down at his watch and winced. "I mean yesterday morning."

"I'm not sure. It could be." Aurora said slowly. She chewed her bottom lip while she thought. She was absolutely adorable. "The man said that someone hired him to kill me. He said that if he hadn't been given specific orders that he would have... fun with me first." She finished quietly. She remembered the way the man had said that and the way he had looked at her, and started trembling.

Jordan felt his temper rise and bit back the harsh words that he wanted to say. That wouldn't do Aurora any good. He wanted to personally beat the guy to a bloody pulp. Just give him five minutes alone with the guy and he would be happy. Jordan couldn't stand the thought of any man treating his girl that way. She looked so alone and vulnerable that he couldn't stand it. He reached out and took her into his arms. She came willingly, which surprised him. She was beginning to trust him more he noted with satisfaction. Jordan wanted her to know she wasn't alone. He would always be there for her.

He could tell that she was reliving what had happened by the shudders that shook her whole body. He felt helpless because there was nothing he could do to stop the memories. He could only hold her and whisper soothing words to her. He couldn't bear to think about how close he came to losing her. He closed his eyes, remembering. He tightened his hold on her. He wouldn't let it happen again. He couldn't lose her again. His heart couldn't take it.

***

Aurora liked being held like this, she could let someone else be strong for her. At least for a few minutes. She never thought that she would be held like this again, especially by this man. For just a little while, she didn't have to be a tough girl for the world. Right now she could trust someone else to handle all the problems, and she could hide from the world.

She started thinking about the break in, but that wasn't why she was shivering so violently. Her trembling was the thought that she had almost lost Jordan. She loved him and she didn't ever want to lose him again, but what could she do about it? She closed her eyes and saw the scene in her living room again.

Aurora remembered waking up to see Jordan being circled by a man with a knife. The same man who had told her he was going to kill her just moments before. Fear, that's all she could call the emotion she felt. Not for herself but for Jordan... at least that's what she told herself. In reality in a way she was scared for herself, terrified actually, that she would lose Jordan forever. She knew that he would protect her, or die trying. That was the only thing she thought about as she shot the man. She couldn't let him hurt Jordan.

That was the same problem she had now. He wanted to protect her. She knew he would get hurt again. That is why she couldn't let him try to protect her. He would be risking his life for her again, and she wasn't worth it. She knew that he would disagree, but she knew the truth. With that thought she pulled away, and he reluctantly let her go.

***

Jordan saw what was coming as Aurora looked up at him. She was masking her feelings. Turning to herself instead of him. Pushing him away. She was going to treat him like she would anyone else, and he couldn't stand the hurt that came from her rejection. It made him feel terrible that she didn't trust him enough to tell him what she was feeling.

"Aurora, please... don't do this." He pleaded, but she didn't seem to notice.

"Thank you. I guess I was more exhausted than I thought." Her voice was professional and impersonal. Not the same as the sweet, caring woman he'd just been talking to and holding in his arms. "I'll drive you home now and then I'll go clean my place up."

Jordan looked around. This wasn't exactly the place or the way he had wanted to tell her this. They were standing right outside the hospital, and she had been having such a hard time with what had happened, but he had no choice. "Aurora, look at me." He said softly, and waited until she complied. "I know you're not gonna want to hear this, but you can't go home now. You know that."

"Jordan, I'm perfectly capable of taking care of myself." The look in her eyes dared him to argue with her. He was smarter than that. She wanted to argue. Get her feelings out, but now wasn't the time or place. He didn't want to make a scene in a hospital parking lot.

"Honey, I know you can take care of yourself. At least against a normal human being, but this is a hired killer. What if he tries again?" He hated seeing the terrified look on her face at the mere mention of that possibility, but there was only a glimpse of it before she again masked her feelings. He was beginning to get frustrated with her lack of trust in him.

"I'll call for backup if he shows up again." She declared defiantly but there was a slight quiver in her voice. He didn't want her to be terrified of the possibilities but she needed to accept reality. She needed help with this one and whether or not she wanted his help, he was going to be there for her.

"Sweetheart, by the time you realized that he was there you wouldn't have time to call for backup." He didn't mean for that to sound the way it came out. It sounded like he was trying to explain something seemingly simple to a three year old that just wouldn't listen. That's the way that Aurora heard it too and her green eyes sparkled with anger. She was beautiful when she was mad he thought absently. Before she could say anything to him, he pleaded, "Please listen to me? I know you don't want to hear this either, but I couldn't stand the thought of you being hurt or killed when I could have protected you."

Her anger vanished and was replaced by something he couldn't quiet name. Finally, she looked up at him and sighed. "Ok. I'll do what ever you need me to. On one condition... you have to stay away from me throughout the rest of the investigation."

He couldn't stop the hurt she must have seen in his eyes. She was pushing him away again.

Seeing the hurt on his face, Aurora knew she couldn't let him go on, believing that she didn't care. So she said quietly, using his words back to him, "I couldn't stand the thought of you getting hurt again or killed while trying to protect me."

She wouldn't look at him. She had just admitted she cared and he couldn't be happier, but she wouldn't look at him. So he put his hand under her chin and tilted her head so she would look at him. "I'm sorry Aurora, but that's not a possibility. I already requested to be your bodyguard throughout the investigation." He didn't mention the fact he had already received confirmation and he had the job. "It looks like you're stuck with me."

"Oh really? What makes you so sure that you'll get what you want?" She sounded only slightly skeptical.

He smiled down at her and her heart fluttered. "Because I'm a very patient man."

"I think that we are talking about two different subjects here, but anyway, I'll just request that someone else guard me." She looked anywhere but at him.

That hurt.

"You don't trust me do you?" His question sliced through her. She wanted to tell him the truth. To tell him now more than ever she trusted him above everyone else, but instead she just stared at some point far away. Refusing to give in to the need to reassure him as well as herself that she did trust him and need him.

After a few moments of silence, Jordan gave up. There was no need to pressure her now about the subject. He had the entire investigation to find out her true feelings for him.

"Fine let's go to the safe house and we can discuss this on the way."

"Gee, I can't wait." She said sarcastically. "Just so you know though, you aren't

gonna change my mind."

"Do you think that I would actually try to do something like that?" Jordan asked trying to sound shocked by her indirect accusation.

She looked at him amused then started walking towards the car, so he followed. *At least she wasn't masking her feelings now*, he thought sarcastically. He wondered how long until she realized that she didn't know where she was going, and that he would have to drive. When she reached the car she turned and looked him straight in the eye and said, "Jordan, I don't want you to guard me because I don't want you to get hurt trying to protect me. You seem to have a habit of that, and being around me tends to get people hurt. I guess that you could say I'm bad luck." That admission of her feelings rocked him on his heels but he didn't hesitate to respond.

Jordan kept eye contact with her, "Then I guess it's a good thing I don't believe in luck. Now, I'm driving." When she started to protest he said, "Don't worry I'll drive safely, and besides you don't even know where we're going."

"You could direct me. You're in no shape to drive."

"Oh you want to talk about shape now?" He asked with a wicked look in his eyes. He looked her up and down and gave a low whistle of appreciation. "I'll gladly talk about that if you want."

There was a silent battle of wills before she gave in.

"Enough Jordan. You drive." She handed him the keys to her car as if they were hot coals. His gazed still lingered on her a minute longer and he muttered just loud enough for her to hear, "Spoiled sport. There for a minute I thought we were gonna have a really interesting conversation."

"That's what you get for thinking." Aurora said tartly as she got into the passengers side of the car, but not before he saw a blush beginning to stain her cheeks.

Jordan threw his head back and laughed, but stopped abruptly when he felt his stitches pull. He was going to have fun guarding Aurora. She certainly kept him on his toes, and didn't let his ego get too big. He thought of the conversation they'd had about egos when he was hurt and smiled. He was happier than he'd been in years.

He got in Aurora's car and started towards his house.

He looked over at Aurora and raised an eyebrow. "Macho show, huh? That's what you call me fighting with a mad man?"

"Don't start with me, Reiley."

CHAPTER 5

"Where exactly are we going?" Aurora asked sounding extremely suspicious.

"To the safe house." Jordan replied evasively. Steering through downtown traffic, he kept his eyes on the road. The fact that he hadn't looked at her when he answered made Aurora even more suspicious.

"And where exactly is this safe house?"

"Outside of town." Again he avoided directly answering her question.

"That wouldn't just happen to be *your* house would it?"

"As a matter of fact it would. What took you so long to figure it out?" He was laughing at her!

She reached over and hit him lightly on the shoulder. She was afraid that if she hit him harder that he would move too fast and pull his stitches. "Why didn't you tell me?"

"Because I wasn't sure you would come with me if you knew where we were going."

"I had already told you that I would do whatever you told me to." She pouted.

He reached over and brushed the hair back from her face. "Yes, you said that, but you also said that I couldn't be your bodyguard. I didn't know for sure what you would do when you found out that the safe house was actually gonna be my house, and that there was no way you could get rid of me. So I just decided to wait until you figured it out for yourself." He at least had the decency to sound slightly sheepish.

Aurora knew she should at least pretend to be mad and keep some emotional distance between them, but she couldn't. Instead she smiled and said, "Are you sure you can handle me through the entire investigation?"

"Absolutely." Jordan assured her with his own smile. "If you give me any trouble I'll just tie you up and gag you."

That idea earned him another hit on the shoulder. This one was a little harder than the first. His smile grew bigger. "Besides can you think of a better safe house? Who would look for you at my house? According to everyone you despise me and don't want to have anything to do with me. It's perfect."

He glanced over at her and couldn't quite read the look on her face, but he knew it wasn't good. He silently chastened himself *think before you speak man*! "What did I say Rorie?"

She reached over and put her hand on his arm. "I've never despised you, Jordan. You know that right?"

She sounded as if she really needed the reassurance. "Aurora, I know that. That's just what people think everyone does when an engagement is broken. They think that we despise each other. I've never thought for a minute that you despised me and I've *never* despised you."

She seemed to think about his answer for a moment not sure whether or not she really believed him. But in the end she smiled and squeezed his arm. "Good." She settled back in to watch the scenery. His house was a ways out of town and if someone did come after her again, he wanted it to be on familiar territory. You could never be too careful. Especially when guarding someone you love.

***

"What happened? I can't believe that you didn't kill her. You're supposed to be a professional! You were paid to kill her not get yourself shot!" Charles was furious.

"She only winged me. I'm fine." Garland ground out, not liking having missed a perfect opportunity to kill a target. Nor did he like having his current employer rub his face in his mistake.

Charles snorted. "She shot you? I thought the man with her shot you and she was knocked out."

"Well, she woke up while I was fighting with the man, found his gun, and shot me."

"I don't guess you happen to know who this mystery man is that showed up to 'save the day' do you?"

"I didn't exactly have a chat with him. I was trying to kill him, and I didn't think he would appreciate me asking, 'oh, by the way may I have your name before I kill you?' It really didn't cross my mind to do that. I'm so sorry." Garland said sarcastically. He was in no mood to have this conversation. His shoulder was aching again, at least the bullet had gone completely through and he hadn't had to have someone remove it. *How could I have let her shoot me?* Maybe it was time to at least think about retiring. But before he could even consider that possibility, he had a score to settle. No one shot him and got away with it.

"Well you couldn't have asked that question since you didn't kill him!" Charles retorted. "I'll call my contact at the police station and see if I can find out who this mystery man is."

As he said this Charles reached for the phone and dialed the familiar number.

***

Aurora stretched as she got out of the car. It had been quite a drive, a little over two hours. Jordan's house was a long way out of town, but the view was worth the long drive in her cramped little car. There were absolutely no other houses in sight. His house sat in the middle of what looked like a field, with a row of trees behind it that blocked the view of any neighbors. Not that there were any neighbors that could be seen if the trees weren't there. The nearest neighbors were about three miles behind the trees. The trees were beautiful, since it was the middle of October all of the leaves were turning colors, and Aurora loved the spectacular view they made. There were even some squirrels playing in them, just one of the amazing things about this area.

Seeing Jordan's house brought her memories flooding back. Jordan had bought the house after they'd started dating. They had been out driving one day and had both fallen in love with the house. The house looked like something out of an old western movie. It was shaped like a horseshoe and had a huge circular driveway. It had needed a good painting but other than that both she and Jordan had thought it absolutely perfect. It was supposed to be where they lived after they were married, Aurora remembered with a lump in her throat.

She remembered painting the house. They had argued over the color, she wanted white with blue trim, but he had said the white wouldn't stay white, they needed to at least paint it off white and he wanted green trim. In the end they had compromised, off white with blue trim. More paint had gotten on them than on the house that day. They'd painted the house and then turned the paintbrushes on each other.

She turned to remind Jordan of the memory, but he was already strolling towards the front door, so she hurried to catch up. She had to keep her memories in check she mentally scolded herself. She wasn't here to get back a long lost love, and she would do good to remember that Aurora told herself tersely. He hadn't really meant what he'd said at the car. He couldn't. Besides, she was here to stay alive, and she had no choice in the bodyguard she had been assigned. She determinedly walked towards the house; she wouldn't let him know she was still in love with him. It would do neither of them any good if she admitted it, they couldn't be together. Too many shadows from the past haunted their relationship. She had to build a wall around her heart where he was concerned.

***

"Do you really think we'll be safe here?" Aurora asked for the third time.

"Yes." Jordan answered patiently. "No one knows where you are except my partner and Cassie. We decided the fewer people that know the better." He didn't want to tell her that they suspected someone she worked with at the LAPD was selling information. He knew she would be upset about that, and didn't want to tell her until he had some solid facts to back up his accusation. He hoped she wouldn't figure it out before he did because he still wasn't sure she wouldn't go after a traitor alone. Especially if she thought there was a connection between them and Lance's murder.

Aurora wondered around his house getting reacquainted with her surroundings. After not having been here in about four years, she had expected it to look totally different. She was surprised at how little had changed. It was clean, but otherwise it didn't look as if anyone had changed a thing in the last four years.

As she was wondering around she was also remembering all the happy times they had spent here. The year they got engaged, Jordan had wanted his whole family to meet her so they had their family Thanksgiving meal here. She and Jordan had spent a week cleaning his house and then four days cooking. They had a good time working together and thinking that after they got married she wouldn't have to go home after they finished for the day. She smiled remembering his mother's surprise when she had walked into the house and seen how good it looked. She had been prepared to cook the whole meal herself, but was glad that Jordan had found someone that could take care of him. The next morning they had all gone to church. They'd gone to the church Aurora had been going to since she was a small child. Everyone had been so happy. She loved his family. They immediately accepted her as one of them because Jordan loved her. She had especially gotten along with his sister, Kerry.

Jordan had a huge family. His mother and father were wonderful people. His grandparents on his mother's side were still living and had treated Aurora great. Jordan had a great relationship with all of his family, especially his siblings. They loved to play pranks on each other just like they were still kids. He had three brothers and two sisters. None of them were married. Jordan had been the first to become engaged so his family had made a big deal of the whole thing. There had been quite a few gag gifts sent and they always kept life interesting. He, according to all his sisters, had the softest heart of all the brothers. Aurora had gotten along great with everyone, but she and Kerry seemed to be made from the same material. She missed being a part of that family.

As she walked, Aurora was mentally checking off the rooms. The house was only one story, but it was huge. There were seven bedrooms on the opposite end of the house. On this end there was the kitchen, study, formal dining room, and living room. The living room was her favorite room in the whole house, with one exception. The living room had a huge fireplace and the room itself was large enough that she never felt 'confined' when she was in it.

She was walking around Jordan's study when she saw the pictures on his shelf. She changed directions and walked closer expecting to see pictures of his family had replaced the ones of her, and she gasped when she saw that the exact same pictures she remembered were still there. She turned and looked questioningly at Jordan. He was leaning against the doorframe watching her. He didn't even try to hide his amusement. "What were you expecting to see?"

"I don't know." She was still surprised. "Definitely not pictures of me. I guess I thought that there would be... um, other pictures there to replace them."

"Why would I want to do something like that?" Jordan asked in an off-handed manner, even though he was dying to hear her answer and suspected she knew how much that answer mattered to him.

She looked cautiously at Jordan for a moment before answering. "Well, because you haven't seen me in years and didn't want a bad memory hanging around." The words were said so quietly that he had to listen carefully to hear her.

"You weren't a bad memory Aurora." Jordan told her with a lazy smile. "In fact some of my favorite memories are of you. Painting the house with you... actually painting each other. You cooking in my kitchen for my family on Thanksgiving. You rushing around here cleaning like a crazy woman." His smile grew as he thought about each memory. "And you complaining that I wasn't doing my 'assigned' jobs quick enough. You worrying that my family wouldn't like you, and spending hours trying to find something to wear. Then having to go shopping at the last minute because you decided that you had nothing appropriate. You were a great memory."

"Were?"

"Yes, were. Now that you're back in my life, I'm gonna have a whole new set of memories to think about. You here with a surprised look on your face when you see your pictures are still on my shelf. You smiling as you walked around the house remembering things that I really wish you would share with me. I'm sure there will be quite a few more memorable moments with you around." His voice held a teasing note that she couldn't resist responding to.

"Most of the memories you just named off were of you laughing at me for something." She noted, feeling her defenses slip. She leaned back against the wall. "So I guess you think of me as a funny memory?"

"Oh, no. Not funny at all." His voice dropped to a husky whisper—a huge change from the laugh it had been just moments before. She shivered as he pushed himself away from the doorframe and came towards her. He reminded her of a panther stalking its prey. Silent and Cautious. He watched her for any sign of retreat, but she didn't move an inch. She should have been annoyed, but instead she was excited.

He continued to stare at her as he slowly walked forward ready to back off if she didn't want him too near. "I have a lot of other memories, but I didn't think that you wanted to hear them." He told her in what sounded like a quiet growl.

She didn't move, couldn't move, his gaze had captured her. She licked her suddenly dry lips, "What kinda memories?"

He smiled and stopped less than a foot in front of her. She should feel crowded with him so close, but that wasn't what she felt. She liked him being this close. There was one problem though: she had to tilt her head back to look into his eyes. She should have worn shoes with higher heels. "I remember the first time I saw you. It was when Lance invited me over for a cookout. When I drove up I saw you by the grill talking to him. You were wearing blue jeans and a yellow shirt. Smiling up at Lance for something he said. You were absolutely beautiful and I couldn't help but stare." He had never told her that story before, and she wondered why. Then he reached out and cupped her cheek, and Aurora swayed towards him. "I remember the look in your eyes when I asked you to marry me. I was so happy. I had been so nervous that you would say no, even though I knew you loved me. I was still nervous. I remember the way you looked me right in the eye and smiling when you said 'Of course. What took you so long to ask?' Then you kissed me, and I knew everything was the way it should be. I have thousands of little memories of you." His voice was soft and wistful. Then he leaned forward and brushed his lips across hers.

She should have pulled back, but she couldn't. She didn't want to. All her defenses were gone. This was the man she was still in love with after all these years, and from what he had told her, he was still in love with her. He pulled back and looked into her eyes, she knew he saw the permission he sought in her gaze. Still he was giving her a chance to stop this if she wanted to. When she didn't make a move to retreat, he leaned down and kissed her again, this time a little harder. She put her arms around his neck and returned the kiss. This was the way it was supposed to be she thought dreamily... the way it could be.

"Excuse me, I hate to interrupt, but that wouldn't be the witness you are suppose to be protecting would it Jordan?"

Aurora jerked away and looked into the eyes of a very amused female she had never seen before. A very beautiful woman. She had a dark complexion, raven black hair, large chocolate brown eyes, and a slim figure. She didn't act the least bit embarrassed at having intruded on a very private moment. Jordan looked up and sighed. "Kami don't you ever know when to keep your mouth shut." He sounded more than slightly annoyed at being interrupted, and if Aurora wasn't mistaken just a little bit embarrassed. *Who was this woman and why was she here?*

"Apparently I'm not the only one with that problem." She returned sweetly.

Jordan turned red and Aurora couldn't help but laugh. He glared at her for a moment and then ran his hand through his hair and sighed. He looked at Kami and said, "You really do have terrible timing. Anyway, yes this is the witness and also the victim I *am* protecting."

Kami's smile grew larger as she said, "Are you sure we don't need to get her more protection?" When he looked at her questioningly Kami explained. "From you." Jordan picked up a pillow from the couch and threw it at her. She caught it and stuck her tongue out at him. The two of them seemed to know each other well and were very comfortable with each other, but Aurora didn't feel threatened by this woman.

Then Kami turned and looked at Aurora. "Sorry. Since Jordan has such terrible manners I guess I'll have to introduce myself. I'm Kami Reynolds, Jordan's partner."

Aurora smiled as Jordan walked off grumbling something about working with rookies, and decided she liked Kami. Anyone that could make Jordan blush like that and set him completely off balance in just a matter of minutes was worth getting to know. Of course being caught kissing a witness you were supposed to be protecting would put anyone off balance. "Hi, it's nice to meet you. I'm Aurora Kavvan."

"Kavvan? The same Kavvan's as Jordan's partner that was killed?"

Aurora cringed at the memory that immediately came to her mind. "Yes, the same. I'm Lance's sister."

"I didn't know your brother personally, but from what I hear he was an amazing man. I hate that I never got a chance to meet him."

"He was definitely an amazing man." Jordan agreed as he walked back into the room. He seemed a little more composed now than he had been when he walked out of the room a few moments before. Aurora couldn't help but smile when she thought about it. She had forgotten how red his face turned when he got embarrassed. She looked at Kami and saw that she was grinning too.

Jordan scowled at both of them. "You two don't have to look so proud of yourselves." He snapped. He was still embarrassed at being caught by his partner. He hadn't even heard her come in, much less realized that she was in the same room with them until she had said something. So much for being a well-trained bodyguard he thought disgusted with himself. Being around Aurora, he couldn't seem to focus on anything but her. He'd been so caught up in kissing Aurora that a parade could have come through his house and he wouldn't have even known it!

"You know, I believe someone is in a bad mood." Aurora said with mock sympathy. "Is something the matter Jordan?" She asked biting back a smile and trying to look confused.

"Maybe you're coming down with something." Kami suggested. She pulled off looking like she was truly perplexed, but Aurora saw the twinkle in her eyes and couldn't help but smile. When Kami looked over at her they both burst out laughing.

Jordan just glared at them and said, "That's enough. Kami I think it is time for you to leave." The suggestion only earned him another laugh. This isn't the way that things were supposed to go. This was his house and he was supposed to be in charge here!

Finally Kami stopped laughing and looked at him seriously, but her eyes were still twinkling. Jordan cringed knowing something was coming that he wouldn't like. "If I leave do you want me to send extra protection in for Aurora?" When he scowled at her she promptly started laughing again.

"That's not funny Kami! Will you two kindly stop laughing now?" he growled.

"We're stopping now." Aurora gasped out, but continued to laugh. Jordan was not very impressed. Not only had Kami come in at the worst possible moment, but also it looked like she and Aurora were going to be giving him fits every time they were together. He'd known they would get along because they were so much alike and apparently they had just found common ground in driving him crazy.

Finally, both of them seemed to calm down enough to have a normal conversation. Jordan tried not to make himself vulnerable to be the center of another joke. "If you two are quite finished laughing at me," he glared at Kami when she chuckled and she just smiled and held her hands up in a gesture of innocence.

She didn't want him in any worse of a mood than he was already. Even though she suspected his wasn't really anger, only frustration. "I think we'd better get a few things straight. First there will be no ganging up on me in my own house."

Aurora snickered. "Yes, your highness. We would hate to disrespect the *king* in his own castle." Seeing her this happy after everything that had happened to her made it hard for him to glare at her. His eyes softened, and she smiled at him, not a mocking smile, but a genuinely happy smile. A smile that he hoped to see more often.

"Oh sure she gets smiled at, I would have gotten chewed out for that comment." Kami complained. "Which room did you put Aurora in?" She asked now in her working mode.

"She's in the second room on the right." He answered without ever taking his eyes off of Aurora. Hearing that, Aurora looked up at him and smiled a huge smile. He felt like someone had just sucker-punched him in the gut; all the air left his lungs in a whoosh. She looked absolutely beautiful when she smiled like that. He had hoped that would make her happy.

That was the room that she had decorated as "her room" when he had first bought and redecorated the house. She had never stayed over night at his home, it wouldn't have been appropriate, but the room she had decorated was still her room in his mind. He hadn't changed a thing about it in the past four years, and now she would finally have the chance to stay in it. She seemed pleased at the thought.

"Where is your room?" Kami asked and waited for his response, but Jordan was too absorbed in Aurora's smile to even hear her words. "Earth to Jordan, come in space man." She waved a hand in front of his face.

"Huh? What did you say Kam?"

"Oh nothing, I was just trying to figure out how to best protect the house, but I don't guess that is a priority right now."

"Okay, okay. You don't have to be sarcastic about it. I'm listening now." Jordan mentally shook himself. He needed to focus on the business at hand, keeping Aurora safe. There was nothing more important than her safety. There would always be time for trips down memory lane later.

"How many bedrooms here?"

"Seven." Aurora answered absently. She was thrilled that she would finally be staying in the room she got to decorate! It was the one room in this house that was her absolute favorite. She was delighted at the prospect of finally getting to stay in it. Then a thought crossed her mind that made her stop. *What if Jordan had changed her room?* Then she paused to consider her musings. Of course he hadn't changed her room! She was positive about that because if he still had her pictures up why would he have changed her room? She doubted that anything had been changed at all. She couldn't wait to get into her room and see if everything was exactly the way she remembered. She looked over at Jordan and he smiled. A warm feeling flooded through her at the warmth she saw in Jordan's smile. It amazed her that he still cared. Still cared enough to keep her pictures around and not change her room at all. She tamped down her warm feelings for Jordan because there was no possible way that their relationship could work. You could try a little voice told her but she squished that thought and turned her attention back to the other two people in the room.

Kami looked up surprised that Aurora had answered her question instead of Jordan, and started to ask something, but then thought better of it.

"Which room is yours Jordan?"

"Second room on the left...right across the hall from Aurora's."

"Good, that means that you can get to her easily if something happens. Now, I'll go get the dogs and bring them by later. You got the security system installed here right?"

"Yes, I had Cassie install it earlier today while we were still at the hospital."

"Who is Cassie?" Aurora asked confused. "And what dogs are you getting?"

"Cassie is a fellow agent. She's an amazing undercover operative and she's one of the best in the FBI. When she is in disguise I don't think even her own mother would know her. She is that good. I trust her with my life. More importantly right now I trust her with yours. And the dogs are for our protection. They will let us know before a security system can warn us if someone is here who isn't supposed to be."

"Okay, you two get some sleep and I'll be back with the dogs about noon. Since it's about two-thirty in the morning right now, you should at least get eight hours of sleep before I get back." Kami smiled at them and then left as quietly as she had come.

CHAPTER 6

"Have you found her yet?" Charles' mood hadn't improved any in the past few hours. No one seemed to know where Aurora Kavvan had vanished, or the name of the man she'd vanished with.

"No," His police source told him sounding uneasy. "But I do think I know the name of the man she was with. His name is Jordan Reiley and he's an FBI special agent. I thought I knew him from somewhere." The cop sounded proud of himself and Charles swore at how stupid his informant really was.

"FBI? How did they get involved with this? And where do you possibly know him from?" Charles raged.

"It seems that Reiley is Lance Kavvan's former partner. It has been about four or five years since the last time I saw him, but he and Aurora were engaged when Lance was killed. Shortly after he died she broke off the engagement, and I've not heard about him since."

"And do you know where she is?"

"No, and Reiley seems to have disappeared too. I called over to the FBI and talked to his partner Kami but it seems no one has seen him since last night, they are claiming that they have no involvement in this case." The cop sounded skeptical about the information he had received.

"Do you believe them?"

"No, but they're stonewalling me. I can't get anything from them."

"Well then, keep looking, someone has to know where they are."

"Fine, but since you are going to be killing one of the best cops here, I think that I should be compensated for the loss. Don't you? I mean if I sell her out the police force will lose one amazing cop. It's also a big risk for me to be asking for this information. Obviously there is going to be someone monitoring the systems. Checking out who wants to know the information on Kavvan and Reiley. That kind of loss and risk is worth a lot of money to me."

"That's what I like about you. You're so predictable because you have no conscience. No heart. You think with your bank account. Don't worry, you'll be well compensated for the department's loss."

"That's all I wanted to hear."

***

"Hey Roar?" Jordan called from the kitchen.

Aurora was lying on the couch in the living room almost asleep and rolled over when she heard Jordan calling her name. She briefly thought about ignoring him and going to sleep; she was exhausted. But instead of going to sleep, she opened her eyes slightly and answered groggily. "Yeah?"

"Do you want anything to eat? I'm starving and I think you've had about as much to eat in the past twenty-four hours as I have."

"Sure." She answered trying to wake up. "I was supposed to have a dinner date last night, but the guy stood me up. He didn't bring dinner like he said he would."

Jordan opened the swinging door between the kitchen and the living room just long enough to give her a look that made her laugh. It was a cross between a grimace, snarl, and laugh. "I did bring the food, but I decided that the neighbors needed it more than you did." He hollered.

She smiled, now completely awake, "Is that a way of telling me I need to watch my weight?" She called good-naturedly.

She wasn't sure exactly what Jordan's answering grumble to that was and thought it was just as well. He had never liked her to joke about her weight she wasn't overweight by any means, but she wasn't the smallest person in the world either. She always stayed in shape with workouts but never gave a second thought to making a joke about not looking like a model. Jordan had always failed to see the humor in her jokes. According to him she always looked perfect and he didn't like her thinking of herself in any other way than he did. Perfect. It had been really great to know that no matter what she looked like, he would think she was beautiful.

She decided to act like she hadn't said that and give a different answer before he came out of the kitchen and gave her a lecture about how she shouldn't put herself down. "Just because I was knocked out was no reason to starve me too! And remember I don't like my food burned!"

He seemed to be willing to overlook her joke and his good-natured humor returned. "If you keep that up you're gonna have to fix your own food. This cook doesn't take criticism very well."

"If I remember correctly you don't take any type of criticism very well!" Aurora retorted.

Jordan walked into the living room and Aurora sat up. He handed her a plate, and she looked at the food and wrinkled her nose. "Grilled cheese? And I thought hospital food was bad. I'll be right back. I think I'll definitely need a drink to wash this down." Jordan watched as she disappeared into the kitchen. When she came back she handed Jordan a Coke she had gotten him. "I thought you would need a little help swallowing too. Oh, and watch out some of the edges are charred." She said and dodged as he swatted at her as she walked by. Then she sat back down on the couch, this way Jordan was sitting in the chair directly across from her. She looked down at her food again with distaste.

"You don't have to eat it you know." Jordan told her trying to keep from laughing at how unhappy she looked with her food. He decided to aggravate her a little by describing the meal he had bought last night. "By the way, if you hadn't lazed out of our date last night you would have gotten chicken fajitas from El Mexicano with white cheese dip on the side."

Aurora groaned. "You actually expect me to eat this after what you just told me. I've not been to El Mexicano since my birthday."

"That would have been about six months ago. This birthday would make you twenty-nine, again?" He teased.

"I'll have you know that this is the first time!" Aurora squeaked as she sat up straighter in her seat. "I'll only be twenty-nine once. Unlike you I don't mind admitting the fact that I'm close to thirty. Of course in your case it's over thirty. Let's see if my math is right, this would be your fourth year at being twenty-nine, right?"

"Exactly." He said smiling with satisfaction. "I'm twenty-nine."

"Which in real terms means that you're thirty-two."

Jordan sighed and sagged dramatically in his chair. "Don't remind me. I'm really starting to feel every one of those years."

Aurora almost choked on a bite of her sandwich when she looked at him. Jordan was hunched over in his chair and imitating the posture and looks of an old man. He looked hilarious. Aurora decided being here with him was good for her after all. She couldn't remember the last time she had laughed as much as she had today.

"What is that smile for?" Jordan asked as he sat up and quit acting like an old man.

"Oh, nothing" Aurora replied grinning mischievously. "I was just remembering that, this old man here," she emphasized her statement by tapping her toe against his shin. "He used to be in pretty good shape. He could even keep up with me on a basketball court. I guess now he is too old for that sort of thing, huh?" Aurora knew for a fact that he was still in good shape. When he'd held her, she had leaned against pure muscle. Obviously he still worked out and kept in shape. For him it wasn't vanity, he had to be in good shape to do his job. That was one of the perks of his job in her opinion because it kept him looking great.

"I do believe I hear a challenge. Am I correct?" Jordan asked leaning forward and propping his elbows on his knees. He was itching to pull Aurora into a hug, but afraid of moving too fast. "I think that this old man still has a few moves, that is if you think that you can keep up with me."

"I won't have a bit of trouble keeping up with you. I will have to take it easy on you though, I wouldn't want you to get hurt you know." Aurora's smile grew bigger and she batted her eyes at him innocently.

Jordan laughed and moved to sit right beside her. "You think you're funny don't you missy?"

"Why sir, whatever do you mean?" She asked with a fake southern accent.

Jordan donned the same accent. "Well ma'am, I just meant that you're in a pretty ornery mood tonight. Is there any reason why?"

Aurora's look sobered a little and she looked Jordan straight in the eye, put her hand on his arm, and stared at him. Jordan thought he'd just ruined everything and was about to apologize when she said, "I'm in a good mood because it has been such a long time since I've felt this comfortable and safe. I don't have to pretend with you, I can be myself. Being here with you, I feel completely relaxed. Thank you." She leaned over and kissed him lightly on the cheek.

Jordan's breath caught in his throat. He was amazed. She had caught him completely off guard. That kiss on the cheek had his emotions swirling. "For what?" He asked his voice a husky whisper.

"Just for being there for me. No matter how hard I tried to push you away, you've been there through everything."

"Why do I get the feeling that we aren't just talking about yesterday and tonight?"

"Maybe because you are an extremely perceptive guy." Aurora tilted her head to the side and studied him for a minute. "Why did you do it?"

"Do what?" Jordan was confused.

"Keep track of me for the past four years. Still care enough to come and check on me when my partner was shot."

Busted.

Jordan's face turned a little red. He hadn't realized that she knew he was keeping track of her. "Because I never have stopped caring Roar." He reached over and brushed the hair back away from her face, and she leaned her cheek into his hand. "Now let me ask you a question." He said softly. "Why did you stop keeping tabs on me?"

Jordan stared at her, but Aurora wouldn't look at him. He hated it when she did that. It made him feel blocked out, like she didn't trust him. They sat there in silence for a few minutes.

"Roar?"

"I'm trying to think of the best way to put this."

"Just tell me, honey. I think I can handle whatever it is." Jordan was braced for her to tell him that she'd stopped caring or she'd wanted to forget him, but nothing prepared him for what he saw when she finally met his gaze. He was startled to see tears in her tortured eyes.

"I didn't want to keep harboring false hopes. False dreams."

"What false dreams?" He turned her to face him.

"Dreams that you would be able to see me the same way you did before Lance's murder." She explained as if he should have already known.

"Honey, you're gonna have to explain this to me. I'm not understanding what you are talking about." He reached over and took her hand, and was startled to realize that she was trembling. He gently put his arms around her and hugged her to him.

"After Lance was murdered, you were so nice to me—treating me like I'd done nothing wrong." He tried to interrupt her but she put her fingers over his lips. "Let me finish before you say anything." She stopped to think about her next words before she spoke again. "I blamed myself for what happened to Lance. I still do. If I hadn't been so careless he would still be alive. I figured since I blamed myself, you blamed me too. I couldn't stand the thought of you with me because you felt obligated to since we were engaged. I knew you loved me before, but I didn't see how you could love me after what I had done. I didn't want you to be unhappy so I did what I thought was best. I broke off our engagement. I thought you would be happier if you found someone who didn't have... quite so terrible a past." She said all of this and then leaned back to look at Jordan's face. She wasn't sure what reaction to expect from him, but the look she saw on his face made her cry.

***

Jordan couldn't believe what he was hearing. He had known by the sound of her voice at the hospital that she thought he blamed her for Lance's death, but it hurt him to hear her say it. He thought she understood five years ago that he would never blame her for Lance's death. He should have made sure that she understood it. He knew she would never do anything to endanger her brother; she loved him too much. How could she have believed that for all of these years? How was it possible that he hadn't known the real reason she had broken off their engagement? He couldn't believe how dense he really was. He was stunned that she could ever think he would be happy with someone else. Hearing that she had left him because she thought it was best for him made him love her even more, even if her logic was somewhat distorted.

When she looked up at him, she looked ready to meet criticism and disgust. What she saw on his face was a mixture of relief and anger, but it was mostly love. When she started crying he just silently pulled her back into his embrace and held her. How could he make her understand? He prayed for the right words.

When her tears finally stopped, he held her a little longer. He didn't want to ever let her go again.

"I think we need to get a few things straight." He whispered against her hair. She nodded against his chest. "I need you to look at me while I say this to you."

"Do I have to?" Her voice was muffled because her face was buried in the front of his shirt. He smiled at her reluctance to discuss the subject that had kept them apart for so long.

"Yes, Roar. I want you to know how serious I am about this." Aurora slowly leaned back. She looked braced for anything. Jordan smiled at her. "Roar, I thought we got this straight five years ago. I have *never* blamed you for Lance's death, and I never will."

"How can you say that? It was my fault." She insisted, pulling farther away.

But he didn't let her go far. "Aurora, honey, *you're* the only one that blames you for Lance's death. I don't know anyone else in the world that does. Lance's death was not your fault. You weren't the one who killed him." When she started to protest he cut her off. "I know you think it's your fault, but tell me why? Talk to me about it. We never did really talk about the night he died, so I want you to tell me exactly what happened to make you think it was your fault."

Her eyes took on a far off look and Jordan knew that she had gone back to the night Lance was murdered. Her voice came out even; not a quiver, but she balled her hands into tight fists against his chest. "When I got to the lake, something seemed strange. I couldn't have told you what, but something wasn't right." She started to shiver so Jordan turned her until her back was resting against his chest and held her. "Lance was late, that was nothing unusual. He always worked late. When his car pulled up, I started walking towards it, but I never made it. Someone hit me on the back of the head. He didn't knock me out, he hit me just hard enough to knock me down and give me a terrible headache. Lance came running to help me. He bent down and helped me up, but the man had taken my gun after he hit me. I hadn't even noticed my gun was missing until I saw that he had it. He had on black gloves. I tried to get him to let us go, but he wouldn't. He told me that because I was a cop, Lance was going to die. Then he pulled the trigger and killed Lance with my gun, and walked away laughing. I tried to help Lance, but he died when the bullet hit him. I couldn't do anything to help him. I couldn't stop the man. They found my gun less than a block away with only one shot missing. The one that had killed Lance."

Jordan's blood boiled when he thought about the man that shot Lance. How could he have laughed? That was too cruel for words. He needed something to hit. Jordan would love to kill the man with his bare hands, but he couldn't right now. He didn't even know who the man was, and besides right now he had to convince Aurora that Lance's death wasn't her fault.

"Honey, nothing you just told me even implies that you had anything to do with Lance's murder. In fact it sounds to me like you tried to save his life."

"But he was killed with my gun. It should have been me." She whispered in a voice thick with tears.

"Roar, I knew Lance really well, and I know that he would have taken that bullet even if it was meant for you. He would never have let you get hurt if it was in his power to stop it."

"I know he would have protected me... that's part of the problem. If I hadn't let that man get my gun, we never would have been in trouble."

"How do you know that? Maybe he had another gun, but wanted to be cruel and use yours?" Her argument was weakening; Jordan could hear it in her voice.

"Why couldn't it have been me and not Lance?" She asked in a tortured whisper.

"The only answer I can give you is, it wasn't your time. I know that's not what you want to hear but think about it. God wanted Lance to come home and be with Him. Lance isn't in any pain, and you shouldn't hurt for him. He is in heaven with God. Don't be mad because Lance is dead. It doesn't do anything but hurt you. I know it hurts and you miss him but he is in a better place now. Aurora that is something I know for sure."

Jordan's argument took all of the anger out of Aurora. The way he told it left her no room to be angry. In fact, it made her feel terrible. All this time she had been mad at God, and she told herself that she had been justified in it. Now she knew she had made the biggest mistake of her life by pushing God out of it.

Jordan turned Aurora so he could look into her eyes and saw that she was thinking about something pretty seriously.

"What are you thinking?"

"I'm thinking that I've been mad for the past five years over something that I can't change. It sounds pretty foolish now. I still want to solve Lance's murder, but it is more important to me that he is in Heaven right now than the fact that he isn't here with me anymore." She answered honestly. "I've been stubborn for the past five years and I'm sorry Jordan. I guess it was just my pride. I couldn't let go. I didn't know who the killer was so I blamed God. Everyone was telling me this, but I wanted to be angry. I have a lot that I can't make up for, but I can fix some things."

"Where do you plan to start?" Jordan whispered not knowing why he was whispering when the house was empty except for them.

"With you." Aurora again surprised him. "I'm sorry that I pushed you out of my life. I'm sorry that I didn't believe you about not blaming me for Lance's death. And I'm sorry that it took me this long to apologize for everything. Forgive me?"

"Of course. What took you so long to ask?"

Aurora smiled as she looked up at him thinking it was ironic that he had used the exact words she had used when she accepted his proposal. "It took a really smart man I know to convince me of how stupid I was being."

She got up and pulled him to his feet.

"I'm going to bed now. Kami will be here in a few hours and I don't want to look like the walking dead. By the way do you have a Bible I could borrow while I'm here?"

"Actually, I had Kami pack you some clothes and things from your house. From the looks of what she brought, there isn't anything left in your apartment. Anyway, your Bible is on the bedside table." He sounded a bit sheepish at that admission.

Aurora hugged him then leaned back to look into his eyes. Gorgeous eyes. "Why did you do that? You know that I've not been going to church or studying my Bible." When he looked a little unsure of how to answer her question she said, "Joe had to have mentioned it as much as you two talk. He told me that you were still checking up on me so I know he told you what I was doing too. He's a hopeless romantic."

"I was praying that you would change your mind about everything. By the way, you might want to start with Psalms 51:12."

"I have changed my mind now and I thank you for being there to listen to me and help me understand everything. I'm going to bed now. Good night." Aurora started walking to her room.

"Sweet dreams Roar." Jordan called with a smile in his voice.

***

Aurora closed the door to her room and went to look for her Bible. She didn't plan on sleeping anytime soon. How could she sleep when there were so many thoughts swirling through her mind? When she looked, her Bible was right where Jordan had said it would be.

Aurora sat down on the bed and curiously turned to Psalm 51:12 (NKJV) and read:

Restore unto me the joy of thy salvation; and uphold me with thy free spirit.

Aurora smiled as she thought about what the verse was saying. She hadn't expected this verse. When Jordan told her the verse, she had expected something about God's forgiveness or repentance, but Jordan had known exactly what she needed to hear. She silently prayed the verse and peace filled her. It may have taken her five years to come to her senses about God, but now that she had, she wasn't going to let herself get pulled away from Him again. She said a prayer of thanks, and fell into a deep, peaceful sleep.

***

Jordan felt like he was walking on air. As he cleaned the mess he'd made in the kitchen, he thought about Aurora and the big step she had taken tonight. She was no longer mad at God for what happened to Lance. She no longer blamed herself for it either. He never would understand how or why she'd ever blamed either of them for it, but he was eternally grateful that God had given him the right words tonight. He was glad that God had been working in her heart and that God had used him as a tool to help Aurora. He had been praying for years for this very thing and he was still amazed when it happened. With that thought he felt ashamed of himself. He should have had more faith that God would answer his prayer. He prayed a silent apology to God.

He smiled. His family would love to hear this news. They had all been praying for Aurora since Lance's death and they had all ached for her when she turned away from God. Especially his sister Kerry. She and Aurora were so much alike that it was scary at times. He decided that his family needed to hear the good news tonight even though it was four thirty in the morning. He picked up the phone and dialed his mother, Abigale. She would appreciate a phone call no matter what time.

"Hey mom! I've got great news you'll never guess what happened tonight."

"Aurora?"

"Yes, how did you know?" He was always amazed by his mother's perceptiveness. Sometimes he was sure she was psychic, but really he knew she was really close to God and He used her to help her family.

"I'm not really sure. I woke up a couple of hours ago and felt this burning need to pray for her. Is everything all right?"

"Couldn't be better."

"You mean...?" She sounded excited.

"Yes."

"That's wonderful. God is so good."

"Yes, He is. Thank you for praying for her."

"I wasn't only praying for her, son..."

"I know, mom. Thank you. I'll call you later to tell you the whole story, but now I need to call Kerry."

"Stay safe, son."

"Always." His mother always had a way of making him smile. She never let an opportunity pass to warn him to be careful. It was the way their conversations always ended.

After Jordan finished the call to his mother and then one to his sister Kerry, he did a security sweep of the whole house before setting the alarm system. They had both been so excited for Aurora. His whole family had been praying for her since Lance's death, but especially his mom and Kerry. They both had a special place in their hearts for Aurora. He was glad that he had such a close family. They understood him without too many questions and he could always count on them for help. Kerry had wanted to talk to Aurora but when Jordan told her that she was in her room hopefully sleeping Kerry had promised to call sometime the next day. Like his mom, Kerry had been awake and unable to sleep when Jordan had called. Kerry and his mother were so much alike sometimes it was scary. They had both known something big was going on, his mom had known somehow that it had to do with Aurora and had prayed specifically for her. Kerry had known it was something to do with Jordan and had prayed for him and whoever else was involved. He was a lucky man to have such a wonderful family.

He checked his watch and groaned. Maybe, if he was lucky, he could get a few hours of sleep before Kami came back with the dogs. He smiled again as he thought of Aurora. She was absolutely wonderful, and he loved her. He just had to pray that he could convince her that they were meant for each other.

***

"It seems that the FBI really doesn't know where Reiley has gone. He and Aurora seem to have vanished off the face of the earth. No one knows where they went!"

"Do you have any idea how much this is going to cost you?" Charles threatened. "If it is more than twenty-four hours before they are found your pay is going to be decreased by a considerable amount."

"I have all my sources working on it. All of my snitches and everyone else that I could possible think of that wouldn't look suspicious trying to find them. If they can be found, I'll find them." Charles thought that the cop sounded a little too sure of himself this time. The man was always cocky but this time he sounded like there was nothing out of his power. That could prove to be dangerous.

"Have you found out any useful information?"

"Only that both of their apartments in town look like they have taken enough stuff to be gone for a very long time, and both of their vehicles are missing."

"Have you checked on family? Maybe they have decided to stay with some family somewhere." Charles was starting to sound a little desperate. The cop smiled at the thought. Maybe Charles being desperate would work to his advantage. Charles was only bluffing about cutting his pay that was something he knew for a fact. It was something that had happened several times before. Actually, with all the extra time he was putting into finding Aurora and Reiley he could probably get at least double the money he had originally asked for. There never could be such a thing as too much money, he thought greedily. He could practically feel all the money he was earning with this little project, if everything went well he could retire early. Somewhere warm and with a lot of sand.

The cop smiled. "I'll look into it. I think that all of his family is scattered across the States, but I know Aurora has no family."

"Keep looking, Aurora Kavvan is a loose end that needs tied up. And she needs tied up *now!*"

"Yes, sir. I'll check and call you as soon as I find something."

"It had better be soon," there was no doubt about the warning in Charles' icy voice. "I would hate for the department to be out two cops instead of just one." And he severed the connection with an ominous click that made the cops blood turn cold. Maybe he had better rethink working for a man like Charles. This man could kill him and would never think twice about it.

CHAPTER 7

"Good morning sunshine!" Jordan greeted her brightly as Aurora walked into the kitchen. Aurora groaned and debated growling at him. It was eleven-fifteen in the morning but they had been up almost all night and it had been a really long day before that.

Jordan looked like he had been up for a while. He was sitting at the table reading the morning paper as if he didn't have a care in the world. No one who saw him would ever dream he was an FBI agent. He looked terrific. Most of the time, he looked like he had just stepped off the cover of *GQ*. And this morning wasn't any different. He had already taken a shower and shaved. When he shaved the scruff off his face, it revealed the boyish dimples in his cheeks when he smiled, and his hair still looked a little damp from his shower. He was wearing a pair of blue jeans that were old enough they fit him like a glove, and a blue shirt that made his ocean blue eyes look even bluer. She had forgotten how much of a morning person he was, she would do good to speak a coherent sentence before her first cup of coffee. She decided it was too good of a day to start off with a growl so she gave him a weak, sleepy smile.

"I see you're still not much of a morning person." Jordan said hiding his smile behind the newspaper, but couldn't hide the laughter in his eyes.

Aurora changed her mind and decided it would be ok to growl after that comment. But she couldn't quite glare at Jordan. When she looked at him his eyes were brimming with laughter, and it looked like he was having a hard time biting back a grin. But he didn't dare openly laugh at her. Smart man.

As she walked by him she smiled sweetly, and took his cup of coffee. "Thank you very much." She sat down to enjoy *her* coffee. She sighed contentedly as she took her first sip. The man could definitely make a good cup of coffee.

Jordan silently smiled at the content expression on Aurora's face. Content. When she glanced over at him he smiled warmly at her and got up to get himself another cup of coffee. He tweaked her hair as he walked past her and she swatted at his hand.

"You do know that you could have gotten your own cup of coffee, don't you? Everything is still in the same place it's always been." He teased as he poured coffee into his new cup.

"I did get my own cup of coffee." She pointed out as she propped her feet up in the chair across from her. "Actually having to pour my own wouldn't have been nearly as much fun, and besides you were expecting me to take yours anyway. It's one of those endearing qualities of mine." He was standing behind her so Aurora had to tip her head back to see him. She smiled up at him and then she picked up the paper he had discarded and started reading.

She didn't see the thoughtful look on Jordan's face as she turned around or she might have asked some questions. Jordan stared thoughtfully at her back for a moment after she turned around. She seemed perfectly at ease sitting at his kitchen table reading the paper. What she'd said reminded him of the times when they used to have coffee in the mornings. Every time that he had gone over to her house to wake her up for something, or when she would come to his house early in the mornings to discuss a case she would always take his cup of coffee. It had never failed. When he first fixed his coffee this morning he wondered if she would take it. It was such a small thing really. Silly. But it meant a lot to him that she had done it this morning.

He walked back over to the table and sat down. "So, do you

want to hear how Joe is doing this morning or would you rather just sit there and read the depressing news in the paper?"

Aurora immediately dropped the paper and sat up. "Of course I want to know how Joe is doing." She snapped, and then looked so contrite that he completely ignored her outburst. It would take her a while to change her actions, he knew. They didn't automatically change overnight just because she was closer to God. It would take a big effort on her part.

"According to Alex he is already proving to be a bad patient."

"Gee, is that supposed to surprise me?"

"No, actually I'm told he's as hard headed as his partner." Aurora grabbed a towel off the table and threw it at him. Jordan caught it and smiled smugly at her. He was gorgeous when he smiled. Of course she couldn't think of a time that he wasn't gorgeous. She mentally shook herself. Now wasn't the time to think about how gorgeous Jordan looks, her partner was in the hospital!

"What did the doctor say about him?"

"The doctor says that he should make a full recovery, but he will have to take it easy for a couple of months. That is already proving to be a challenge for him, as soon as he woke up he wanted to know if you were all right. He couldn't remember anything except looking out the window and hearing a gunshot. He thought maybe you had been shot too. Alex assured him you were fine, but then she told him about the man breaking into your house. Apparently he's a little protective of you. Alex said he tried to check himself out of the hospital. He wanted to make sure that you were protected. The only reason he stayed was that Alex told him you had been put into protective custody... by me."

"I really don't deserve a friend like him." Aurora's voice was soft and she sounded on the verge of tears. "For the past four years I've been trying to push him away, the same way I tried to push you away, but both of you are stubborn men. I guess that is why you are both so special to me. You never gave up on me, even when I had given up on myself."

Jordan stood up and pulled Aurora to her feet. He pulled her into his arms and quietly held her. "I'll never give up on you, Aurora. That's a promise."

"Thank you. That means more to me than you'll ever know."

Aurora relaxed in Jordan's embrace, trying to absorb some of his strength. He seemed to have enough strength for both of them at the moment, and she wasn't sure that she could stand right now without his support.

"I talked to mom and Kerry after you went to bed this morning."

"Really?" Aurora sounded excited. "Do you think that I could call and talk to them?"

"Sure. They'd love to hear from you." He shifted to where he could see her face when he told her the reason for his call. "I called last night to tell them about you."

"What about me?"

"I told them about all the trouble you've been getting yourself into." He teased gently, and she gently touched his chest where his stitches were.

"Don't you mean the trouble that I've been getting *us* into?"

"Hey, no more blaming yourself remember?"

"I know. It's an old habit I'm trying to break. So what did they say when you told them that I was staying here and that I've changed my mind about God?" She asked insightfully.

"They were both thrilled." He admitted. "How did you know that was really why I called them?"

"Remember I know your family. Now that I think about it they have probably been worried sick about me for the past few years."

"We were all praying." There was such warmth in his voice that she knew he was telling the truth and she felt horrible for making his whole family worry.

"I miss your family. They were great. I miss being able to talk to Kerry about absolutely nothing and her understanding. You have a very special family."

"Yes, I'm a very lucky man." He tightened his hold on her, unsure of her reaction to his next words. "Mom said to invite you to

Thanksgiving dinner. It's gonna be at Edward's house this year. It seems he has a special announcement that he wants to make."

"Would you happen to know what kind of announcement?"

"It seems that he has been dating a woman for the past year, Amy, and I think they are getting pretty serious. At least that's what my inside source tells me." Aurora laughed at his antics.

"How's the rest of your family?" Jordan noticed she hadn't given him an answer about to the invitation to Thanksgiving yet, but he wouldn't pressure her right now. She had enough on her mind. Besides, Thanksgiving was almost a month away. He could wait.

"They are all doing great. Edward's obviously doing great seems a little worried about turning thirty-six next month. He thinks that we will embarrass him at work or something. I think he is remembering some of the gag gifts he sent to us and cringing when he thinks about how I will retaliate. He still likes working at the hospital, but I think he wants to open his own private practice outside of Los Angeles. Kerry is good. She's a little frazzled. This year she is teaching thirty second graders."

Aurora groaned for her friend, but smiled. "She's having the time of her life. She loves little kids."

"True, but you won't get her to admit that right now. She still wants to move back to LA, but she really loves the kids she is working with in Colorado. I think she just likes the skiing. JJ is designing a new building in New York. He says it's a dream assignment. Rick is gone somewhere on assignment and I think mom is gonna kill him when he gets back. She says just because he is CIA, there is no reason not to tell his mother where he is going. She thinks he enjoys making her worry. He promises that he'll be back before Thanksgiving though. And Tiffany is working hard tracking down cheating husbands and missing people. I'm told she's one of the best PI's in the business. Right now she says that she's on a high profile case and that it will probably get huge media coverage when all the facts are known, but right now she can't tell me any details because of confidentiality. It's really driving me nuts. I want to know what she's getting herself into just in case I need to help her get out. She even thinks she might have to take on a partner to handle all of her business if this turns out the way she's expecting." Aurora could hear the frustration in Jordan's voice. He hated not being involved, especially where a sibling was concerned. He wanted to be right in the middle of everything to help and Tiff wasn't allowing him to. She switched subjects to get his mind off his youngest sister.

"How about your parents? Are they still doing well?"

"They are still in Arkansas. The farm is doing well. Dad says that one of us kids will have to settle down one day and take over for him when he gets too old to do the work. Personally I don't think he'll ever get that old."

"I agree." Aurora smiled remembering each one of Jordan's interesting family members. Even though they were all completely different, there was nothing they wouldn't do for one another. She laid her head against Jordan's chest content to just let him hold her for a while. After a few minutes she leaned back and smiled up at him. "I think we had better find something else to do."

"Why? I'm enjoying what we are doing." Jordan pulled her back against his chest and rubbed his chin against her hair.

"So am I, but it's almost twelve and Kami will be here any minute."

"So?" Jordan sounded like a pouting three-year-old and Aurora had to bite the inside of her cheek to keep from smiling.

"So, I would hate for your partner to catch you in an embarrassing situation two days in a row. I think we put on enough of a show for her last night, don't you?"

"What's wrong with shows?" Aurora glared at him, but her eyes were twinkling with laughter. "Ok, ok. I guess you're right. I mean I wouldn't want you to get embarrassed again." Jordan said, but still didn't release her.

"*I'm* not the one who turned about ten different shades of red yesterday." Aurora pointed out sweetly, and Jordan acted shocked.

"I only did that to protect you. I didn't want Kami to notice how embarrassed you were at being caught in that situation."

"Oh, now I see. You were just trying to help me." Aurora had just a hint of sarcasm in her voice.

"Exactly." Jordan sounded proud of her for finally understanding.

Aurora rolled her eyes. "Right." She said sarcastically.

"What? You actually think that I was embarrassed to be caught kissing you?" Jordan practically growled but it was a playful growl. So Aurora couldn't resist playing along.

"Yes." She answered without hesitation.

"Well then, I think we should test that theory." Jordan leaned down towards her as he spoke.

Protesting never crossed Aurora's mind. She tilted her head to accept his kiss. Jordan's lips had barely brushed hers when she heard a car door slam. She pulled back, and heard him sigh in frustration. She knew exactly how he was feeling. Jordan leaned his forehead against hers and closed his eyes.

"I guess that means you don't want to test your theory?"

"Not really. I don't like putting on shows for people."

"I'll try to remember that from now on."

Aurora laughed and pushed lightly on Jordan's chest, careful not to hit his stitches. He didn't seem to be hurting too bad, but she didn't want to accidentally hurt him. He loosened his hold on her, but she was still standing in the circle of his arms. Aurora didn't want to move, but she knew Kami would walk in any second.

"You go help Kami with the security dogs and whatever else you two are gonna do. I'll be in the living room when you get done." Aurora turned as she heard the front door open. Jordan's arms were still around her but she didn't mind. It was nice to feel safe and in his arms she definitely felt safe.

"Hi, Kami."

"Good morning, Aurora."

"I'll be back in as soon as we get the security completely set up for the house and surrounding area." Jordan whispered softly in her ear and then turned her to kiss her gently on the forehead.

Aurora smiled up at him, then turned and walked down the hall towards the living room. She laughed silently as she heard Jordan say, "We are gonna have to work on your timing, Kam."

***

"So, are you going to tell me about her?" Jordan glanced over at Kami. He had been expecting her questions, and was wondering what had taken her so long to ask. Kami was usually very straightforward when she wanted to know something. So much so that some people might call her pushy. She had waited until they were almost completely done with all of their security set up before she asked anything.

"Sure. What took you so long to ask?"

"I wasn't sure you would want to talk about it."

"So what do you want to know?"

"Anything that you want to tell me. I'm just a little curious because that is the first time I've ever seen you with a woman and it didn't look like the two of you had just met."

Jordan ignored her teasing. "Oh that narrows it down. Anything I want to tell huh? Let's see... she's absolutely gorgeous. Red hair..."

"Ok let me qualify my statement. Tell me about *you* and Aurora."

"Good thing you qualified that, otherwise you would have been out here for days listening to me tell you about all of her good qualities." Jordan told her only partly teasing. He really could talk for days about Aurora. She was an interesting subject for him.

"Now I know you're in love." Kami muttered.

"What?" Jordan questioned, sure he hadn't heard her right. He couldn't be that transparent. Could he?

"Nothing, just thinking out loud. Go on with your story." She said with a dismissive wave of her hand.

"Aurora and I were engaged when her brother was murdered." All the teasing had left his voice. Kami's jaw almost hit the ground but she didn't interrupt him. "She blamed herself for Lance's death because he was killed with her gun. She thought I would do the same, and also that I would be happier with someone who had a less complicated past. She was wrong on both accounts." His voice was deadly serious, more serious than Kami had ever heard.

"And you're going to convince her of that." Kami summed up his thoughts with her words.

"I've already convinced her that I don't blame her for Lance's death, but I'm not sure I can convince her that I'll never want anyone but her."

"I don't think that it will take too much convincing."

"Why?"

"Because it is obvious the two of you are still in love." She told him, sounding as if she were stating the obvious. Okay, maybe he was that transparent.

"Really? You think she is still in love with me?" Jordan's hopeful voice made her want to laugh. He was one of the smartest men she knew, but apparently he was dense when it came to women.

"From what I saw yesterday, you shouldn't have to ask." Kami told him dryly.

Jordan turned a little red at the obvious reminder that Kami had walked in on him kissing Aurora yesterday. Kami chuckled at his sheepish look.

"Mind telling me why you let her go when she broke off the engagement?" She asked in her normal direct manner. Jordan had never mentioned being engaged before. Kami vaguely remembered some gossip around the office but she'd dismissed it as nothing because Jordan had never mentioned it to her. Now she was dying to hear something about the woman who her partner hadn't been able to get over in all these years.

Jordan considered his words carefully before he answered. He knew that he could trust Kami and because she was a good friend he didn't want to say anything that would make her think badly of Aurora. He finally decided that with Kami, honesty was always the best policy. She wasn't one to judge people harshly with out reason.

"She was having a hard time dealing with Lance's death, and she blamed God for letting him die. She wouldn't talk to me about it and I thought she just needed some time alone to work things out. It just seemed like I was making things worse for her. When I let her go she stopped speaking to me, and that was four years ago. The first time she spoke to me again was two days ago. It seemed like at the time she wanted nothing more than me out of her life, and that really hurt my pride." At the look Kami gave him, he quickly went on to avoid a lecture he knew would be coming. "I know that wasn't a good reason, but by the time I figured it out, it was too late. I had already let her get too far away from me. She wouldn't let me back in her life."

"Does she still blame God?" Kami gently prodded. He knew she was worried about his and Aurora's future. A difference in religion could tear even the closest of people apart.

"No," Jordan said and told her the highlights of what had happened last night. He knew Aurora wouldn't mind. In fact, he thought that Aurora and Kami had really hit it off yesterday. He would be in deep trouble if he ever let Kami, Aurora, and Kerry all in the same place. They would gang up on him and there would be nothing he could do to protect himself.

"I think you need to talk to Aurora about this." Kami informed him in a tone that told him not to argue.

"I want to but I'm not sure now is the right time."

"Why is now not the right time?"

"I'm supposed to be protecting her. She is a victim and a witness."

"That really mattered yesterday didn't it? Besides, that's just the excuse you are using and you and I both know it."

"Ok, fine." He admitted frustrated beyond words. "I'm afraid that she won't believe me. That she'll say that she would rather just stay friends."

"So, basically you're being a chicken." Kami stated matter-of-factly, and Jordan scowled at her.

"Trust you to put it in those terms." He muttered.

"I don't think that Aurora is the kind of woman who would lead a man on. I think she kisses you because she loves you, and I think she doesn't want to let you go again. I think she hopes you are in love with her, but she's afraid that it is more an obligation on your part than love. Convince her it isn't. Also think about it this way, maybe this is God giving you a second chance at the love of your life. You at least have to tell her how you feel."

"Actually I already have."

"When?"

"Yesterday, as we were leaving the hospital. But that was before she changed her mind about God. She seems to have changed her mind about me too, now that I think about it." His cocky voice was far more confident than he felt. Kami laughed.

"Then you have to tell her again, and pray that she is God's will for you. I'll be praying for the two of you." Kami promised.

"Thanks Kam. I needed to talk about this." Jordan gave her a hug, and Kami laughed again.

"I think this girl is good for you, you've not been this happy since I've known you. Go find Aurora and talk to her, I'll finish here." Kami gave him a push towards the house.

"Well, if you insist." Jordan smiled and took off for the house at a jog.

Kami was happy for her partner. He deserved to be happy, and Aurora seemed to be the one to make him happy. She silently said a prayer for both of them. From what she'd seen of Aurora, she was a great person. She hoped everything worked out for her partner; he needed something to go right in his life right now. She turned and scowled at the security monitors. She hated this part of her job. Gadgets weren't her strong suit. She sighed. The things she did for a friend she thought ruefully.

CHAPTER 8

Jordan stopped in the doorway of the living room to admire the view. Aurora was sitting on the couch, her legs folded pretzel style underneath her. The sun was shining directly on her, and in his mind Jordan saw that as a sign from God. She was writing in a notebook, and seemed to be lost in thought. He wondered if now was the right time to bring up their relationship. How should he approach the subject? He didn't want to push her into something she wasn't ready for, but then again, he wasn't sure of her feelings for him. Okay, he was pretty sure that she still loved him, but could she get past Lance's death?

He hadn't been this nervous since the day he proposed. As he watched her, she stopped writing and tapped her pen on the notebook, and he decided that now was as good of a time as any to talk to her about their future.

"I've been thinking," Aurora said without looking up as he walked into the living room. He wondered if she'd known he was standing there staring at her before he walked in, but didn't dare ask.

"That sounds dangerous." Jordan teased. He was trying to think of the best way to approach the subject of their future, and was more than a little preoccupied. Aurora didn't notice. She was still lost in her own thoughts.

"It's about last night's break in and Joe being shot." Jordan's smile faded and all thoughts of talking about the future flew out of his head. He sat down beside her and gave her his complete attention. "I think that maybe they're both related to Lance's murder."

"What makes you think that?"

"I don't know," Aurora admitted looking a little perplexed. "I guess that it's more of a gut feeling than any real evidence right now, but I know that there is some connection. The obvious connection is Charles. When Lance was murdered I was undercover with Joe trying to get evidence to convict Charles of drug manufacturing and supplying. Then Joe was shot when we were on the stakeout at Charles' main drug lab. Again we were trying to get evidence to convict him of drug manufacturing and supplying. We were trying to do the same thing and something went wrong both times. It is just too much of a coincidence that on the same day Joe was shot I was attacked in my home. It's obvious that Charles is connected but I think there is someone else involved as well. Someone we haven't thought to look at."

"I'll look into it." Jordan's voice was all business as he started to stand up. "I trust your instincts over most people's 'proof' any day."

"No," Aurora put a hand on his arm and he sat back down. "It's a lovely compliment that you trust my judgment, really it is. But I would like to get all my files and notes over Lance's case and this last stakeout at Charles'. I think if I look I will find that there is something that I've missed."

"I don't know if that is such a good idea, Roar. You're supposed to be here as a witness and victim, not as a cop." Jordan scratched the stubble already growing on his chin as he thought.

"Being a cop is a big part of who I am, Jordan. I can't change that. I think like a cop and I act like a cop. I can't turn that off just because I'm a witness now." He noticed that she left off the victim part, but didn't mention it.

Jordan blew out a frustrated breath. "I know that and it's not that. I just don't want you to, well…"

"Don't worry Jordan. I'm not gonna work myself to death over this. I just want to look at the files and see if anything jumps out at me. Something I've not noticed before."

"And what if nothing does?"

"Then I'll be no worse off than I was before."

"I just don't want you to get another promising lead that turns out to be nothing." Jordan voice and words were protective, but instead of irritating her, they warmed Aurora's heart.

"Jordan, I've been working this case for years, I'm use to going down dead end roads. Don't worry, I'm not relying on only myself like I use to. Now that I have God back in my life, He will help me." She smiled at him. "Thank you for worrying and trying to protect me, but I really want to do this. I think it would be good for me to have something to do with my time, even if it turns out that nothing important comes from it. I can't just sit here and do nothing."

"You don't know how good it is to hear you say that." Jordan took her hand and laced his fingers through hers. "I've been praying for you these past five years hoping that you would come back to God, and it is wonderful now that you finally have."

"You don't know how good it feels to say that God is here with me now. After five years of trying to get along without His help, I've realized that I can't do anything on my own. I need His help for everything." Aurora tugged his hand and smiled. "Oh, and there is something else."

"What?"

"I've got you here to lean on too." She demonstrated her willingness to let him take some of her load, by leaning her head against his shoulder, and he released her hand to put his arms around her.

"Lean as hard as you like, I think I can handle your weight." Jordan assured her.

"What about the weight of the world that I have on my shoulders?" Aurora asked teasingly as she nestled snugly into his embrace. Jordan smiled, noticing that her head fit perfectly under his chin, like it was suppose to be there.

"I think my shoulders are broad enough to take the weight off yours for a while." Jordan flexed his muscles to prove his point.

"Oh, you're so strong. My hero." Aurora put her hand to her

forehead and sighed dramatically. Pretending to swoon. Someday she would have to tell him about her thoughts of him as a knight in shining armor coming to her rescue when that man broke into her house she thought amused, but now wasn't the time.

"Well, everyone has to be something. Being your hero is fine with me." Aurora sat up and giggled. Jordan loved her giggle—it made her sound like a carefree child. He wanted her to be carefree, and he would do everything in his power to keep her safe.

"So, are you gonna get my files for me?"

"Of course."

"Thanks."

"No problem. The sooner you figure this case out for me, the sooner I can throw the bad guys in jail and save the day. You know, your everyday hero stuff."

"So if you're the hero, but I solve the case, what does that make me?"

"The brains behind the brawn?" Jordan suggested slyly.

Aurora pondered his suggestion and then shrugged. "I guess that will have to work."

Jordan considered carefully how to approach the next subject that he needed to talk with her about. "Aurora?"

"Hmm?"

"How are you doing with the morning Joe was shot?" He asked the question casually but Aurora heard the worry that lay beneath the words.

"What you're really asking is how am I doing with taking another human's life, right?"

Jordan winced at how bluntly she had put the question but nodded.

Aurora thought for a moment before answering. "I feel bad for killing that man, but I would do it again in an instant if it would save Joe's life. Yesterday it hurt me deeply to know that I had killed someone, and it still does today but not as deep. Today I've talked to God about it and he is helping me deal with it. I'm praying that everyday the pain will get less and less. The main problem is my not knowing whether or not the man was saved." Jordan nodded knowing how she felt. He'd taken a few lives in his line of duty and knew exactly what she was going through. Now for the tough part.

"They've identified the man as a *Randy Cossack*." He watched her closely anticipating her reaction.

"He's one of Charles's known thugs! Why would he send someone so obviously connected to his organization? He shouldn't have taken that risk. Even if he expected Randy to kill both of us, that was still a big chance to take." Her eyes were flashing fire and Jordan could practically see the ideas flowing though her mind.

"I don't know but I intend to find out. Maybe he just got impatient and made a mistake. It wouldn't be the first time something like that had happened."

Aurora chewed her thumbnail as she considered all the implications of what Jordan had just told her. "He knew we were there and didn't want to stop business any longer than absolutely necessary? This was a warning to leave him alone? There are thousands of reasons for his wanting the stakeout gone." She blew out a frustrated breath.

"We'll figure it out, Roar. Now, are you really gonna be all right?"

"I will always carry the knowledge that I killed a man, but I will also carry the knowledge that I killed him to save my partner's life. That makes it easier to handle. Thanks for worrying about me. I really appreciate knowing that I can talk to you if I need to."

"Anytime you need me I'm here." He promised.

"You'd better watch it or I'll hold you to that."

"I'm counting on it."

Aurora looked stunned for a moment but then smiled at him.

"Do you want to come and meet the new arrivals?"

"Who else is here?" Aurora was worried about meeting some of Jordan's friends. What would they think of her?

"Sally and Frank."

"How do you know them?"

"I guess you could say we sort of work together. They are a good team to work with. They seem to notice things that no one else does." He told her as he helped her to her feet and led her towards the back door.

"Sort of work together?" She looked up at him speculatively as they walked outside. "How can you sort of work with someone?"

"Well, they aren't on payroll or anything, but in my opinion they excel at their job." There was an unmistakable twinkle in Jordan's eyes and Aurora couldn't help but wonder what she'd missed. Jordan smiled at her then raised his fingers to his mouth and let out a shrill whistle.

What on earth?

She spun around to see two huge German Shepherds racing towards her. They stopped in front of Jordan and waited patiently for his command. He reached down and patted them still smiling.

"They're beautiful." Aurora had always loved animals and these dogs were gorgeous. "Which one is Sally and which is Frank?" She asked finally catching on to his private joke.

Jordan's eyes shone with laughter but his smile was now hidden. Aurora wanted to smack him for playing this trick on her, but it really was amusing. "This one," he pointed to the largest dog. "Is Frank, and this little beauty is Sally."

"Little beauty? There is nothing little about that dog, Jordan." She pointed out

"She has a point. Neither of them is small." Kami agreed as she rounded the side of the house to join them. "But they are the best guards in the state."

"Remind me to thank Cassie for getting them for me. I don't know who owed her such a big favor, but now I owe her one."

Aurora squatted down to get a better look at her guardians. Sally came up and greeted her with a slimy tongue across the face. Aurora crinkled her nose.

"It looks like you've made a new friend." Jordan chuckled.

"Lovely." She smiled as she wiped the drool off her face.

"She was just being friendly." Jordan admonished.

Aurora grinned up at him. "I hope she is a little more vicious than this when there is someone here that isn't supposed to be. On the other hand, maybe she could lick them to death."

"I think she's telling you, you need a tic tack Sally girl." Kami told the dog with a smile.

"It will take more than one." Aurora informed Kami and they both laughed.

"I can't believe they're picking on you girl. The nerve. I thought all women stuck together. Didn't you?"

"Will you show me the other security measures you've set up?"

"Sure." Kami agreed quickly. "Jordan you can go and work on something else." She shooed him into the house. He shot a warning glance over his shoulder at Kami. She ignored it and waved him into the house.

"Now that he's gone, I want to know all about you and Jordan." Kami informed her linking arms with Aurora.

"There's not a lot to tell."

"Then it shouldn't take long." Kami smiled at her and Aurora knew she'd just made a good friend. A friend who would be great in an interrogation room. Her manner could make someone talk to her without her saying anything. There was just something about her that made you want to confide in her. Aurora guessed that worked to Kami's advantage in her line of work. Get a suspect to trust and confide in you and you'll have all the evidence you need.

"Well..."

***

Jordan was sitting on the couch in the living room pretending to be absorbed in a file he was reading when Aurora came in. She knew he was really waiting to question her. She'd seen him at the window watching her and Kami as they'd walked around the yard.

"So, did Kami interrogate you?" Jordan asked nonchalantly.

Aurora grinned and pointed to his file, "You know it's usually easier to read if the words are right side up."

Jordan knew he'd been busted so he threw the file down on the coffee table and stared at her waiting patiently for her to answer. She didn't say a word but Jordan saw the smile that flickered across her face. "You are gonna tell me aren't you?" He persisted.

"Tell you what?" She asked innocently.

He didn't buy it. "Whatever you told Kami." Aurora's smile was devious to say the least. He was glad she and Kami got along but wanted to know exactly what she'd told his partner. He had to get the information out of Aurora because heaven knew it would be easier than getting anything out of Kami.

"I plead the fifth."

"Remember, you'll want me to tell you something one day soon and I'm not gonna." He warned.

"Yeah, right. You're an old softie, I'll only have to ask you once and you'll give in."

"Dream on, missy." He laughed. It felt good to be able to joke with her again. Maybe now was the time he should bring up their future... no. Not tonight. Everything's going too right to potentially mess up.

"I think I'll call and check on Joe if you don't mind?"

"Go for it. He'd rather hear your voice than mine anyway. Want me to leave?" He started to rise to his feet to give her some privacy. She put her hand on his knee and he sat back down.

"No. I won't tell any secrets that you can't hear." She teased. "By the way how is your stomach?" She asked as she dialed the hospital.

"Hungry. How about yours?"

"Very funny. I meant how are your stitches."

"Still there."

"Jordan..." she turned towards him exasperated when someone answered the phone. "Oh, hi, Alex." She made a face at Jordan while she spoke to her friend. "No of course not. He would never be infuriating." She spoke the words sarcastically to Alex but was looking at Jordan. He held up his arms in question and she shook her head at him and went back to her conversation. She was extremely aware of Jordan sitting beside her listening to every word she said and was somewhat glad when he got up and went into the kitchen. It wasn't that she minded him hearing her conversation; it was that he stared at her while he listened.

She talked to Alex for a few more minutes after he left and then hung up.

"How's he doing?" Jordan asked as he walked back into the room a few moments later carrying two plates with sandwiches on them and two glasses of water.

"Alex says he's still not being a very good patient, but the doctors say it might be a good sign. It's driving him nuts to have to lay in bed when he wants to get up and catch the men behind all this. The doctors said his restlessness means he is feeling better and is well on the way to a speedy recovery. They gave him something to make him sleep for a while so his fidgeting didn't cause any damage to his wound." She told him as she took the plates and sat them on the coffee table in front of them.

"I feel his pain. I would hate to be laid up while the investigation was still going. I would want to be right there in the middle of it tracking the bad guys." Jordan sat down next to her ready to enjoy a long talk.

"How is your stomach feeling where your stitches are?"

And she dared to call him stubborn? He knew she wouldn't give up until he answered but it had been fun to watch her glare at him earlier when she wanted an answer but was talking to Alex on the phone.

"It really doesn't hurt that much. I figure one more day and I can do anything I normally do." Aurora's eyes widened in disbelief and she started to lecture him so he quickly changed the subject, "What did Alex think about your news?"

"What news?" Aurora asked around the bite of sandwich she'd just taken.

Jordan was surprised by her question. "About last night." He reminded her.

"Oh, I completely forgot." From the dejected look on her face, Jordan thought she was going to cry. "I was gonna tell her, but then we started talking and I forgot."

"Call her back." He suggested.

"I would but she was fixing to go to sleep and she didn't sleep well last night. I don't want her to miss anymore sleep."

"I don't think she would mind being woken up for that news."

"I'll let her sleep for now." Aurora thought as she chewed. "Do you think Kerry or your mom would be home right now?"

Jordan checked his watch. "Kerry should be home by now but mom will be out with dad checking the cows and feeding all the animals."

"Do you think Kerry would mind if I called her?"

"No. In fact she is planning on calling you later, but you can go ahead and call her now if you want." Jordan offered.

"Okay." Aurora almost sprang out of her seat in her eagerness to talk to her old friend.

"You could at least finish your sandwich." Jordan called to her as she reached the door.

"I'll eat later." She told him, not even slowing down or turning around. So much for that long discussion he was planning on having with her. Jordan grinned to himself. He had no doubt that Kerry would be happy to hear from Aurora. His only fear was that Kerry would ask some questions that he and Aurora hadn't discussed yet. He should have talked to her already. *Face it buddy. You're scared.* Jordan was almost disgusted with himself. He would find the right moment to talk to her. Soon.

CHAPTER 9

Aurora hurried to her room excited at the prospect of talking to Kerry Reiley again. Amazing! She'd never expected to talk to Kerry again. They had become such good friends when she and Jordan were together that it had really hurt Aurora to lose the friendship when she had broken up with Jordan. She picked up the phone and dialed the number from memory.

"Hello?"

"Hi, Kerry. You'll never guess who this is."

"Aurora?" She squealed. "I was just fixing to call you. How are you? Are you all right? Why are you staying with Jordan? Is he behaving himself?"

The questions came quicker than Aurora could answer and she laughed. Her friend still talked as fast as ever. "I've missed you too Kerry. It seems like an eternity since I last talked to you."

"It has been an eternity." Kerry confirmed. "Oh, I'm so happy that you finally are back to your old self. I can't wait to come and see you. So, how are you doing?"

"Great. I don't think I've ever been better." Aurora said as she lay on the bed. She hit her head on the headboard. "Ouch."

"It really sounds like you're doing great." Kerry teased. Her sense of humor reminded Aurora very much of Jordan's.

"I just banged my head on the headboard and hit an old bruise."

"How old of a bruise?" Kerry asked with keen insight into Aurora's not quite truth.

"About eighteen hours."

"That explains why you're staying with Jordan. Someone's after you aren't they?"

"I think we need to hire you on down here. The LAPD are always looking for people with good instincts."

"You didn't answer my question." She accused.

"They're also always looking for persistent people." Aurora teased.

Kerry let the silence linger until Aurora knew she wouldn't give up until she knew the truth. "All right. Your brother will tell you if I don't. Yes, someone is after me, but I don't know why. That's the main reason I'm stuck here. Well, that and Joe is in the hospital because he got shot the morning before someone tried to kill me. We're trying to figure out exactly what I did to hack someone off enough to try to kill me. You think it was something I said?"

"That's a real possibility." Kerry agreed good-naturedly. "I'm guessing you can't go into details right now, but when you can I want the whole story."

"Will do. So how are the second graders this year?"

Kerry groaned. "Only about seven more weeks until Christmas break. They're driving me crazy."

Aurora laughed. "It's going that well, huh?"

"Don't tell anyone, but I love it. I can't think of anything I would rather do. The kids I have this year are so smart. I love teaching them. They're gonna go far in life, I can tell."

"That's what you say every year." Aurora pointed out.

"Only because it's true." Kerry defended. "Anyway, tell me, how are you and Jordan?"

"We're both fine." Aurora answered knowing exactly what Kerry meant but not willing to answer that question. In fact, she wasn't sure how she should answer that question.

"You know what I meant. Now spill or I'll pester you until you do."

"To be honest, I'm not really sure."

"You mean he finally got you to talk to him and even has you in the same house with him and he hasn't even told you how he feels about you?" Kerry sounded astonished.

"Well, he basically told me last night that he still loves me, but that was right after I was attacked and I don't really think he knew what he was saying at the time." Aurora twisted the phone cord around her finger in her agitation.

"Trust me Aurora, the man is still crazy in love with you and he's an idiot not to tell you that every day. He was telling the truth last night."

"I'll tell you what. If he tells me again, when he's not in pain or under the influence of drugs, I'll believe him."

"Okay, I'll take that for now because I know he will tell you again soon. So has he kissed you yet?" Kerry sounded like a teenager who was getting the scoop on her best friend's date.

Aurora felt herself blush and was extremely glad that Kerry couldn't see her at the moment. It would cause way too many questions. "Kerrrryyy..." Aurora moaned and Kerry squealed. "He has! Tell me." Aurora couldn't help but laugh at her exuberance. "You know you're not supposed to kiss and tell." Aurora admonished with a laugh. It was so good to have her friend back.

***

"You still haven't found her?" Charles' voice was more threatening in person than over the phone. When Charles looked at you with his beady black eyes they seemed to pierce right through and see your deepest thoughts. All the secrets hidden where no one else can see. The cop fidgeted in the black leather chair in Charles' office. Maybe he should forget the whole thing and skip the country. If he thought for a minute that Charles wouldn't be able to find him, he'd be gone. As it was, he was stuck. Charles had people everywhere. He would be dead before his plane ever touched the ground. He needed a lucky break. Anything to get him back into Charles' good graces.

"I still say let me kill him and find Reiley and Kavvan on my own." The officer shivered as Charles' hit man slid a finger across his throat as a gesture of how he wanted to kill him. Garland. A man every officer in the world had tried to get a profile on. They had tried every way they could to arrest Garland, but he'd always managed to escape. Now he was sitting less than three feet away. This officer had done his fair share of looking for the elusive Garland and now wished someone, anyone, had him in custody right now. It would make him feel a whole lot better if Garland wasn't looking at him with murder in his eyes. He was sure Garland wouldn't mind killing another cop if Charles ordered him to and paid him a little extra. In fact, Garland would probably enjoy doing it. He was a very sick man. He needed to be in a psychiatric ward somewhere for the criminally insane.

"I'll find them soon. A couple of my people have some very promising leads." Lying came easy now, especially if it would possibly save his life.

"For your sake I hope you're right. Now go. You don't want to be seen here associating with someone like me. Especially when there is so much at stake." Charles dismissed him and the officer left as quickly as his legs would carry him.

"Are you sure about him?" Garland questioned motioning towards the door that the LAPD officer had just left through. It was amazing that Charles had been able to get a seemingly loyal police officer to work for him. Garland knew the way the cop had been looking at him that given the opportunity that cop would throw him in jail. Charles had to have some kind of incriminating evidence or something solid to make a man like that work for him.

"Are you questioning my judgment?" Charles snapped.

"I am if it's going to get me killed." Garland replied evenly.

Charles couldn't argue with his logic. The cop had been awfully nervous tonight. Was he hiding something? No of course not. He knew the consequences of betrayal. "He has been on my payrole for years now. He knows it wouldn't be smart to cross me. Besides if he becomes too much of a risk I'll have him eliminated."

Garland knew another name would soon be added to his list of hits.

***

"What are you doing out here?" Jordan yawned as he walked out onto the front porch. He'd heard Aurora get up about ten minutes before and walk towards the front of the house. He'd assumed she was getting a drink or something from the kitchen. When she hadn't come back he'd gotten worried and gone looking for her.

She jumped at the sound of his voice. Apparently she'd been lost in her own thoughts. "Sorry. I didn't mean to wake you." She apologized but it was obvious her thoughts were still on something else.

"Want to tell me why you can't sleep?" He scrubbed his hands over his face in an attempt to wipe away some of his drowsiness. It didn't really seem to help.

"Nothing. I just couldn't sleep."

"That's why you're sitting on my front porch swing at three a.m. petting Sally?" He sounded unconvinced and Aurora couldn't blame him. Her excuse was lame to say the least. How do you tell someone that every time you close your eyes you see your brother's lifeless body lying at your feet? That you wake up and know it's just a dream but you're still scared beyond all reason? Having problems breathing. Paranoid that every shadow could be a murderer waiting in the shadows with a gun to kill you the same way he killed your brother.

Jordan saw the haunted look in her eyes. "Come on, Aurora. Talk to me." He coaxed as he sat down beside her and put a hand on her shoulder. "You can trust me."

"I know I can trust you, Jordan." She assured him reaching up to hold his hand. He couldn't believe the relief he felt at hearing her say those words. He hadn't been sure he would ever hear those words from her again.

"Then talk to me, honey. Tell me what's wrong."

"Bad dream." It was all she could say. She wanted to tell him, but couldn't find the words or the energy. Her dream hadn't been anywhere close to as terrible as it had been on the stakeout but it was still horrible. It amazed her how a dream could drain all of her energy as if she'd worked out all day and she'd only been sleeping.

Jordan watched her for a moment and then got up and offered his hand. He saw the truth. She was reliving that night at the lake and was too shaken to speak.

She looked at his hand suspiciously but took it and he tugged her to her feet. "I think there's a good movie around here somewhere. Want to watch it with me?"

Her relief was visible and Jordan felt a surge of possessiveness. The man who haunted her dreams would pay. There was no doubting it, Jordan would make him pay.

"Sure." She quickly agreed and Jordan was glad he hadn't pushed her for answers. He should have known the best way for her to deal with it right now was to distract her and the only thing he wanted right now was Aurora to be happy. He wanted that haunted look in her eyes to go away soon and he would do everything in his power to make it go away.

"You get to pick the movie." He told her as he held the door for her to walk in.

"Nothing serious."

"Okay. How about a comedy?"

"Sounds good, but nothing too corny."

"Have you ever seen *Ice Age*?" When she shook her head he continued. "Well then that's the movie we've got to watch. I think you'll like it."

"As long as it's good."

"If you stay awake long enough to see the whole movie, I think you'll enjoy it."

"I don't think I'll ever be able to go back to sleep after that dream." She said quietly, but Jordan thought she looked as if she would fall asleep at any minute.

***

Jordan looked over and smiled. Aurora didn't even make it halfway through the movie before she was sound asleep. Jordan debated letting her just lie there and watch her sleep all night but commonsense won in the end. If he was going to be able to protect her, he had to get some sleep. He picked her up, only wincing slightly at the momentary pain from the pull of his stitches, and carried her to her room. He hoped now she would be able to sleep through the rest of the night. He brushed her hair back from her face marveling at how beautiful she was. She looked like an angel when she slept. He would have to tell her that, it would make her smile. Heaven knew his woman needed some happiness in amongst all of the sadness in her life and he wanted to be the one to bring it to her.

He straightened and left the room. She was one of the most important people in his life and he couldn't let himself loose his focus on this assignment. He might be on his home turf, but Aurora's life depended on him staying alert.

***

Aurora woke up and stretched lazily. She looked around slightly confused. The last thing she remembered was lying on the couch watching that silly movie Jordan had picked out. It was morning and she was lying in her bed. Jordan must have carried her in here after she'd fallen asleep. She smiled and got up to go find him.

Finding him wasn't hard at all. He was sitting at the table eating. No surprise there. The man could eat more than anyone she knew and still not gain a pound. It was annoying, she had to exercise to keep in shape and not gain weight, he could do whatever he pleased and still look great.

"Hey. You look well rested."

"Thank you. It must have been the boring movie that made me sleep so well." She teased.

"That movie will be a classic. It's great."

She scoffed at his comment. "It's corny."

"It wasn't that corny. Besides that's part of its appeal."

"I guess I'll have to watch the whole thing before I reach a final verdict on it. So what's on the agenda for today?"

"I've got to do research."

"What about me?"

"You can have a lazy day and do nothing." He knew that doing nothing would drive her crazy. Aurora had to be doing something otherwise she felt like a burden. But he just couldn't resist after the way she'd just bashed his movie choice. That was one of his favorite movies.

She walked over and smacked him. "What was that for?"

"For being a brat." She put her hands on her hips and glared at him. Jordan was amused by her display of temper but didn't dare smile. He didn't want to actually get on her bad side today, just antagonize her a bit.

"I think I'll take that as a compliment."

"You're just asking for it this morning aren't you, Reiley?"

"You know you're cute when you're aggravated?"

"Reiley." Her voice warned him not to go there. Especially since she hadn't had her coffee yet. It was dangerous to irritate Aurora before her first cup of coffee. People had been known to lose limbs over it.

"What did Kerry say to you last night that put you in such a difficult mood?"

"I'm not the one that's being difficult."

Jordan held his hands up in a gesture of innocence. "What did I do?"

"You're just trying to annoy me this morning and I was coming in here to thank you for putting me to bed last night."

"You're welcome. I thought it might be a little more comfortable than sleeping on the couch."

He watched as Aurora puttered around the kitchen getting herself a cup of coffee and breakfast. He was glad that she felt comfortable enough in his house to help herself to whatever she needed. If he got his way she would soon be around here a lot more often.

"So are you ready to get to work now?"

"I thought I was getting a lazy day today." Aurora said as she sat down at the table to join him.

"You can if that's what you want to do. I just thought you might want to get to work so we can get this man caught and you're life back in order."

"That would be nice." She agreed eagerly.

Jordan ignored the pang of disappointment. Aurora wanted to go home and back to her life, but that didn't mean he couldn't be a part of it. A big part if he had his way. He shouldn't take it personally that she wanted to get her freedom back. He pasted a smile on his face and spoke with a lightness he didn't feel. Even though logically he knew that her eagerness to get home shouldn't disappoint him, it did. He wanted her to want to be here with him.

"Good then let's get to work. After you eat breakfast." He pointed to the food in front of her.

"Bossy man." She mumbled as she took a bite of her toast.

Jordan turned to hide his smile. She definitely had spunk. That was part of what he loved about her, a small part.

CHAPTER 10

Aurora wasn't overly surprised to look up on the third day she was there and see Rick Reiley standing in the living room doorway. It was evening and she'd had a pretty boring day up until then. She hadn't even heard him come in, but then again he was CIA and loved to tell people he was quiet as a ghost. In reality he just got to play with all the neat toys that the CIA got. Well, maybe it wasn't all the toys; the man might have a little talent too. She wasn't sure how he'd gotten in the house without setting off the alarms or alerting the dogs, but he'd done it. A chill ran up her spine. If Rick could do it, so could someone else. He wasn't the only person in the world who'd had that kind of training and some of those people weren't the good guys.

His showing up wasn't a surprise because that was just the way Jordan's family was. Jordan had talked to his mother and told her something was wrong. She would have called the family and had them praying. What would surprise Aurora was if Rick was the only one of Jordan's siblings that showed up.

"Hi, Rick." She gave him a smile as she stood. He walked across the room and gave her a hug.

"Hey, Roar. It's been a long time. How are you?" His eyes searched her face and she felt almost shy under his intense gaze.

"I've been better." She saw a flash of surprise in his eyes at her honest answer but he quickly recovered. He pointed back to the couch where she'd been sitting, reading a file. "Sit back down. Relax." She obeyed and he took the chair straight across from her.

"I hear you and Jordan have been keeping things interesting." He teased his blue eyes sparkled. All of Jordan's family had blue eyes, but they all reflected different personalities. Jordan and Rick looked the most alike but there was a family resemblance in all the siblings. Jordan was only slightly taller than his older brother and that was a running rivalry between them. Well, that and the fact that Jordan was FBI and Rick was CIA. Often times, there was a good-natured argument between them about which agency was best. The whole family was fun to be around.

She looked over at Rick and was shocked to realize just how much she had really missed this family. She studied him. He hadn't changed much over the years. His dark brown hair, the same shade as Jordan's, was beginning to get just a touch of gray at his temples, but it made him look sophisticated instead of old. She would have to tease him about that later. Right now it felt good to just talk to him.

"We've been trying." She felt lighthearted as a child joking with him. She didn't ask how he knew about the case. She figured he couldn't tell her anyway. "Jordan just went to take a shower but he'll be back in a little while." She informed him.

"Good. That gives us time to talk." Leave it to Rick not to beat around the bush. He settled himself better into his chair getting ready for a long chat.

"Sure what do you want to talk about?"

"Is my brother treating you good?"

She blushed. "You know Jordan has always treated me good, Rick."

"All right. I know Edward and Amy are gonna make an announcement at Thanksgiving. Is there possibly gonna be another announcement?"

"I don't know. Who else do you expect an announcement from? I didn't know another of your siblings were in a serious relationship." She would have expected this line of questioning from everyone else, but she'd expected Rick to wait a little longer. Be a little more subtle than she knew the others would be. She was wrong. That whole family was nothing but a bunch of matchmakers! She didn't mind, but it did strike her as rather amusing. She'd probably get the same questions when she talked to the others. Kerry had already questioned her, now Rick, only three more left and then his parents. The only thing was, she wasn't sure what to tell them. Her and Jordan's relationship really hadn't been defined yet.

Rick looked at her for a moment but she couldn't read his thoughts. "Okay. I won't press, but you are at least coming to the farm for Thanksgiving, right?"

"I've been invited." She answered evasively.

"You didn't answer my question and you know it." Rick told her with a straightforwardness that didn't surprise her in the least.

"Is anyone else coming or just you?" She tried to change the subject.

"Yes, JJ is on his way. He'll be here in an hour or so. Now are you coming or not?" He wasn't detoured by her change in subject.

"I don't know, yet." She told him without looking at him. She was suddenly very interested in the file she'd been holding. Rick was amused. His brother definitely had a keeper in Aurora Kavvan. She was not only beautiful, but she was smart and fun too. Now, if Jordan could only convince her of that. Right now her cheeks were tinted pink and she looked like she would rather not have any more questions. Too bad. He was curious.

"Aren't the two of you back together?" He knew he should really stay out of their business but he also knew Aurora wouldn't be mad at his questions. She'd been like a part of the family when she and Jordan were together, and he felt comfortable enough with her to pry.

"No." She answered slowly. "Not really."

"What does 'not really' mean?"

She laughed. "You definitely sound like a seasoned interrogator." She looked at him, judging how much she should tell him. It was useless to try to avoid his questions; he was as persistent as Jordan. It definitely ran in their family. She'd just opened her mouth to answer his question when Jordan walked into the room. She quickly snapped it closed.

He smiled. "Hey Rick! What took you so long to get here? I figured the whole family would have been here by now." Jordan walked across the room and the brothers embraced for a long time.

"I would have been here sooner but I thought you might like some time to take care of some unfinished business." Rick looked pointedly at Aurora and there was no mistaking his meaning. Jordan choked and Aurora gasped. Rick ignored their reactions and went on. "I thought Kerry had to have been mistaken."

Jordan groaned. His family always had good intentions, but sometimes they didn't know when to back off. Or be quiet for that matter. He glared at Rick who smiled wickedly and he felt like groaning again. This would be a long visit if he didn't get the conversation back under control.

"So, are you all that's coming?"

Rick took his change of conversation in stride. "No, JJ is on his way and by the way he's picking up dinner. He didn't want to have to eat your cooking."

"My cooking is good!" He sounded outraged.

Aurora laughed and he turned to glare at her but she'd already looked back down at her file again. "Besides, Aurora has been cooking dinner."

"Maybe I should call him and tell him to forget it. I've not had a home cooked meal in forever."

"How about if I cook breakfast in the morning?" She offered.

"That sounds good." Rick agreed quickly, awarding her with a warm smile.

The men sat down and began talking and catching up. "I thought you were gone on an assignment until Thanksgiving."

"Well, I'm only back in the states for a week and then I'm gone again. I plan to go to mom and dad's tomorrow night."

"I'm guessing you're staying the night?"

"If it's not too much trouble."

"You're definitely trouble." Jordan told him with a smile. "But you're welcome to stay. Do you know how long JJ is planning to stay?"

"We're catching the same flight tomorrow night."

"Do you feel like you've been invaded, Roar?" Jordan teased.

"No. It's your house." She reminded him. "Besides I like Rick and JJ. It will be good to catch up with them."

If it hadn't been his brothers she was talking about, Jordan would have been jealous. As it was, he was glad she wanted to talk to his brothers. He'd heard the end of her and Rick's conversation earlier and had wondered what her answer to that last question would be but had decided they needed to discuss it before his family got the answers. He hadn't even asked the questions yet and *they* were demanding answers. Somehow that seemed a little off to him.

***

The Reiley men were in the kitchen talking over the details of the case and Aurora really didn't feel like going through all of it again so she wandered into the living room. There was no particular reason she'd come to this room except it made her feel peaceful.

JJ had arrived about half an hour after Rick and there had been constant talk and banter between the brothers since then. They had all been very kind and included her but she thought they would like some time alone to catch up. Do some 'male bonding.'

She'd seen something earlier that intrigued her. They had been talking about the case earlier and Jordan had said something about Cassie and if she wasn't mistaken, and she was pretty sure she wasn't, she'd seen a flash of interest in Rick's eyes. It was something new and different to think about. Something besides the case.

Where had Rick met Cassie? Had something happened between them and they parted on bad terms? She didn't think that was possible because she couldn't see Rick being in 'outs' with anyone. Especially not a woman he had dated. All the Reiley men were gentlemen and treated their women well. She couldn't fathom a reason any of them would be rude to a lady.

She was still thinking this over when JJ walked in the room. He was the quietest of the family. The thinker. Of course to be able to design the beautiful buildings he did, she figured he had to think a lot.

"Get tired of the cop talk?"

"Yep. I'm sorry someone's after you, Aurora." She knew he was sincere. He was a Reiley. "Whoever it is, he's gonna be sorry if Jordan ever gets a hold of him."

Aurora didn't comment. She knew Jordan was protective of her. Obviously he'd shared some of his feelings with his brothers. That was a good sign. Well, maybe. She hoped they could work things out between them and maybe his family's curiosity would finally be ended.

"So, are you two back together yet?" The quiet question didn't surprise her, but it did make her want to laugh. Two brothers in one day questioning about the same thing. They really should get together and plan this better.

"No." She was in a playful mood and decided to tease him. "But what about you? Is there someone special in your life?" At twenty-eight, JJ was still single and Aurora couldn't figure it out. All four Reiley men were great looking. Edward was soon to be thirty-six and just now settling down. Rick was thirty-four and as far as she knew hadn't been in any serious relationship in years. His job wasn't the best for a family man, she conceded. A woman would have to be very understanding. Jordan was thirty-two and would have been married by now if he'd had his way, but at the moment he was still single. Well, sort of. If she had her way he wouldn't stay that way long.

The women of this world had to be crazy to let these men get away. Of course, she was one of them. But soon she hoped she and Jordan would be able to talk and work things out.

"Not at the moment." His gaze was direct and she wandered exactly what answers Jordan's family was looking for from her. "So, you and Jordan haven't discussed the future yet?"

She shook her head and he continued. "My brother must be getting slow in his old age to not grab you before someone else does.

If he isn't careful some younger man will notice how beautiful you are and come steal you from him."

She smiled. It was a nice compliment but not possible. She was in love with one man. Jordan. "I don't think you have to worry about that happening JJ." She assured him and he smiled.

"That's all I wanted to know."

They talked companionably until Jordan and Rick joined them then the conversation turned to different things. Aurora decided to call it a day around ten-thirty but the brothers stayed up to talk.

***

"What's wrong with you?" Rick demanded as soon as he heard Aurora's door close.

"Yeah, Jord. You've been wanting this woman back for the past four years and now you're not even going after her?" JJ put in.

Jordan held up his hands to stop the questioning. "Okay, you two. Take it easy. I'll answer your questions but you don't have to jump down my throat to get the answers."

"Sorry. We didn't mean for it to seem like we were." JJ apologized.

Rick looked at his youngest brother. "Yes we did." All three laughed and then Rick and JJ turned their questioning gazes to Jordan.

"Well, I know I'm still in love with her." Jordan started.

"Tell us something we don't know." Rick mumbled and JJ shot him an amused look. Jordan ignored them and continued.

"What I don't know for sure is how she feels about me. I'm pretty sure she is still in love with me, but it could just be this whole mess has thrown us back together. Not that I'm complaining. But I don't want to ask her now because I'm supposed to be protecting her and she's vulnerable. I don't want it to seem like I'm forcing her to make a decision."

Rick gave a low whistle. "I hadn't thought about that."

JJ looked as though he were weighing his words very carefully. "Go ahead and spit it out, kid." Jordan told him.

"Well, Aurora and I were talking earlier and I got the distinct impression she knows her feelings towards you and they are real." He told them exactly what was said and Jordan could have whooped with joy but as it was he sat here smiling like an idiot. JJ shook his head. Leave it to Jordan to be head over heals in love and not realize the woman he loves is completely in love with him too.

"I think it's time we head to bed." Rick interrupted the conversation. "We will have all day tomorrow to talk. Our flight isn't until eight-thirty tomorrow night."

"All right. Thanks you two. For coming down here, not for the third degree in questioning." Jordan smiled and bid them goodnight.

***

"You're up early." Jordan commented as he walked into the kitchen and saw Aurora already busy preparing breakfast.

"I promised Rick breakfast and I thought he might want it in the *morning*." She said the word as if it was something vile and he laughed.

"What are we having?" She looked at him sheepishly but didn't answer. "Okay, out with it, woman."

"Well, I couldn't decide so I decided on a little bit of everything."

"What is a little bit of everything?" He asked as he crossed the room to inspect the dishes already on the counter. Amazed at the amount of food, he looked at her curiously. "Are you trying to feed an army?"

"Close enough." She laughed. "Three Reiley men." He inspected the dishes more closely and gaped. He turned and crossed the room in three easy strides and caught her around the waist.

"You're incredible." She blushed at his compliment. "You remembered what each of our favorite breakfasts was and fixed it. There was a lot of thought put into this meal so don't act like it was something you just couldn't decide on."

She opened her mouth to protest but her eyes betrayed her.

She'd done this just for him and his brothers. "Thank you." He said as he bent and lightly covered her mouth with his.

"Oops. Sorry." Rick said as he and JJ entered the room. Neither of them looked it in the least. In fact, they both looked very interested in what was going on.

"No problem." Aurora said, her voice coming out a little lower than usual as she tried to turn back to her cooking, but Jordan's arms tightened and she couldn't move. She laughed and swatted his arms. He let her go reluctantly and turned to glare at his brothers. Rick shrugged and JJ smiled.

"Jordan would you get the plates and you three can fix your food while it's still hot." She told them indicating the dishes of food on the counter. Jordan moved towards the cabinet with the plates as his brothers came to see what she'd fixed.

"Homemade biscuits and white gravy. My favorite." Rick said as he raised the towel and uncovered the biscuits.

"Blueberry pancakes." JJ said with wonder as he surveyed the number of them. Maybe she'd gotten a little carried away. It did look like the food could feed a few more people than were here.

"I wonder who the ham, eggs, and hash browns are for." Rick said in a teasing voice that dared her to answer.

She smiled sweetly at him. "There is enough for anyone who wants them."

It was not exactly the answer he'd been hoping for but Rick let the subject drop. He was persistent but chose his timing.

"I'll say. Are you sure there aren't a few more people coming to help us eat this feast?" JJ asked still amazed by the amount of food.

"Okay, so I got a little carried away." She admitted. "But you three had better eat all the food." She told them raising her spatula in warning. They fixed their plates and headed into the dining room.

She was last, behind Jordan. Before they got to the door he stopped and turned to look down at her. "Thank you for remembering and for making all three of us feel special."

"You *are* all special." She told him, meaning every word. She thought the world of Jordan and his family.

He leaned down and quickly brushed his lips across hers. Aurora stood there for a moment after he left stunned. She'd been expecting the other kiss, but this one had caught her off guard. She hurried into the dining room so they could begin the meal. When she sat down, Jordan gave thanks and they began eating. Aurora looked up several times to find Jordan's eyes on her and she smiled. He was definitely one of a kind. There wasn't another man like him in the world.

***

The rest of the day passed quickly and soon it was time for Rick and JJ to leave and catch their flight. They both hugged her and JJ gave her a kiss on the cheek as they left. Rick had jokingly warned him that Jordan might not take too kindly to him kissing his woman. Both Jordan and Aurora ignored his comment and said their goodbyes. But after they left the house was quiet. It was strange but having JJ and Rick here had made her feel like nothing out of the ordinary was going on. That the only reason she was here with Jordan was they enjoyed each other's company.

"Hey, Jord?" She called as she looked through the house. Where in the world could he be?

"Ouch!" She heard him holler and then heard mumbling. "Yeah?" He called just loud enough for her to hear.

She followed the sound of his voice and found him under the sink fixing the leak she'd mentioned earlier that morning. All she could see of him was his long, blue jean clad legs. Not a bad sight.

"Did you knock yourself out?" She teased as she settled into a chair to talk to him.

"Very funny. You're the one who insisted this leak needed fixing." He grumbled.

"I did not!" She told him indignantly. "I just said that your water pressure would be better if the leak was fixed!"

He leaned out to grab a tool and looked at her. "Same difference." He stated before going back under the sink. "If I hadn't gone ahead and fixed it you would be nagging me about it for days." She didn't take offense at his words because she heard the laughter in his voice.

"I guess you aren't really where we could talk huh?"

He leaned out and gave her an amused look. "You do pick the oddest times to have discussions." When she started to rise he put his hand out to stop her but pulled back when he realized it was covered with grime. "Stay. I can talk to you while I fix the sink."

"I don't want to mess with your concentration." She told him sounding unsure.

"Why worry about that now? You've been blowing my concentration for years." He told her honestly and she blushed slightly.

She chose not to respond to his comment, but steered the conversation to the topic she came to discuss. "What I came in here to talk about is Rick."

"You want to discuss my brother?" He sounded suspicious. Like he had anything to worry about! She was completely hooked on him, not even the brother who looked similar could turn her head from Jordan.

"Well, more specifically I want to discuss Rick and Cassie." She supplied quickly.

"I didn't know there was a Rick and Cassie." He replied evasively as he leaned back under the sink.

"That's kinda what I was wondering about." She had been curious before when Rick's interest had been piqued at the mention of Cassie's name, but now she knew there was something going on. Jordan was refusing to come out and admit or deny it!

"What made you start wondering about them?" His voice was muffled by the cabinets, and she couldn't tell what he was thinking.

"I saw the interest in Rick's eyes when Cassie's name was mentioned last night and just got to wondering. So what's going on between the two of them?" She insisted.

Jordan sighed and scooted from under the cabinet. "I wish I knew. They both seem interested in each other, and have for years but for some reason they've never done anything about it. They've been friends but one or the other usually is in a relationship. Never anything serious... well not usually." He amended. "Cassie went head over heals for this guy a few while back but he turned out to be a jerk. Other than that I've not seen any reason for them not to get together."

"Maybe they're worried about the geography. He does live all the way across the US."

"I don't really think that's a factor. Well, at least not a big one. I think they are afraid of what they might lose if they give love a try."

"All right." Aurora said lost in her own thoughts. Jordan could practically see a plan forming in her mind. Leave it to them to be working out someone else's love life when they hadn't even established exactly what theirs was. It was sort of funny in a way. Before Jordan could voice his thoughts, Aurora stood up.

"I guess I'll leave you alone so you can fix the sink, but be careful. The top of the cabinet needs a sign on it that says 'objects may be closer than they appear.'" She giggled and hurried out of the room before he could reply.

"Smart aleck." He muttered as he rubbed his forehead where he'd hit it earlier.

CHAPTER 11

"It's been a long five days." Aurora plopped down on the couch and kicked her shoes off. As usual she got her shoes off at the first opportunity. Jordan had gotten used to finding them all over the house. Wherever she was when she finished and could take them off is where they stayed. It had been an amusing morning because of her forgetfulness about where she left her shoes yesterday.

Apparently she'd kicked them off in his study after they'd come in from a walk and this morning she had been in a tizzy because she couldn't find them. She'd thought they were in the living room and he figured they were at the front door. They'd spent thirty minutes looking for them and she'd received a good amount of teasing from him about wasting time because of her bad habits. He really didn't mind it had been an amusing break in a tedious investigation.

"I think I might take offense to that." Jordan said as he handed her a bottle of water and sat down beside her.

"Why would you do something like that?"

"Because apparently being here with me is an ordeal that you're having to live through. Is it really that bad?"

"Jordan, being here with you is... complicated." That was putting it mildly.

"Complicated huh?" Jordan rubbed his chin as he considered her words. "Complicated good or complicated bad?"

Aurora smiled. The past few days here with Jordan at his house had been enlightening to say the least. He was still the best man in the world. He'd treated her like a princess and made her feel useful at the same time. Every time she turned around he was checking to make sure she didn't need something.

Just as Kerry had said, Jordan still loved her. For some unknown reason, this absolutely wonderful man loved her. Aurora was sure of it. He hadn't mentioned it again since that day at the hospital. He hadn't needed to. As the saying goes, actions speak louder than words. For the past five days Jordan's actions had been speaking volumes. He treated her great and kept her involved in the investigation. They worked well together. Their relationship was definitely more than friends but she wasn't sure exactly what you could call them at the moment.

Sometimes she was sure he was going to bring up the subject but something always seemed to happen. He seemed unsure of her reaction to the subject. At the hospital she hadn't exactly been forthcoming with her feelings. At the time it seemed any relationship between them was doomed. Now it was a different story. If he asked, she would tell him the truth. She wanted them to have another chance.

It was as if he didn't want to push her into something. He was giving her time to make up her own mind about their relationship. She knew he didn't want to put any pressure on her but she also knew that they needed to talk soon.

The past few days they had fallen into a routine. Jordan fixed breakfast, with the exception of the morning she fixed breakfast for him and his brothers, they researched through the day looking at files, or checking information via the phone or the Internet. So far their searches had turned up nothing. It didn't look like anyone had missed her. No one had been checking up on her. Kami had given a story to everyone at the station that Aurora had gone to visit a sick friend out of town.

Aurora knew that her friends wouldn't believe it but she also knew they wouldn't do anything to jeopardize her safety. She was starting to get disheartened. None of their research was giving them any hard evidence on who was behind the attempts on hers and Joe's lives. She knew who it was. Charles. Now if only they could find the evidence to prove her right.

Aurora looked at the piles of files around her and grimaced. Jordan hadn't been able to get his hands on her personal files yet but she was sure he soon would. He'd given Kami the mission of locating and attaining those files and if anyone could get them it would be her.

Aurora's favorite part of their daily routine was after a full day of deskwork, she used her culinary talents to cook amazing meals. She wasn't bragging, just stating the facts. Then she and Jordan would talk or play checkers. Sometimes they just sat in the same room and read. It was nice to just have someone who understood that sometimes silence was the best.

She glanced over at Jordan and saw he was waiting expectantly for her to answer him. "I guess you could say... good complicated."

Jordan's smile was cocky. "Since you've so obviously enjoyed my company this week maybe we should talk about..." the phone rang interrupting him and Jordan glared at it accusingly.

Aurora giggled. "Glaring at it won't make it stop ringing. Most people answer their phones to make them stop ringing." She suggested not even trying to hide her amusement.

Jordan grabbed the receiver. "Hello?" He barked and she had to hide her smile at his obvious irritation. She didn't blame him but it was amusing that every time he tried to bring up the subject in their conversations something like this happened.

She went back to her file. She'd read this one at least ten times and still nothing jumped out at her saying *I'm the evidence you need*. She wished it would really be that easy.

She was putting the file in the reject pile when Jordan handed her the phone. She looked at it a moment, confused before she took it. Who would be calling her here?

"Hello?" She asked uncertainly.

"So, do you know anything yet?"

Kerry.

Aurora should have known Jordan wouldn't give her the phone without knowing who was on the other end.

"Like what?" Aurora pretended ignorance.

"Roar." Kerry's voice was a warning and a plea all in one.

"Nothing has been said yet." She glanced guiltily at Jordan. There was no way he could know what they were talking about but she still felt uneasy having this discussion with him sitting next to her. What would he think if he knew what she was discussing with his sister?

"Give the phone back to my bonehead brother so I can straighten him out."

"No!" Aurora's voice came out sharper than she'd meant for it to and Jordan raised a questioning eyebrow. She felt her face flood with color but tried to give him a reassuring smile.

Kerry relented somewhat, but Aurora knew Kerry was as stubborn as her brother and wouldn't ever fully give up on the subject until she had the answers she wanted. "I'm disappointed in him. He should have said something by now. If he doesn't say something soon, I really am gonna have a talk with him."

"I don't think so." Aurora was proud of herself. Her voice came out even and there was no trace of the panic she really felt.

"Well, has he kissed you again?" Kerry couldn't restrain her curiosity and Aurora laughed.

"I'm pleading the fifth." It seemed like every time Jordan even thought about kissing her, they got interrupted. Most of the time it was Kami inadvertently interrupting them. Sometimes she seemed apologetic and sometimes she seemed amused. Aurora wasn't overly sure what went on in that woman's head and figured no one else knew either. It hadn't helped that both JJ and Rick had walked in on him kissing her the morning before. Now the whole family probably knew.

"I really am gonna have to have a sisterly talk with him now aren't I?"

"I don't see why you would." Aurora noticed Jordan hadn't even picked up a file. He was sitting there listening to the one-sided conversation with open curiosity.

"I think I'll call you back later, Kerry."

"Oh, the phone police telling you that you're time is up?" She sounded amused at Aurora's haste to get off the phone.

"Something like that. Talk to you later."

"Bye."

She hung up the phone completely ignored Jordan's questioning look and grabbed the file she had just discarded and began reading.

"So how's Kerry?"

"Fine." She sure wasn't going to volunteer any information.

"What were you two talking about?"

"Nothing you need to worry about." She assured him but the blush staining her cheeks told him a different story.

Jordan decided not to push her. "Okay have it your way, but that's two."

"Two what?" She asked him completely confused.

"Well, first you wouldn't tell me about your and Kami's conversation and now it's Kerry. That makes two."

"You won't do it." She told him putting the file down.

"You're sure about that, are you?"

"Yep."

Jordan grinned and leaned back against the couch, pulling her with him. He propped his feet up on the coffee table, and then seemed content to just stare at her. Aurora fidgeted feeling extremely self-conscious under his watchful gaze. She sat up and pulled away from him a little. When he continued to stare at her, she cleared her throat. "Um, you do know that isn't good for your furniture don't you?" She said indicating his feet on the coffee table.

"It's a lot more comfortable though." He looked at her through half open eyes. "I'm making you uncomfortable right now. Why?" His laid back tone aggravating her.

"No you're not. Why would you think that?" Her denial came too quickly. Jordan smiled and pointed to her hands. She was wringing them in her nervousness.

"Ok. A little uncomfortable." She admitted reluctantly.

"Why?" Jordan prompted.

"Because you're staring at me."

"So?"

"So, it's a little unnerving to have someone just sit and stare at me." Aurora said pointedly.

"I'm sorry." He said, not sounding it in the least. In fact he sounded amused. "I didn't mean to make you uncomfortable. I was just enjoying the view."

"Right." She said turning a little pink. "So, what's on the agenda for today."

"You just can't stand it can you?"

"What?" Aurora asked sounding surprised.

"Sitting down and relaxing. Taking a day to do nothing but enjoy the day."

"I don't know why, I just can't stand to sit and do nothing. I think I would go absolutely crazy if I had to just sit here." Aurora said and she continued to fidget.

"Well, what do you say we try to work off some of your energy?"

"Absolutely." She immediately agreed.

"Basketball in ten minutes?"

"What about your stitches?"

"It doesn't hurt besides I need to workout or I'll get out of shape."

"You're sure?"

"Yes."

"Great. Court out back?"

"Yep."

"See you in ten." Aurora said as she got up and practically ran to change clothes. Jordan watched her go, and silently scolded himself. He should have thought of this sooner. It was a wonder she hadn't gone crazy the past five days. He should have thought about her needing a way to release her pent up energy. She had been under a lot of stress lately and he hadn't even thought of it until now. He shook his head and went to his room to get ready.

CHAPTER 12

Less than ten minutes later, Aurora was walking towards him, basketball in hand. She looked absolutely adorable. With her red hair up in a ponytail she looked like a teenager. Her cheeks were already a little pink from the cool breeze, but her eyes were sparkling with a challenge. She looked comfortable in her t-shirt, sweats, and a pair of old tennis shoes. How in the world could this woman make a t-shirt and sweats look so appealing? She looked relaxed, but her eyes told him that she was restless and ready to start the game.

She needed a way to release her frustration. Seriously, he needed a way to release his frustration, he thought with a grimace. He didn't like someone trying to kill *his* girl. It was frustrating him that he couldn't even get a lead on who it was. He would like to get this over with as quickly as possible so he could pursue a relationship with Aurora that wasn't haunted by this investigation.

"Well old man, think you can keep up with me?" She taunted.

"All I can do is try."

"What are we playing to?"

"Fifty ok with you?"

"Are you sure you can last that long?" Aurora asked sounding shocked.

"You're asking for it, you know that?" Jordan asked enjoying their light-hearted banter.

"Let's play." Aurora threw him the ball.

It was a fast paced game. After twenty minutes both were dripping with sweat. Aurora shot a ten-foot jump shot that Jordan blocked with little effort. Her green eyes flashed fire and he grinned. "Still don't like being blocked, huh?" He sounded a little out of breath. "Hate it." She panted. Aurora made a move to steal the ball, and Jordan spun left around her and shot. Nothing but net. Aurora winced. "Ouch."

***

"Thirty-nine to thirty-five. I'm surprised." Aurora said trying to catch her breath. She had barely beat him in a race after the three-pointer he just bricked.

"What surprised you?" Jordan noticed he sounded out of breath himself. Maybe he shouldn't skip his workouts anymore. It definitely didn't look like Aurora had been skipping any. He grinned. She was, without question, easy on the eyes. Aurora caught him checking her out and shook her head in a silent reprimand but her eyes were smiling.

"The fact that you're beating me, and still breathing." She answered in a voice that sounded surprised that he'd had to ask.

"Very funny smart aleck." He muttered and she smiled. "Just for that I'll stop giving you easy shots."

Aurora stopped. "Easy shots?" she sputtered. "I'll show you easy shots, mister." With that she drove straight at him, and at the last second cut right for an easy lay up. When she turned towards Jordan she had a smug smile on her face. He couldn't help grinning at her victory.

***

After what seemed like an eternity to both of them, Jordan sunk the winning shot.

"Good game." Aurora said as she picked up the basketball.

"Yea, not bad for an old timer huh?" Jordan said as he sat down exhausted on the grass.

"Don't gloat or next time I won't take it so easy on you. By the way it's October the ground will be cold."

"I noticed."

"Then get up."

"I'm not sure I can." Aurora howled with laughter and almost fell over at the pathetic look on his face.

"Come on old man." She said as she pulled him to his feet. "I'll take the first shower and fix dinner while you're taking yours."

"Can't beat a deal like that." Jordan agreed immediately.

***

"Something smells good." Jordan sniffed appreciatively as he entered the kitchen. The domestic scene he saw made him stop and a satisfied smile curved his lips. Aurora stood in the kitchen, barefoot, stirring spaghetti sauce. She was wearing jeans and a yellow sweater. Her hair was still a little damp from her shower and was beginning to curl as it dried. The whole scene looked so natural. For about the hundredth time in the past two days he thought this is the way life is suppose to be, Aurora here with him.

"Good timing." Aurora said without turning around. "The spaghetti is almost done and the garlic bread is done. By the time you set the table the spaghetti will be done, and I'm more than ready to eat. By the way, I was wondering. Won't whoever is after me know where you live?"

"Well, yes and no." He answered as he got the plates down and put them on the table.

"Oh, that's about as clear as mud."

Jordan chuckled and snapped a towel at her. She stuck her tongue out at him when he missed. "Ha ha!"

"Once they figure out that you're with me, which I'm pretty sure they've already done, they'll have to search for a while to find out where I live."

"Or they could just look at anything that you've filled out that asks for you're address." She pointed out, sounding as if she thought he had lost his mind.

"That's the beauty of it... I still have my apartment in town. It's the address that I use on everything. I stay there when I'm on a case and only a few people know about this house." It took Aurora a minute to grasp what he had just said.

"So how far will they have to dig before they find this place?"

"It's not really that far to dig, you just have to know the right place to start. I'm hoping that they're attempts at digging lead us to them before they figure out my little secret. Table is set."

"Good plan. Now lets eat, I'm starving."

"Yes, ma'am." They ate in silence. Both were lost in their own thoughts and were comfortable in the companionable silence that surrounded them. They finished almost the same time but both seemed in no hurry to move.

"Great dinner, Roar." Jordan finally broke the silence.

"Thank you. I'm glad you like it because you get to clean up."

Jordan made a face at her. "How did I know you were gonna say that? Come on, I'll wash and you can dry." He pulled her up and started cleaning off the table.

"Nope, I cooked."

"But you wouldn't want me to do all this work by myself would you?" Jordan asked pouting, his bottom lip quivering.

"Yes." Aurora answered, but started gathering up dishes.

"See, I knew you cared." He said triumphantly.

"I've never stopped, Jord." She said quietly as she walked past him to the sink and put the plates in.

Jordan stood stunned for a moment and then regained his composure. "Good because I was wanting to talk to you about us." He began cautiously.

"Ok, but first can I call and check on Joe?" Aurora turned around in time to see a look of pain cross Jordan's features before he turned his back to her and began gathering up glasses and silverware.

"Sure, go ahead." His emotionless voice and the fact that he kept his back to her told Aurora more than any angry words he could have said. It took Aurora a moment to realize what she had done wrong. She'd hurt his feelings. She should have explained herself a little better. She wanted to check on Joe and then she could give her full attention to their discussion. Aurora was determined to convince him that she wanted to talk about their relationship just as much as he did. "Jordan?"

"What?" He still hadn't turned around to look at her so she put her hand on his arm and pulled until he looked at her. He was a stubborn mule.

"What's wrong?"

"Nothing." He answered gruffly as he grabbed the glasses and walked past her to the sink.

"Yeah, right. I know better than that."

His shoulders slumped in defeat and he turned around to face her. "It's just that every time I try to bring up the subject of our relationship, it seems like you try to avoid it." And then he looked away, out the window towards the woods behind the house.

Aurora tentatively put her hand on his arm and waited until he looked at her again, then she held his gaze. "I'm sorry. I know I avoided talking about our relationship in the past, but that's only because I didn't think we could have a relationship. Now, I wasn't sure exactly what you wanted and still had some doubts, but I *do* want to talk to you about us. I want to see where we are in our relationship. I promise that after I check on Joe we will talk about this."

A look of pure relief covered Jordan's face. "Good because I've been trying to think of how to bring up the subject and I never came up with anything. I'll clean up in here while you go call Joe."

Aurora smiled up at him, and Jordan felt all the air rush from his lungs. She was beautiful.

Aurora just couldn't resist. He still looked so relieved about being able to talk to her about their relationship that her heart went out to him. She stretched up on her tiptoes and kissed him lightly on the lips. She had only meant for it to be a quick thank you kiss, but Jordan had other ideas. He immediately put his arms around her and pulled her closer, deepening the kiss. Aurora didn't resist, she put her arms around his neck and relaxed in his arms. This is where she most wanted to be after all. When Jordan pulled back, he smiled. "Finally." He sounded a little bit out of breath.

"Huh?" Aurora asked her thoughts were a little fuzzy at the moment.

"I've been trying to kiss you for an eternity now, and every time I got up the nerve we got interrupted."

Aurora giggled self-consciously. "I expected Kami to walk in at any second." Jordan chuckled and looked around.

"Nope she's no where in sight."

Aurora leaned her head against his chest and felt the reassurance of his steady heartbeat. She snuggled closer as Jordan started rubbing her back. "I thought you were gonna do something."

Aurora pulled away. "Oh, yeah. I, um, got a little side tracked."

Jordan grinned wickedly. "What could have possibly side tracked you?" He asked innocently.

Aurora tilted her head to the side and tapped her teeth. Pretending to think hard, and then shrugged. "Gee, sorry I can't remember."

Jordan growled and pulled her back to him. "Then let me refresh your memory." He murmured against her lips and then covered them with his own. This kiss was a sweet, soul-stealing kiss. When Jordan finally released her lips and raised his head she said, "I think I'd better go call and check on Joe now. I'll be back soon and we can finish this, um, discussion."

Jordan smiled as she walked away; he definitely enjoyed *discussing* things with her.

***

Aurora sat on the couch for a few moments trying to settle her pounding heart before she called Joe. The nurse had told Aurora that Joe would for sure be awake if she called back tonight. So far all she'd talked to at the hospital were nurses and Alex's sister. She still hadn't been able to share her news with Joe or Alex.

She knew that if she sounded even the least bit odd Joe would be suspicious. That was the last thing she needed. She wasn't even sure where her and Jordan's relationship was going, so how would she explain it to Joe if he asked?

She dialed Joe's hospital room and he answered on the second ring.

"Hi Joe." She said quietly.

"Hey beautiful." Joe answered enthusiastically. "It's great to hear your voice. I've missed you." Aurora thought that he sounded tired, and maybe a little drugged, but she smiled at the old greeting. Ever since they had first become partners Joe had answered her phone calls like that. At first it had irritated her, but now it felt good to hear the familiar words from her friend.

"I've missed you too. I hear you've been being a bad patient since I'm not there to keep you in line. You'd better start being a good patient." She warned. "You would hate for me to have to come out of hiding and force you to be good wouldn't you?"

Joe laughed and then groaned. "Roar! Don't make me laugh, it hurts too much."

"Sorry. Next time duck and maybe the bullet won't hit you." She suggested.

"Very funny, Rorie."

"So tell me, how are you feeling?"

"Wonderful." He said sarcastically. "The food here is really great."

Aurora snickered, but said seriously, "Joe, really how are you feeling?"

"Honestly? I feel like a Mac truck hit me. I'd feel a lot better if my favorite nurse was here though." He sulked.

"You feel that good huh? Where's Alex?"

"She went home to shower and get some clothes. How are you handling all of this?" Joe tried to sound offhanded but Aurora heard the concern and worry in his voice.

"Better than you would think." She answered honestly.

That seemed to pique his interest. "Something you want to tell me?"

"Yes." Aurora said and went on to tell him about how Jordan

had showed her how unreasonable she was being by blaming God. And that she was just being stubborn and irrational. Then she told him about the verse that Jordan had told her to read and how it had made her feel wonderful and terrible at the same time. "It made me realize that I could have the joy of my salvation back, but it also showed me that for a long time I have been being very stupid for hanging on to my anger. It was such an enlightening and convicting feeling. Now I know how Paul must have felt on the road to Damascus.[1] Completely horrible for the wrong he had done to so many people. Joe, I'm so sorry for the rotten way I've treated you the past five years. You're one of the best friends I have and I treated you terribly. Please forgive me?"

Joe sounded choked up. "Aurora, I forgave you a long time ago. I'm just happy that you've changed your mind about God. Alex and I have both been praying for this very thing."

"I know you have and thank you for not giving up on me, Joe. Will you do me a favor?"

"Anything." Joe promised.

"Brave man, agreeing before you even hear the favor." Aurora trying to lighten the emotion that was so vivid she could almost feel it, but she was feeling so loved that she almost started crying.

"I figure you are worth anything, Roar. And besides I knew you wouldn't ask for too much since I'm lying in a hospital bed." Good old Joe, Aurora thought. He knew she was on the verge of tears and he was kind enough to ignore it and tease her.

"Will you tell Alex I called, and tell her to call me as soon as she gets in? But don't tell her why. I want to tell her. I would rather have told both of you face to face, but I don't think my jailer would let me." Aurora said as Jordan walked in the room. He made a face at her; apparently he didn't like being referred to as a jailer. "I've had hostage negotiation training but it doesn't work on this particular man." She couldn't help but throw another barb at him for the face he'd just made.

Joe chuckled. "No problem, Roar. I promise I won't spoil your surprise."

"Thanks Joe. And I really am sorry for the way I've been acting. I couldn't believe you got shot. The only thing I could think was that the last words I had said to you were in an argument. I never should have said those horrible things to you. I'm sorry Joe."

"Aurora, don't worry about it. I knew you didn't mean those things. You were mad at me for being so overbearing. I have my faults too you know. I should have *interrogated* you a little differently. It's forgotten." He said with finality. "So, how are you and Jordan really getting along?" He asked slyly.

Aurora was amused at how quickly Joe had switched the subject, and was even more so at his choice of topic. She had been trying to ignore the fact that Jordan was sitting right beside her, but there was no way she could. Apparently he had decided the couch was a loveseat and had sat down right next to her and seemed content to just sit and stare at her. Again! The man just couldn't resist seeing how much he could get her off balance. In a way it was kind of fun.

"Are you trying to play cupid, partner?" Her voice was barely audible but her partner had good ears.

"Absolutely. You did the same thing for me."

Aurora looked over at Jordan then shifted to where her back was to him. "Point taken. I guess you could say pretty well." She answered evasively.

"That's all you're going to tell me?" Joe sounded exasperated.

"At the moment yes."

"I was expecting a little more than pretty well, Rorie."

"Let's say things are working out."

"That's even worse. Is Jordan there with you?"

"How did you ever guess?" Aurora asked sarcastically, shifting uncomfortably on the couch. She was getting good at carrying on these kinds of conversations in front of Jordan and keeping her answers vague. Now if only she and Jordan could have the same kind of discussion that would be progress. If only he knew how often she discussed him with other people he would be surprised.

Or would he? Did these same people talk to him about her? Probably. They were all trying to make sure she and Jordan were happy. Everyone was playing cupid these days. Oh well. Nosey friends were the best kind. At least she hoped that was true because that was the only kind of friends she had.

"Well, your answers are even more evasive than normal. Let me talk to him."

"Are you serious?" Aurora asked incredulously.

"Yes," Joe said patiently. "I want to talk to him." Aurora didn't trust the sound of his voice. It probably wasn't a good idea to let Joe and Jordan discuss her, but against her better judgment she handed Jordan the phone.

He took it seemingly unsurprised. "Hi, Joe. How you feeling?"

Aurora listened to one side of the conversation, but couldn't tell what they were talking about. Mostly Jordan said yes or yea. It was driving her crazy, especially since Jordan was leaning back staring at her while he was talking. After a few minutes Jordan reached around her and hung the phone up.

"Well?" Aurora said impatiently.

"Well what?" Jordan asked innocently.

Aurora felt like screaming. They had been talking about her and now he wasn't going to tell her what was said? He couldn't do that! It was just wrong!

Isn't that what you've been doing to him? A little voice taunted her. She silenced her thoughts and continued her questioning.

"What did Joe want to talk to you about?" She asked with a little less patience.

"Sorry, but that would be telling." Jordan's eyes gleamed wickedly as he leaned back and laced his fingers behind his head. He looked as if he could sit there all night and not tell her.

Aurora squealed in frustration and Jordan couldn't choke back his laugh. That earned him a swat on the arm, but he slanted her a satisfied half smile. "Cocky is not very becoming." She warned him.

"I thought we were gonna finish our discussion." He reminded her in a husky whisper and put his arm across the back of the couch behind her. He tried to pull her to him but she put both hands on his chest and pushed. He flinched. His cut only hurt occasionally now. Only when pressure was directly applied to it and Aurora was sorry she had inadvertently caused him any pain.

She quickly removed her hands from his chest and said, "I'm so sorry Jordan."

They'd both been so careful earlier, playing basketball not to pull his stitches but he seemed to be fine and she'd forgotten he was still hurt.

"It's ok. I honestly forgot about the stitches too. Now can we finish the discussion we started earlier?" Jordan grabbed her hand and again tried to tug her to him but she still resisted.

"Not until you tell me what the two of you were talking about." She insisted. Jordan put his hand over hers and rested their hands on his chest. His eyes were twinkling, but he didn't laugh.

"Remember, I still owe you two."

"No, that's not fair." She argued.

"Oh, really? How so?"

"That was something you wanted to know that I didn't want to discuss. This is something I want to know."

Jordan looked at her skeptically. "And?"

"I really don't want to tell you what Kami or Kerry and I were talking about. It was personal and you're just not telling me about your conversation with Joe because I won't tell you what my conversations were about." Her eyes were pleading with him and snapping fire at him at the same time. She had the most amazing eyes. Not everyone could be angry and beg at the same time with only their eyes.

Jordan had a short debate with himself. The stubborn side of him wanted to goad her and not tell her what she wanted to know until she told him what he wanted to know. The more sensitive and loving side of him wanted to tell her not to worry and keep whatever secrets she wanted and he would tell her what she wanted to know. He chose somewhere in the middle of the two extremes.

The truth with a devious twist.

"We were talking about you." It was obvious her patience was wearing thin.

"I gathered that much. What about me?"

"Well, if you want to get technical, we were talking about us."

"Jordan, please just tell me." Aurora pleaded.

"Impatient aren't you?" Jordan smiled at the warning in her eyes. "He wanted to know if I planned on talking to you about how I feel."

"What else?" Aurora didn't believe for a minute that was all that they had talked about.

"You'll have to wait until later."

"Why?"

"Because you promised me that we would talk about our relationship after you got off the phone with Joe." He answered promptly.

"Ok. What did you want to say?"

Her immediate agreement caught him completely off guard. He had expected more of an argument from her. "Well... um..." Jordan started to fidget and look really uncomfortable. Dang! He had rehearsed this speech a million times but for the life of him, Jordan couldn't remember a single word he had prepared.

"That's a good start." Aurora couldn't help but tease him. He looked too cute; it was like he was a high school kid asking a girl out on a first date. All that was missing were books and lockers she thought with a satisfied grin. She'd off balanced the most stable man she knew. It was a great victory. One she would bask in for a while.

Jordan scowled at her, but then quickly changed the look to one of uncertainty. "I don't really know how to say it."

"Say what?" Aurora prompted.

"That I want you to give us another chance. To see if you still love me as much as I love you." Jordan said in a rush. He was searching her face for the answer, and she let him see what she was feeling. Love.

"Of course I'll give us another chance. What took you so long to ask?" She said with a twinkle in her eyes. Jordan released the breath he hadn't known he had been holding, and gave her a dazzling smile. Aurora's stomach turned to mush.

"I was scared senseless that you would say no." He looked a little sheepish at his admission.

"I believe the senseless part, but did you really believe that I would say no?"

"Yes... I mean no... um," Jordan stammered. He was never this off balance. He could interrogate men and get them to tell him what he wanted to know. That was easy. He was the tough one that always had the answers and he was babbling like an idiot. Only this woman could do that to him. She messed with his whole focus.

He took a steadying breath that seemed to calm his nerves, and then tried again. "What I mean is I wasn't really sure that you still wanted to give us another chance. I knew you still cared, but I guess it was like the first time I proposed. I was pretty sure I knew what you were gonna say, but I was still scared to death."

"I can't believe that my knight in shining armor is scared of anything." Aurora said amused that he had been so worried about her answer. She also noted that he had said *first time he proposed* and hope soared through her.

"Knight in shining armor? I hope you are gonna explain that one to me." Jordan said looking at her quizzically.

"Maybe after you tell me what else you and Joe were discussing." She bargained.

"You are nothing if not persistent Roar." Jordan laughed. He was more than ready to tell her about his conversation with Joe. It would lead into the discussion he'd been trying to have with her since the day he'd brought her here.

***

"I've found them." The cop was ecstatic that one of his informants had finally found Jordan Reiley's home outside of town. Of course that informant would never again be able to inform him of anything else. It wasn't smart to leave witnesses behind that could possibly testify about the information he had been wanting.

"Where?" Charles asked sounding relieved.

"Reiley owns a house and some land about two hours outside of

Los Angeles. It seems that he rarely stays there and not many people know about it. I found the deed in some information a source gave me."

"Good work. I'll see that you are rewarded for how swiftly you got the information I needed. I honestly wasn't sure you could deliver the information I needed. I really expected if you could that it would at least take a full week. I'm impressed by your capabilities. They will be taken care of tonight." Charles hung up thinking the same thoughts his police informant had thought earlier, it isn't good to leave people who can testify against you. He handed Garland directions and a note that had three names on it, when Garland read it he smiled an evil smile and walked out the door whistling a happy tune.

Strange man. Charles thought. He took perverse pleasure in killing people.

Not a man you would want mad at you.

"Actually Joe asked me when I was planning on proposing to you. And I told him," the ringing of the phone interrupted Jordan and he looked apologetically at Aurora as he reached to answered.

Could this really be possible? It was the second time in one day that their extremely important conversation had been interrupted by a phone call. Of all the rotten luck! If it had been any other conversation Aurora would have thought it was funny. As it was, she could have screamed in frustration. Jordan was so close to telling her what she wanted to know and someone *had* to interrupt!

"Reiley here." He heard nothing but static for a moment and started to hang up, but then he heard a familiar voice. "Get out of the house now!" Kami yelled, and then all he heard was static. Jordan's blood ran cold in his veins.

CHAPTER 13

Jordan dropped the phone into its cradle and jumped to his feet. As he did, he grabbed Aurora by the hand and pulled her to her feet. He took off at a run for the front door pulling her along behind. He hesitated before opening it, and thought maybe they should go out the back. "Jordan what's wrong?" Aurora asked, with her eyes round as saucers. What in the world had been said that had made him change so drastically right before her eyes? They had gone from a personal conversation to guns?

Jordan pulled his gun out and checked his clip. Full. His back up weapon was still in the glove box of his truck, but his truck was still parked behind Kami's house. Kami and Cassie had hidden it while he was bringing Aurora home. Dang! He would really like to have his backup weapon right now. It had saved his life more than once in a tight spot like this.

Aurora tugged his arm to get his attention. "Who was on the phone?"

"Kami." Jordan answered in the voice she knew as his working voice. It was very formal and stiff. Frustrating.

"I'm guessing they have found your house?" Good grief! It was like pulling teeth to get him to answer questions Aurora thought slightly aggravated, but she understood his detached manner. She couldn't fault him for being distant. He didn't need any distractions. He had to focus on getting them out of here, fast and alive.

"Apparently." At his answer Jordan watched in amazement as Aurora went back over to the couch and reached into her bag and pulled out her Glock. He had no idea she had her weapon here. He thought she had left it at her apartment the night of the break-in. She checked her clip and nodded in satisfaction then reached back into the bag and pulled out another full clip. "I'm ready. What's the plan?" She asked walking back towards him. Jordan was staring at her with disbelief written all over his face.

"Where did you get that?" He asked motioning towards the gun.

"Kami brought it with all of my other stuff. She put in the drawer of the bedside table and left a note in my Bible. Anyway, you do have a plan don't you?" Aurora was starting to look a little concerned.

"I'm working on it. I'm having to make this up as I go. The man that was sent to your apartment was a professional assassin. We pulled his file and his name is Garland, he doesn't miss, and he has never been found by any law enforcement agency. He has too many disguises and is too good at his job to be in one place very long. That makes him impossible to find. I figure he'll be the one sent here, and I don't know if he's ahead of my people or not." Jordan looked worriedly towards the front door and then down at her. He was obviously torn on what course of action he should take. "I don't want to walk you out the front door, and into a trap."

"If it were just you here what would you do?"

"Thinking like that is not an option. It's not just me here, you're here too and I don't want you to be hurt." He looked at her with such love that she reached up and hugged him. "Jordan I know you're worried about me getting hurt, but I'm a police officer as well as a witness. I can handle myself better and you'll be in less danger if you quit trying to protect me. Think of me more as backup than someone you have to protect." She said with a wink and reached around him to open the front door. She knew without his answer that if he were alone in this situation, he would rush out the front door because that would be the last thing someone waiting for them would expect.

Jordan sighed and leaned down to give her a quick kiss before he stepped cautiously out the front door. He quickly scanned their surroundings. No one in sight, but the hair on the back of his neck was standing on end. Something was wrong very wrong, or maybe it was just that Kami's phone call had rattled him. He prayed that was the case. He didn't want Aurora to be hurt. Especially not on his watch.

He signaled to her the coast was clear, and she silently came outside. Aurora pointed towards her car and they both dashed towards it. They reached it at almost the same instant, Jordan just a step behind. Even though Aurora had told him that she didn't want him to try to protect her he was going to. Not because she was a witness or someone he was paid to protect, but because she was the woman he loved.

When they reached the car, Jordan pushed Aurora through the driver's door and into the passengers seat. They both prayed as he turned the key in the ignition. The car started on the first try and Jordan drove quickly down the driveway. They both fastened their seatbelts; not knowing what was coming, but preparing for the worst. He was amazed that Garland hadn't been outside the house waiting on them. He was also thanking God that they had been able to get out before he had arrived.

"How did you find out about Garland?" Aurora asked. He had been so absorbed in his thoughts, worrying, that it took him a minute to understand her question.

"What do you mean?"

"Neither of us saw his face, the description I gave of his voice and eyes wouldn't have been helpful in getting his name, so how did you find out who he was?" Sounding totally confused, and a little bit suspicious.

"I had my team check out your apartment after the police left." He told her the truth without telling her everything. "The bullet went completely through him and they were able to get a DNA match from the blood left on the carpet. He had been hit one other time and that's why his DNA was in the system. Otherwise we still wouldn't know who he was."

"Why would you have your team check my apartment?" Aurora asked more to herself than to Jordan. And then, reality hit her like a lightning bolt. "You suspect a LAPD officer is dirty, don't you?" Aurora asked, praying he would say no, but knowing the truth from the tension showing on Jordan's face before he answered. He silently sighed and looked straight ahead as he answered her as if he couldn't bear to watch the pain he knew he would inflict on her by answering her question.

"Yes." He answered quietly. He knew she would have eventually figured it out, but telling himself that didn't make Jordan feel any better. He had known she would be hurt by the news that one of her fellow officers was dirty. But there was no way to soften the blow. He chanced a glance at her while he was on a straight stretch in the road and saw several emotions cross her face. First disbelief and denial, then confusion, and last anger.

"That explains why you wouldn't tell any of the LAPD officers where you were taking me. You wouldn't even let me tell Sergeant Nickels. How did you know?" Aurora voice was tight with controlled anger.

"Honestly, we've suspected one of the Los Angeles PD was selling information to Charles for years, but never could pin-point who it was, until now. Joe getting shot on the stakeout only confirmed our suspicions of a dirty cop and narrowed our suspect list considerably. The stakeout at Charles' drug lab was a highly classified operation. There were only six people total who knew about it, Sergeant Corey Nickels, Joe, JD, Daniel, you, and Cassie. Cassie was the only person at the FBI who even knew about the stakeout. It was a professional courtesy so that both agencies would be working on the same page. I only found out when I called to check on you, and was told Joe was in the hospital. After I left the hospital, I wanted to see what I could find out about your investigation and got stonewalled. I couldn't do anymore investigating, so I did the next best thing. I made such a scene in Cassie's office they had to tell me what was going on."

"Those men you just mentioned are all men I would trust with my life." Aurora sounded torn between loyalty to her friends and the truth. It hurt to know that one of her friends could have betrayed her. Someone she trusted with her life. Someone Joe had trusted with his life, and trusting that person had almost gotten him killed. Aurora felt her anger rise at the thought of her partner lying in a hospital bed because of this man, and she was going to find out who he was, and he would pay. She'd do everything in her power to make certain that he paid. There were only three suspects it could be because it wasn't Joe, Cassie, or her. That left Daniel, JD, and Corey. Jordan seemed to read the turmoil her mind was in by the expression on her face. He reached over and took her hand in a reassuring grip. She was glad that he was going to be with her during this.

"I know you trust them honey, and I'm sorry but it's the truth. I know how close you feel to the LAPD officers that you work with." He gave her hand a gentle tug and she undid her seatbelt and slid across the seat to lay her head on his shoulder. Jordan slid his arm around her and they sat in a comfortable silence, both lost in their own thoughts.

Jordan still wasn't comfortable with how easy it had been for them to get away from his house. Something wasn't right. From the sound of Kami's voice it was urgent that they get out. So what was going on? Which direction would the trouble come from? He shifted uncomfortably in his seat as a set of headlights flashed in the rearview mirror, and tensed, as the headlights seemed to speed up, quickly catching up with them. Aurora noticed his tension and turned around.

"Whoever is in that car is coming up fast, Jord." He heard the panic in her voice as she reached for her seatbelt.

"I noticed." Someone was chasing them. It had to be Garland. "Maybe it's just some kids out acting stupid."

"I think you believe that possibility about as much as I do." Aurora tried a laugh and failed miserably. She was terrified. She put her life in danger everyday on the job, but this was different. Someone was trying to *kill her*. Their sole intention tonight was to take her life. Jordan's too if he got in their way. She glanced at Jordan, the man she loved, and knew without a doubt he would die trying to protect her. He would put his life on the line for her.

Jordan pressed a little harder on the accelerator, but it didn't seem to matter. The car stayed with them. In what seemed like slow motion, a black car pulled up along side them and a man leaned out the passenger side window. Jordan shoved Aurora's head down at the same instant he saw the man had a gun. Bullets pinged off the car. Jordan tried to maintain control of the car to avoid wrecking, but it was a wasted effort. One of the bullets blew out a tire and they sped into the ditch, towards a tree. Aurora closed her eyes and prayed they would both live.

Aurora felt her body being jerked and heard the crash but didn't open her eyes. Thankfully, both she and Jordan had put on their seatbelts and hadn't been thrown from the car. She felt his arm across her back still holding her down. Aurora's back hurt, whiplash, she mentally checked her body and didn't think anything was seriously injured. Hopefully, Jordan was fine too. She slowly opened her eyes to find Jordan struggling to get his seatbelt off. "Roar, you ok?"

"Yes." She said as she to started trying to unfasten her seatbelt. Nothing worked. She tugged and pulled, but couldn't get it to budge. "Jordan I'm stuck."

"Move your hands." She looked as he took a knife from his belt and slashed the seatbelt. "We've got to move. They'll be back soon, and I don't want to be here waiting for them."

Aurora needed no encouragement to get away from these men. She hurriedly got from the car and looked around, confused. It was dark out tonight. There was very little moonlight most of the time. Thick clouds cloaked any brightness but sometimes they moved and the moonlight shone bright. The darkness would be a great asset for their escape but if the clouds moved at the wrong time…

There were trees on both sides of the road. Which way should they go?

Jordan answered her question before she had a chance to ask; he took her hand and led the way into the woods on the opposite side of the road. He prayed that their assailants would check the other woods first and give them a head start to get away. A thought stopped Jordan in his tracks, and Aurora ran into his back. "Jordan? Hello? Bad guys behind us remember?" Aurora said walking past him and tugging on his hand.

"They wouldn't have left us without making sure we were dead. Those men are here somewhere." Jordan quietly spoke his thoughts, but it was loud enough for Aurora to hear. He saw Aurora's face pale in the soft moonlight.

"Very good detective work, Reiley." Aurora gasped as a strange, yet familiar voice came from the woods directly in front of them. She spun to face the coming threat, but saw no one. Her stomach lurched. She knew that voice! "Scared officer Kavvan? You should be because I'm going to kill you." The voice, Garland, taunted her mercilessly.

"Over my dead body." Jordan said in a fierce growl. Aurora looked up and saw pure rage in his eyes. She had known he would protect her but seeing him ready to kill for her was scary.

"Absolutely." The voice agreed. "She will have to watch you die before I kill her. That part is purely for my enjoyment."

"You're a sick man Garland." Aurora said with pure hate in her voice. *This is the man who has been trying to kill me and now he says I have to watch Jordan die first?* She was enraged at the very thought. "You're supposed to be the best assassin in the business. If you're such a great professional killer why not show yourself and at least give us a taste of your best work. As I recall last time we met, you lost. Speaking of which how is your shoulder?" She baited, hoping that it would be enough to make him come out. His voice sounded as if he were all around them, it was very alarming.

"That was pure luck on your part. I won't make that mistake again." Garland said in an unconcerned voice. And before their eyes, he seemed to materialize in the moonlight directly in front of Aurora. She jumped, and then looked up into the same hate-filled brown eyes that had almost taken her life only days before. As she involuntarily shivered, Jordan pulled her behind him and protectively shielded her body with his.

"Do you think that will do much good Reiley?" Garland chided. "Good show, but seriously you will both be dead in only moments. So why waste the energy on a foolish effort to save her life, that won't work."

"Call it instinct Garland." Jordan's voice was harsh. He looked around for any way out, but there was nowhere to run or hide. No way to protect Aurora. He had failed. As he realized it his heart broke. He couldn't save the woman that he loved. "I'm sorry." He whispered in a voice full of emotion.

"I love you, Jordan." Aurora said in a soft but sure voice from behind him. He turned and looked down into her eyes and saw the love, and also the realization that it would take a miracle for them to live through this. He momentarily forgot his anger and everything else except his love for this woman. "I love you too, Roar."

"How touching." Garland said with sarcasm dripping from his voice. "Any last requests?" He asked as he slipped a gun from the inside pocket of his coat and made a show of putting a silencer on it.

"Yes. Where did the other men from the car go?" Jordan asked.

"What, no begging for your life or hers, Reiley?" When Jordan shook his head Garland seemed to consider his request. "You surprise me. Not many people can manage that. I usually expect the unexpected from everyone that way I avoid surprises. Your request is an intriguing one though. All right, I'll tell you what you want to know. It won't do you any good since you'll never be able to use the information anyway. I sent the men back to my employer's home to await my return."

"Oh, that short of a walk, huh?" Even if he died he wanted to know who was behind this. If only Garland would tell him and stop playing this stupid game.

"Walk? Perish the thought. I was planning on *borrowing* a car from one of the nice people who drove by. Clever don't you think?"

"Oh, very original." Aurora said sardonically.

"Enough chit chat." Garland snapped. "I hope you have both made your peace with God because He is the only One who can save you now. Now, Aurora you get to watch your boyfriend die." He smiled evilly and aimed the gun at Jordan's heart.

Jordan's hand tightened on hers and she closed her eyes and leaned into Jordan awaiting the inevitable. Then she heard a shot. She opened her eyes tears running down her cheeks, expecting to see Jordan bleeding, and then stopped. She'd *heard* a shot. She looked up into Jordan's surprised eyes. He was alive and unhurt.

She frantically searched for Garland, and finally saw him. He was standing exactly where he had been with a shocked expression on his face. When she looked harder there was a hole exactly where his heart should have been, even though she didn't believe he ever had a heart. Then as she watched he fell. He was now laying face down in a pool of blood, exactly where he had been standing only moments before. There was no reason to check for a pulse, Garland was dead.

"What happened?" Aurora's voice was trembling. Jordan turned and hauled her into his arms for a hug, and she sagged against him in relief. He looked over her shoulder.

"Thanks, Kami." He said in a hoarse whisper. "What took you so long to get here?" He joked to keep from crying in relief. "You could have been a little faster and saved us from the last five minutes of thinking it was the end of our lives. My life actually flashed before my eyes."

"You're welcome, but it isn't me you should be thanking." Kami told him as she stepped out of the shadows she had been hiding in. "I was only backup on this assignment."

"If it wasn't you then who?" Jordan asked confused, still holding Aurora tight. He wasn't sure he would ever let her go again. She was too precious and life was too short.

"Me." A soft voice from their right that Aurora had never heard before. She turned towards it, and saw a tall, slender woman with beautiful auburn hair holding a gun still trained on Garland.

"Cassie? What are you doing here?" Jordan asked in disbelief as his longtime friend stood up out of a bush that couldn't have been five feet away from him. Talk about surprises, Cassie was supposed to be out of town working on another assignment.

"Well, you're welcome." Cassie teased.

"Thank you, Cassie. I owe you more than you'll ever know." Jordan said seriously, and he turned back to Kami and asked, "But how did you two get here so fast?"

"We were well over halfway here when I called. We'd been told a little late that someone had hacked into your personnel records and we were let's just say exceeding the speed limit slightly to get here in time. I saw Aurora's car in the ditch over there and figured you wouldn't mind terribly if we crashed the party. I knew you wouldn't go the obvious way into the woods by the car so we came this way. When we heard the voices we decided to stop and see if we could lend a helping hand." Kami was smiling mischievously at them. "It seems like at least one good thing came out of all of this though." She indicated Aurora still in Jordan's arms. "You do know, Jordan, that your arms will get tired if you continue to hold her up in the air like that."

"I don't think my arms will ever get tired of holding her." Jordan argued as he hugged Aurora tighter to him.

"I like the sound of that, but Kami is right." Aurora said as she leaned back a little. "Besides you know how I don't like to put on shows for an audience." She smiled into his eyes, and Jordan couldn't stop himself, he kissed her in front of Kami and Cassie. And even though Aurora said she didn't like to put on a show for an audience, she didn't resist his kiss.

"So do you two want a ride tonight or not? I think Aurora might need a new car, her last one isn't exactly in any shape to be driven." Kami said laughing the whole time. Jordan reluctantly pulled away from Aurora and looked at Kami with a mock scowl, it was too good a night to be in a bad mood. They were all alive and well.

"Kami, have I ever mentioned that you have bad timing?" Jordan asked good-naturedly.

"Only a few times in the past few days." Kami answered still laughing at him, but he didn't mind. He'd just seen a miracle occur. There should have been no way he and Aurora should have lived tonight. Only God's grace had saved them. "Now can we please go? I'm getting a little bit cold out here."

"Absolutely." Aurora agreed. "Let's get out of here. It's getting chilly, but mainly because these woods are creepy!" Everyone silently agreed, and quietly they walked to Kami's waiting car.

CHAPTER 14

When they got to Jordan's house, everyone spread out and quickly checked the house for any sign of an intruder. Even if they thought Garland had killed Jordan and Aurora, Charles would have wanted any evidence against him found and destroyed. Everyone was especially wary of the silence in the house. Nothing looked disturbed but there could be someone waiting somewhere inside the house. The dogs were calm so that seemed to put everyone a little more at ease, but it was still a nerve racking task.

As Aurora searched the rooms, she thought about her situation and thought it was a little strange. She knew very little about Kami and absolutely nothing about Cassie but she trusted them completely because Jordan trusted them. That was something new and different to her; she was used to trusting people because she knew them and knew how well they could back her up. Trusting someone just because someone else did was completely foreign to her, but at the same time, trusting these women just felt right. But then again who was she to judge who could be trusted and who couldn't? Right now she was afraid that one of the men she trusted from the LAPD was behind all the attempts on her life.

They all met back in the living room and everyone reported happily that there was no one there but them. Cassie was stationed at the door as a look out to make sure no one came up to surprise them, while Jordan and Aurora packed. Kami was looking at the security system and the videotape from the outside camera for any sign that someone had been there.

"Pack your things quick, okay Roar?" Jordan called as he hurried to his room to pack his own clothes.

"I still don't see why we can't just set a trap to catch whoever it is trying to kill me. They already know where this place is and that I've been staying here. I could stay here and wait, you know, be the bait to lure them out." Aurora said as she leaned against the doorframe in Jordan's room. Jordan was packing but stopped with a stack of jeans halfway to his suitcase and swung around to look at her. His eyes were blazing with suppressed fury and his mouth was a grim line.

"Or they could send another professional assassin to finish the job." He ground out, his voice as well as his face showed how angry he was and Aurora wanted to retreat as he stalked towards her, but she stubbornly stiffened her spine and held her ground and waited. She tilted her chin defiantly, ready to meet his challenge. If he hadn't been so mad at her for suggesting they use her as bait, Jordan would have been amused at her obvious display of defiance. Didn't she know how precious her life was to him? He would never let her be bait, no matter how bad he wanted to catch this man.

She was expecting Jordan to argue or at least ask her not to set herself up. She was totally unprepared for what he did. Instead of yelling at her or arguing, he gently grabbed her chin and brushed a kiss across her lips. Aurora stood there looking up at him completely dumbfounded. "I will not allow you to be bait for any reason. I love you too much, and I've come too close to loosing you twice in the past few days." Jordan's voice was soft but there was steel behind the words that warned her not to argue.

Jordan's face softened and the steel disappeared from his voice. His blue eyes darkened as he looked down at her. "I want to grow old with you Aurora, not lose you only days after I've finally found you again."

Aurora felt tears behind her eyes, but stubbornly blinked them back. She had cried more in the past few days with Jordan than she had in years. She did not cry! This was one time she would not cry. "I really want to catch this guy Jordan," his eyes hardened and she hurried to finish her sentence. "But after that confession I couldn't possibly argue farther." Aurora conceded and she leaned against Jordan's chest.

She sneaked a glance at his face and noted that it was more relaxed and there was none of the earlier hostility showing. She decided to tease him a little. "You know, Reiley, it sounded like you were planning on sticking around for a while."

"Only the rest of my life. Do you have any objections?" Jordan asked raising a questioning eyebrow.

Aurora snuggled closer putting her arms around his waist. "Absolutely none." She sighed as Jordan's arms came around her to hold her close. She was content. She felt loved, protected, and safe. There was nowhere in the world she would rather be and when she was in his arms she felt as if she were the most important person in the world. That together they could do anything.

"Good because there is something that I need to ask you." He told her as he pulled away from her and walked to his dresser. He reached into the top drawer and took something out. Aurora wrapped her arms around her waist and hugged herself. She suddenly felt alone and abandoned without Jordan's arms around her. *This is ridiculous!* she told herself, *he's just across the room.* It wasn't as if he'd deserted her.

"You say you have to talk to me, and then walk away to finish packing. Typical male." Aurora grumbled as she watched him take something out of a box and then put the box back into the drawer. She couldn't see what he'd taken out and apparently he didn't want her to see because he slipped it into his pocket before he turned around.

"Stop grumbling at me." He teasingly chastened. "I wasn't packing, I was getting something and I'm already back. See." He stopped in front of her and held out his arms to her for another hug. It had been a very emotionally trying day for both of them and he needed the hug as much if not more than she did. Aurora eagerly stepped into his embrace and he smiled. He held her. Something he'd been dreaming of doing for the past five years. Praying he would get the chance again and now he never wanted to let her go again.

A few moments later Jordan asked, "Can I ask you a question now?"

"Does that mean that I have to let you go?" Aurora asked as she hugged him a little tighter.

Jordan laughed at her obvious reluctance to let him go. She was so different from the woman who he had seen at the hospital only days before. That woman would never have willingly let him know how she was feeling, but this Aurora loved him and let him know it without a doubt. She seemed like a whole new person, and he definitely liked the change. He silently thanked God that she was back in his life.

He didn't want to let her go, but just had to ask her this question. He couldn't let another minute go by without letting her know exactly how much she meant to him. He'd come to learn that life was short. You shouldn't waste any time.

"Yes, you'll have to let me go, but only for a minute." He promised. When she didn't immediately release him he gently coaxed, "You'll like the question."

Her curiosity obviously got the best of her as she slowly released him and stepped back. "Okay, but it had better be good." She finally agreed. Then watched in amazement as Jordan knelt down on one knee and took her left hand in his.

"Aurora Kavvan, will you marry me?"

Aurora was shocked. She knew that he loved her but she hadn't expected him to propose this soon. She thought they would at least date for a while before he proposed. They'd never even finished the discussion about their relationship. Everything was happening so fast.

She looked down into his eyes and saw the love shining from them and also the fear that she would reject him and knew there was only one answer she could give him. She didn't make him wait for her answer. She squeezed his hand and looked deeply into his eyes as she answered him smiling. "Of course. What took you so long to ask?"

Jordan broke into a huge smile and slid a ring on her left hand. Aurora slowly looked down at the ring and gasped. She looked questioningly into Jordan's eyes and saw that they were dancing merrily. "Why did you keep it?" She asked astonished at the ring she was seeing. This couldn't be possible!

"Because I knew that I could never marry anyone but you and this ring was perfect for you. Even though you said that you never wanted to see me or this ring again, I knew that we were meant for each other." He answered seriously.

Aurora realized that she was crying and ruefully shook her head, *so much for not crying tonight*. She smiled down at Jordan through a veil of tears, "That was beautiful Jordan." She said, with her voice thick with emotion.

Jordan stood and gently wiped the tears from her face. "I love you, Aurora. I always have and I always will." He bent and softly kissed her.

***

Kami smiled to herself from the doorway and then turned and quietly walked away. This was the one time she wouldn't interrupt her partner. He deserved some privacy with his new fiancé now because he wouldn't get much in the next few days if they didn't get a break in this case. Besides maybe she would catch the bouquet at the wedding.

***

"Where is Garland?" Charles thundered as he paced behind the desk in his office. "He should have been back hours ago!" His anger turned on his second in command Jim.

"He *did* have three people to kill." Jim reminded him in a calm voice. He had been trying to calm Charles down for the past couple of hours and nothing had worked. Charles had turned the full force of his fury on Jim.

"And why exactly did you drop him off instead of making sure that he finished his job?" He lashed out.

Jim gave a careless shrug. He'd seen Charles in these moods often enough to know not to antagonize him but he couldn't resist. "You said he was a professional. In your words, *he's the best that money can buy*. I figured you knew what you were talking about and he could handle the job all by himself."

Charles face turned red in anger and he took a deep breath, ready to shout at Jim when the door burst open and Chris ran into the room. "Your cop just called. Garland is dead, but apparently all three of his targets are still alive."

"How is that possible? He was a professional assassin!! They aren't supposed to miss or get caught. He should have had no trouble taking out two cops and an FBI agent." Charles was in a rage and Jim wouldn't be a bit surprised if things suddenly started flying through the air. Charles really needed to control his temper because when he got mad, it didn't matter who it was around him, they got hurt.

"Sorry, dad." Chris said backing towards the door. Watching them, it was obvious to Jim that the kid knew his father's temper and wanted no part of it.

"I guess this is a case that I will have to handle personally. This woman will not win, but she is getting to be too much trouble. I thought when I killed her brother five years ago that would be the end of her, but she is nothing if not persistent. I have to give her credit for that." Charles fumed, even though it sounded like he admired that trait in her, as he grabbed his coat. "Call and set up a meeting with the cop. One hour at his house, and after that Jim I want you to get Chris away from here. Take him to the house in Florida. If something goes wrong and I'm taken away, I want him to be able to still run the family business."

***

Jordan leaned his forehead against Aurora's and swayed gently back and forth. "I think that we're gonna have to postpone this until later and finish getting ready to go. We need to already be out of here." He admitted reluctantly.

"Okay. We don't want to be still here if someone shows up to kill us, right?" Aurora gently prodded, hoping he wouldn't change his mind, but ready to set a trap so her life could get back on track. She was ready for a normal life. She wanted to plan her wedding with this man.

"Right." Jordan agreed quickly. There was no way that he would change his mind and let her be bait. Her life was too precious to even consider letting her take such a great risk. "Now go finish getting packed, I don't want my woman to be here if the bad guys show up." He waited a moment expecting her to argue. She didn't.

"I guess we will have the rest of our lives to finish this." Aurora agreed, secretly happy that Jordan was so protective of her. One week ago she would have been offended at the thought of a man thinking of her as 'his woman,' but now it felt good. "By the way tell your mother that I would love to come to your family's Thanksgiving if the invitation is still open."

"It's absolutely still open. Besides we wouldn't want to let Edward hog the spotlight, would we?"

"Nope. I think we might give them something to talk about. Two engagements in your family at the same time? That is unheard of." She stretched up for one last kiss and then quickly went to her room to finish packing.

"Come on you two. We haven't got all day!" Cassie called from her perch at the front door.

"We're coming, oh impatient one." Jordan said as he walked into the front hall carrying three suitcases. Two were his but the other was Aurora's. It was the only one she had finished packing by the time he walked by her door.

"Someone's in a good mood. Mind telling us why?" Kami asked coming into the front room carrying an apple.

"I would but for some reason I think you already know, Kam."

"Know what?" Kami feigned innocence as she flopped down

on the couch, opening her eyes wide and looking at him in mock confusion.

"Don't even try to play innocent with me. I know you too well to believe it. Besides I saw your shadow in my doorway as I was putting the ring on Aurora's finger." He pointed out casually and watched amused as Cassie's jaw dropped when she it registered what he had just said. Kami laughed gleefully at her reaction.

"You should have heard him Cas, it was *so* romantic. He got down on one knee and proposed. Then he put on her engagement ring, it was the same ring from their first engagement. He's kept it all these years! Then he explained to her how she is the only woman he has ever loved, and he could never even think of marrying anyone else." Kami finished in a rush and sighed longingly.

Jordan shook his head, he'd known she was there part of the time, but he hadn't realized that Kami had been there listening to the *whole* proposal. He was going to have to put a cowbell around her neck so he could tell when she was coming. He really didn't mind that she'd heard his proposal, he would never be embarrassed for anything he said to Aurora when he proposed, but he hadn't meant for anyone except Aurora to hear him. He hoped she didn't get mad at his overly curious partner.

He smiled at Kami good-naturedly. "You have no shame Kam, listening in on a very private moment and you don't seem the least bit apologetic about it."

Kami smiled unabashed. "I'm not. I have to listen in on your proposal because heaven knows a man will never propose to me like that." She took a big bite of her apple to emphasize her point.

"That's because the guys you date don't deserve you." Jordan answered promptly. Cassie nodded her agreement. "The last guy you dated turned out to be a bigger jerk than most of the men we put in jail."

"I did a background check on him, and no, he didn't have a record." Jordan informed them with a twinkle in his eyes. "You definitely deserve someone better than him though. Maybe you should let one of us pick out a man for you to marry."

Kami smiled, "You didn't really do a background check on him did you?" When Jordan didn't answer she let out an exasperated sigh. "I swear, it's like having a big brother at work, always checking out my dates and intimidating them when he doesn't think they are good enough for me. Cassie can't you keep him in line?"

Cassie looked at her with amusement. "Like anyone can control him."

"Well, at least having you two around is good for my ego, and no thank you, I think I can find a man on my own. Even if there are a few frogs before I find my prince."

"Like she needs any help with her ego," Cassie muttered, and they all laughed.

"What's so funny?" Aurora asked as she strolled into the front hall carrying the rest of her luggage. Jordan was mesmerized by the way she walked. She was as graceful as a model and she had absolutely no idea what effect she had on men. When she walked through a room every man strained his neck to look at her. She was completely oblivious to all the attention she attracted. That was something he didn't understand. She was gorgeous and she had no idea. She thought she was plain that she was just like any other woman. She didn't know how wrong she was! But that was part of her appeal. She didn't try to attract male attention. Her appeal was completely natural.

He sat the suitcases he'd been holding down and pulled her to his side. "Just two of the nosiest FBI agents in the world discussing my proposal." He watched her reaction, not sure what to expect. He was relieved when she sat her suitcases down and turned to Kami and Cassie with a delighted twinkle in her eyes.

"You heard?" She looked back and forth between Kami and Cassie. Kami nodded and Cassie smiled. "Wasn't that the most romantic proposal in the world?" Aurora beamed at them.

"That's exactly what I was saying." Kami looked over at Jordan and smiled smugly, "See I told you. Now I want to see this ring, Aurora."

Aurora proudly held out her left hand for inspection and reveled in the compliments that flowed freely from Kami.

When Kami was done inspecting the ring, Cassie silently

inspected the ring. She smiled softly at Aurora and said quietly, "It's beautiful. It's just perfect for you." She met Jordan's eyes above Aurora's head and nodded. It meant a lot to him to have Cassie and Kami's support. Of course he didn't believe that anyone could dislike Aurora. He gazed down at her, right now she would perfectly match the description of a blushing bride he thought happily and pulled her a little closer to his side.

He really hadn't planned on proposing today, but after what had happened he didn't want another minute, much less another day, to go by without making sure that Aurora knew exactly how much he loved her and wanted to be with her. He had known for years that she was the only woman for him, but the night she came home with him, he felt the full force of his love. He knew that he still wanted to marry her but debated about buying her a new ring. He wasn't sure how she would feel about him keeping her ring, but never even considered getting rid of the ring. In the end, he decided that he would never find another ring more perfectly suited for Aurora. It wasn't a normal engagement ring, it was actually quite unusual. That is why this ring was perfect for his Aurora. The center stone was a heart shaped diamond. Outlining that diamond was a row of tiny, bright red rubies. They sparkle like fire when the light catches them just right. On the left side of the diamond and rubies is a smaller dark green emerald heart, and on the right side is the same size dark blue sapphire heart. All this was set in a gold and silver swirled band that perfectly accented the stones.

It was a beautiful ring, but not near as beautiful as the woman who was wearing it. He stared down at her, enjoying just watching her interacting with his friends. Not paying any attention to the conversation going on around him.

"Right Jordan?"

"Huh?" He said jerking his attention back to what the women were saying.

All three of them were staring at him waiting for his reply to a question he didn't even hear. Jordan felt a little self-conscious being the center of attention all of a sudden and having nothing to say. He cleared his throat his shirt collar feeling suddenly too tight, "Can you repeat the question?" All three women stared at him in seeming disbelief for a moment and then Kami asked, "Where exactly did you go spaceman?"

He squirmed uncomfortably and avoided the question. "I think we need to get on the road now. Someone could come any minute and we wouldn't be ready for them."

Kami and Cassie nodded looking at him strangely. They let him off the hook easily, too easily he thought. Aurora looked at him quizzically but didn't ask any questions. When he saw the amused expressions on his friend's faces before they turned and led the way out the door he leaned down and whispered in Aurora's ear, "What did I miss?"

Aurora hid her smile and whispered back, "They had just been discussing how quickly we needed to leave, and asked your opinion. What exactly were you thinking about?"

Jordan felt a blush creeping up his neck and onto his face, but there was nothing he could do to stop it. He really should have been paying attention to the case and not how beautiful his bride-to-be is.

"I'm more intrigued now than ever, why are you blushing like that?"

"I was actually thinking about you, and how beautiful you are." He answered her honestly.

"Oh."

"What no smart comebacks?"

"Only that you had a good subject to think about." She smiled contentedly at him and he kissed the tip of her nose.

"You'll get no argument from me. Now we'd better hurry and catch up with those two before they leave us. Otherwise we'll never hear the end of it from those two. Believe me, they know just how and when to bring up things to cause the most embarrassment possible."

Aurora grinned and they hurried to catch up.

***

"Where are we gonna stay now?" Aurora questioned as she saw the lights of Los Angeles appearing before them. A sudden sense of panic welling up in her, even though she knew that she wasn't in any immediate danger. She tried to shake off the feeling.

"My house." Cassie answered without turning around. Kami had let Cassie drive her car back to Los Angeles. Both she and Jordan had agreed that Cassie was by far the best driver if a crisis came up.

"It's a beautiful house." Kami turned and enthusiasm lit her face as she explained. "Cassie decorated it herself and I personally think it's the most beautiful house in Los Angeles."

"You're just saying that so I'll come out and help you decorate your apartment." Cassie accused.

"No I'm not." Kami denied sounding offended. Cassie slanted her a look that everyone knew meant she didn't believe a word of what Kami was saying.

"But a little help never hurt anyone." Kami finally admitted.

"See, I told you that you had an ulterior motive." Kami made a face that luckily Cassie didn't see. Aurora laughed at their humorous byplay, her uneasiness fading, and she leaned back into Jordan.

***

"It really is a gorgeous house Cassie." Aurora said as she walked back into the living room. Being a cop she liked to know all the ways to get in or out of any place she was in, but when she had looked through the house she had been amazed at its beauty. Kami had given her the royal tour while Jordan and Cassie sat up a state-of-the-art surveillance system. Kami had told Aurora that her favorite room was the dining room because of the beautiful chandelier that hung directly over the table. The dining room was very formal, even though it was beautiful, and after her tour, Aurora silently agreed with Kami on her choice of rooms.

"Is everything set?"

"Almost, Cassie is working on the last of it. You can go to bed and sleep through the night without a worry." Jordan told her. "There isn't an inch of this place that isn't covered by a camera."

"I'm not sure if that is good or bad." Kami muttered looking around suspiciously, and Aurora giggled.

"You must be tired." Jordan slanted her a sideways look.

"What makes you say that?"

"That giggle."

"You don't like my laugh?" She pouted, hiding a smile at his uncomfortable look. She really shouldn't tease him in front of his friends like this, but he was so cute when he didn't know what to say.

"I adore it, but that's not the point. The point is I know by the sound of that giggle, you're tired." Jordan explained patiently. "You need to get some sleep."

Aurora waved a dismissive hand at his comment but couldn't cover up the yawn that followed. Jordan gave her an 'I told you so' look and she smiled sheepishly at him, but made no move to go to bed.

For safety reasons, all four of them had agreed to stay at Cassie's house throughout the rest of the investigation. Since her house had five bedrooms there was more than enough room for all of them. Each room was decorated in a different theme and there were colorful paintings on every wall. Kami's room had a Spanish theme with sombreros and decorative rugs everywhere. Cassie's room was girlie. It was the only way Aurora could describe it. There was pink and frills everywhere. She wasn't sure how that room fit her image of Cassie but then again she really didn't know the woman.

Jordan's room was decorated in a sort of gothic style. There were pictures of gargoyles and the room was a dark gray. Aurora would never have thought to use those as a decoration but the room had its own appeal. The room Aurora was staying in had a western theme to its décor. There were paintings of cowboys and old barns covering the wall, and the border was tan with black and brown horses trying to buck cowboys off. She wondered who had decorated the rooms. Whoever it was had a wide range of tastes.

"I love the room I'm staying in; it makes me feel like a cowgirl."

Kami looked over at her amused. "Have you ever even seen a cow?"

"Yes!" She answered indignantly pulling herself up to stretch out her meager inches.

"Where?" Kami quizzed, obviously not believing her.

"When I went down to meet Jordan's parents. They live on a farm, and it had cows and horses, and everything." She told Kami enthusiastically. Kami smiled and exchanged a look with Cassie. "It must be love."

"Definitely, if she is this excited about seeing a cow." Cassie agreed.

Aurora ignored their teasing, but sneaked a glance at Jordan. He seemed to be enjoying watching their antics. "How did you ever get a house like this in the middle of Los Angeles?" Aurora asked to change the subject. Cassie and Kami looked amused at her obvious change in subject but luckily they didn't resume their teasing. In reality, Aurora was awed by how large the house was, especially for one person.

"My parents owned it, but gave it to me when they found a house they liked better and moved to Florida." Cassie answered distractedly. She was setting up the last of the cameras in the living room.

"That was sweet of them." Kami said.

"I thought so. Anyways, it's time for bed everyone. We've got to be rested so we can catch bad guys tomorrow." Cassie said in an authoritative voice. She was only slightly older than the rest of them, but she definitely held all the authority in the group.

"Yes, *mother*." Kami teased, but immediately got up to comply when Cassie gave her a look. "Good night everyone." She said sweetly.

"Good night."

"I'm exhausted." Aurora said falling back into the couch.

"I told you earlier to go to bed." Jordan pointed out.

"That's why I didn't. You know I don't take orders well." She said smiling impishly. Jordan smiled down at her and then reached down and grabbed her hand. Then he pulled her to her feet as if she weighed nothing, and right into his arms. He gave her a quick hug and kissed the top of her head.

"Now go to bed."

"You're bossy." She mumbled as she turned and walked towards her room. Jordan didn't take his eyes off of her until she went into her bedroom and shut the door.

"You're love-struck." Cassie commented when she caught him watching Aurora walk down the hall.

"Guilty." He answered with an easy grin then reluctantly turned his gaze to Cassie.

"It's good to see you this happy Jordan."

"Thanks, it's good to be this happy. I feel like I'm flying." He said as he started dancing around. He knew he looked crazy but he didn't care.

"And you're acting like an idiot." She laughed.

He stopped mid step, and looked over at her in mock concern. "That's a good thing right?"

"Absolutely." She agreed quickly. "Now go to bed so I can finish setting this thing up." She pointed to the camera. "Oh, and get someone out to your house to pick up those dogs."

"Need any help?"

"Nope. Only peace and quiet." She told him pointedly, and Jordan was slightly concerned. She'd been prickly ever since her boyfriend of over a year, Sam, had left her for some bimbo at his office, some secretary or something. But who could blame her? She'd been head over hills for the guy and he'd been scum. Actually lower than that but that was the only thing that came to mind at the time. When he'd left her, Jordan had wanted to kill the guy for his stupidity.

She had told him at the time that the guy wasn't worth it and she had been right, but he knew how much it had hurt her to admit that fact. They were supposed to be married in less than six months but Sam hadn't gotten her a ring yet. He said that he couldn't find the right one for her and she had believed him. They had the whole wedding planned out a date set and were supposedly going to order invitations the week he left her.

She never once had any clue that he was cheating on her the whole time. The man was a first class idiot. No man could find a better woman than Cassie Williams, well except Aurora. The guy had used her job as the excuse that things hadn't worked out and Jordan always thought that Cassie had blamed herself. Thought that she wasn't good enough. They always joked with Kami about the men she dated because she was a bum magnet. If there was a bum anywhere around, she attracted them. Cassie was a quieter, more self-reliant person when it came to matters of the heart.

He loved Cassie like a sister and the jerk had made her cry. He would love to make the guy feel pain over the tears that he had seen Cassie shed. He'd never liked the guy and even told Cassie he wasn't good enough for her but she'd just brushed his comments aside. Jordan had put up with the guy only to make Cassie happy. He and Cassie had entered the FBI about the same time; she was just a little before him. They'd become instant friends even though at the time he and Lance had been inseparable. Both he and Lance had relied on her different times to cover their backs. Now she was one of the few people he trusted without question.

It was strange but the whole time she'd been with this guy, Jordan had never even believed they would get married. Even when the wedding date was set, he hadn't believed it. He'd acted happy for her but he'd never really felt it. He supposed it could have been because he never liked the guy, but in reality the reason was because he'd always thought Cassie and Rick would get together. They were a perfect match even if they wouldn't admit it. He hoped someday they would realize it but until then he would try to be careful, but give them every opportunity to spend time together. It was a devious plan, especially when Cassie was still supposedly getting over that scum Sam, but Jordan thought maybe it had been long enough.

Jordan really had forgotten in his happiness that Cassie was possibly still hurting. It had been over a year, but he believed that she really believed she loved Sam and you don't just get over love over night. He knew that from experience. He would have to be a little more careful so it didn't seem like he was rubbing his and Aurora's love in her face.

She'd been there to help him through difficult times and now she was clammed up and wouldn't talk about the jerk at all. But when she wanted to talk, he hoped she knew that he would be there for her. He silently studied her for a moment more and then nodded.

"Ok. I can take a hint. Good night Cas."

"G' night, Jordan." She was relieved for some time alone. It wasn't their fault but Jordan and Aurora had reminded her of happier times. She was happy for them really; it was just that she wanted the same happiness for herself. She'd thought she found it with Sam but she'd been wrong. It might have worked out for her, if only she wasn't an FBI agent, but that was nothing she could change now. Nothing she wanted to change. It was better this way. At least they hadn't gotten married and had kids when he decided to leave. At the time, she'd been so sure she was in love with him, but now that she looked back on it, she thought maybe he was just who she got comfortable with. It was time to move on. A man with dark hair and blue eyes flashed through her mind. If only she was strong enough to take the chance…

CHAPTER 15

Jordan jerked awake at the sound of Aurora's scream. It was a blood-curdling scream that scared him to death. *Oh Lord, please don't let anything happen to her.* He prayed as he sprang out of bed and raced across the hall. Cassie and Kami came running out of their rooms and they all met at Aurora's door. Each of them with guns ready. Cassie nodded and Jordan flung the door open and peered inside. It was completely dark and nothing looked wrong. Jordan's brow wrinkled in concern.

"Aurora? Honey are you alright?" He called, but the only noise he heard in the room was the pounding of his own heart and whimpering coming from the vicinity of the bed. He glanced back at Kami and Cassie with a questioning look and Cassie nodded towards the light. With Kami and Cassie covering his back, he flipped on the light and stepped into the room.

Then he saw her. Aurora was lying in the middle of her bed still deeply asleep, but thrashing violently. The sheets were all tangled and she seemed terrified.

"*Lance!*" Her strangled cry tore at Jordan's heart. Aurora had tears streaming down her cheeks and she was sobbing, reaching out towards some unknown something. Jordan felt like he'd been punched in the gut. She looked so helpless and alone. He knew she was dreaming about that night at the lake and there was nothing he could do to help her in that dream. He'd seen the after affects from one of her nightmares when they'd been at his house. It had completely drained her of energy and it hadn't been nearly as bad as this dream obviously was. He wasn't sure he wanted to see the terror in her eyes when she woke up but he knew he had to be there for her. No matter what, he would always be there for her.

He turned back to Kami and Cassie and met their sympathy filled gazes. He was completely at a loss. What should he do? He'd never seen her like this and didn't know how she would react to anything.

"What do you want us to do?" Kami asked sympathetically her eyes filled with silent tears of her own. Even though Kami seemed to have a very flippant attitude, it was only to disguise how empathetic she really was. Right now she was feeling both Jordan and Aurora's pain. He was so thankful that he had her for a partner.

He struggled with her question for a moment before answering. "I'll handle it. You two go back to bed, I'll yell if I need any help. I know Aurora well enough to know that she would rather you two not be there when she wakes up. She'll be embarrassed enough as it is because she woke everyone up."

"Ok, Jordan. We'll leave. Just call if you need us." Cassie told him quietly and put a reassuring hand on his shoulder.

He nodded to them silently and turned back to Aurora while they walked slowly back to their rooms. Aurora was lying still now but she was curled into a ball in the middle of her bed whimpering pathetically. He silently wondered how often she had this kind of nightmare. He felt so helpless. He couldn't do anything to help her with this. His heart ached for her as he moved to her side and sat on the edge of the bed. He was afraid that he would scare her if he touched her. So he called to her softly, "Aurora?" When she didn't answer he said her name louder, but still got no response. "Honey, you've got to wake up." He told her as he reached out and laid a hand on her arm. He immediately wished he hadn't.

The moment he touched her, Aurora sprang up and knocked him off the edge of the bed. Jordan's head barely missed the bedside table as he fell. Then she landed on top of him with her fists flying. He lay there completely stunned for a moment, and then his training took over. He rolled and pinned her with his own body weight. She struggled against him and he had to be careful not to hurt them both while he was trying to calm her down. He looked down into her face, hoping to see some recognition in her eyes. Maybe after she realized it was him she would settle down. He was shocked when he realized that her eyes were still closed and there were still silent tears falling down her cheeks. *She's still completely asleep! She doesn't even know it's me here, but she's fighting someone or something from her nightmare!* He realized completely baffled, but anger surged through him at the man who'd put her through this. He would really like to get his hands on the guy before he was arrested. He would beat him to a pulp.

"Aurora wake up!" He commanded in a voice that made most suspects cringe in fear. But whenever he talked to her she grew more violent. So, Jordan gently but firmly held both of her hands above her head with one arm and reached out and lightly slapped her face.

Her eyes flew open at the light contact. "Jordan?" She asked in a scared, confused whisper her eyes were completely unfocused as they darted around taking in her surroundings. He could see she was completely disoriented and terrified at being in such unfamiliar surroundings.

"It ok, honey. It was only a dream." He assured her as he released her and moved off of her so she could breathe. She gratefully sucked in a full breath of air, and sat up. She wrapped her arms around her waist and rocked herself quietly.

Jordan watched as she fought for control. She was doing her best to hold back the sobs, and he couldn't bear to watch her fight for control of her emotions in front of him. He reached out and gathered her into his arms and rocked her as he would a small child, and she gave in to the sobs. After a few moments, she calmed down but her sobs had turned into hiccups.

She pulled back to look at him. She still looked too pale for Jordan's liking, but dreaming about your brother being shot in front of you when there was nothing you could do to stop it, would do that to anyone. Especially someone like Aurora. Lance had been the only family she had and they'd been the closest siblings Jordan had ever known. There was nothing they wouldn't have done for each other.

"Did I wake everyone up?" She asked miserably between hiccups, he would have laughed out right if she hadn't looked so pathetic. He was so relieved that she was all right and thinking about how crazy it was that she was worried about waking everyone else up when she was the one who was obviously having the problems. When he'd heard her scream he had feared the worst. He thought maybe someone had gotten to her and was trying to kill her again. That fear had made his blood run cold in his veins. He never wanted to have that fear again, three times in less than a week was more than enough for his lifetime.

"Yes, but Kami and Cassie went back to bed when we realized it was a nightmare. They thought you might appreciate them not being here when you woke up."

"Remind me to thank them later. At least they didn't see me attack you. Are you ok?" She asked rubbing the blood from a small scratch on his cheek.

"I'm fine." He assured her, although, he was pretty sure that he would have a black eye in the morning. That would definitely take some explaining. He could just see the looks on the faces of the men he worked with when he told them that his fiancé gave it to him. Not to mention the fact that she gave it to him the same night that he proposed to her, he thought ruefully. Maybe he should leave that part out. He would get ribbed enough as it was without throwing that extra detail in.

"I'm so sorry." She moaned pitifully, sounding on the verge of tears again.

"There was nothing you could do about it. You were asleep." He pointed out, trying to make her feel better but that didn't seem to ease her gloomy mood.

"I've not had that bad of a nightmare since the morning Joe was shot. He woke me up about the same way as you did except he pinned me *before* he tried to touch me." She told him pointedly.

"Smart man. I'll bet that he didn't get socked in the jaw, but he could have passed on the information. It would have been useful." Jordan teased, trying to lighten the mood.

"On the stakeout I had these dreams almost every night." She whispered and leaned her head back against his shoulder. "This one was different. I'm not sure what, but I think I remembered something in this dream I've never remembered before. Something important to the case, but I can't put my finger on what." Her brow puckered in concentration. Then she sighed, aggravated that she couldn't remember such an important detail. "Can we go for a walk? I can't just sit here and think about it or I will go crazy." Her look was hopeful.

Jordan knew she already knew the answer to her question but still felt like a heel having to refuse her. He wanted to be able to give her anything she asked for.

"No we have to stay within the secured area, I'm sorry." When he saw the defeated look in her eyes, he remembered something. "But Cassie does have a workout room in her basement. You could beat up on a punching bag for a while or jog on a treadmill. Whatever you'd like." Her mood visibly brightened, and Jordan felt good that he was the one who made her happy at a time like this.

"Beating up something other than you, sounds wonderful at the moment. My muscles feel so tense that I think they're gonna snap." She said rolling her neck. Jordan stood up and helped her up. "Get ready and I'll meet you in the living room in a couple of minutes. After you have used up all your frustration, I'll massage your back, if you'd like." He offered, knowing how much she loved massages.

"You don't have to. It's three in the morning, go back to bed." She coaxed him, but it was obvious from the look he slanted her that he wasn't going to take her advice.

He completely ignored her pleading and leaned over and kissed her forehead, "Hurry up, Lady."

As he walked out she smiled to herself. She hadn't really wanted to be alone right now but she hadn't wanted Jordan to miss sleep just because she had a nightmare. She shivered involuntarily as she thought about that night at the lake. She definitely didn't want to be alone. All the memories seemed so much worse when they were the only thing to think about, when there was no one there to distract her. Jordan had known her well enough to know she hadn't wanted to be alone, and that's why he hadn't gone back to bed. He knew she needed someone there with her while she was dealing with this dream... not someone *him*.

She was a really lucky woman to have a man like Jordan. He was there for her when she needed him. She glanced down at her ring again still unable to believe that they were actually engaged. Was it only a few days ago that they had met again at the hospital? It seemed like an eternity ago. One thing was for sure; she wasn't going to let him get away again.

***

J.D., Daniel, and Corey, the names kept circling over and over in her mind. One of these three men was a traitor! How could that be? She'd trusted all three of these men with her life since she'd joined the force. All three of them had already been LAPD before she graduated from the academy. She swung harder at the punching bag, letting her frustration show. *Something in my dream was important! Why can't I remember?* Aurora punctuated that thought with a quick jab that stung her hand even through the glove. She continued to pound the punching bag, lost in thought.

She glanced at the man holding the punching bag for her. Jordan was so good to her. He didn't try to break the silence at all, but she knew he was there if she needed to talk. He knew right now she was trying to figure out the importance of her dream and he wasn't trying to distract her. She was grateful for his presence and his silence.

She had tried to remember every part of her dream. It had been the same as always, but there was something not right about it. She was at the lake, Lance had driven up, she was hit on the head, and the man had her gun. All of that was still as clear in her mind as if it were the day it happened. Then the man had shot. *That's it!* She mentally cheered and cried at the same time. This time she had seen a man's face when he pulled the trigger. She knew it hadn't been his voice at the lake, but it was a sign that she knew who the traitor was. Somehow she knew that the man's face she had seen in her dream was responsible for all the trouble in her life: Lance's death, Joe being shot, and even the attempts on Jordan's and her life. She knew she had the evidence somewhere in her files. She just had to find it.

***

Jordan had been holding the punching bag for over a half an hour while Aurora took out her frustration on it when she suddenly stopped mid swing. She looked at him with startled eyes.

"Did you ever get my files?" Her question came out in a rush.

"Kami was supposed to be bringing them. Why?" He didn't understand her sudden question, and then it hit him she'd remembered something from her dream. "What is it, Roar?"

"Nothing for sure... I need to look at my files." She was breathing a little hard from her workout, and felt like she needed a shower. But at the same time she felt wonderful, she was pretty sure that she knew who the traitor was. This meant her problems weren't almost over, but just beginning. The man she'd seen in her dream and starting to believe to be a traitor was one of her closest friends. She would not only have to find evidence against him, she would have to testify against him when it came to court. That would be one of the hardest days of her life. She bit her lip as she began to think. Her thoughts were running ninety to nothing. So many people had trusted that man with their lives so many times, it was a wonder her whole department wasn't dead! How could he have done this?

She silently scolded herself, *innocent until proven guilty. You need to remember that.*

"I'll go wake Kami up so she can tell me where they are." Jordan told her as he headed towards the door.

"No, don't wake her up. We can look for them ourselves, and if they aren't here we can wake her up later. We've all had a long night and I would hate to wake her up again. Especially if this turns out to be nothing."

"But that wouldn't be nearly as much fun." Jordan pointed out, grinning. "She's been spying on our very personal moments and interrupting us at very inopportune times these past few days. I think for all the trouble she's been being that she deserves to be gotten up early, don't you?" He asked with a wicked gleam in his eyes.

Aurora grinned mischievously. "Yeah. I totally agree. Wait on me and I'll help you." She walked towards him as she took off her boxing gloves.

"So should we use water balloons or a bucket of water?" Jordan asked as they climbed the stairs. Aurora laughed at his silly antics and the sound was music to his ears. *For us to have both come so close to being killed so many times in the last few days we are in extremely good spirits, thank you Lord.* Jordan prayed with a smile.

***

"This had better be good." Kami grumbled as she rolled out of bed to answer the persistent knocking at her door. If it had been an emergency they wouldn't have knocked so why in the world would someone be getting her out of bed at such a ghastly hour? She slowly opened the door and glared at Jordan and Aurora's smiling faces. She groaned.

"What are you two so happy about at almost four in the morning? Any normal person would be asleep right now."

Jordan didn't bother to answer her question. "Where did you put Aurora's files I asked you to get?"

"There still in the trunk of my car, why?" She asked sleepily, not bothering to hide her yawn. As soon as this discussion was over, she was going back to bed for at least a few more hours. If they didn't hurry up and tell her what was going on, she might just fall asleep leaning against the door.

"I may have remembered something." Aurora informed her smiling. Now that she thought about it more she was almost positive that she knew the identity of the traitor, all she needed now was the evidence to prove it. She was happy and sick at the same time.

Hearing that news, Kami was instantly wide-awake. "I'll go get them for you."

"Would you rather me go?" Jordan offered. "It's kinda cold out there tonight and I've already got my shoes on."

"Well, if you insist."

Jordan's steps were hurried as he walked towards the garage. They had put Kami's car in the garage and left Cassie's in the driveway. That way if anyone did suspect they were all staying here it wouldn't be as obvious, and if they came onto Cassie's property looking around, a camera would catch them. They really didn't expect to get that lucky but sometimes even the smartest criminals made a mistake. They'd already made the mistake of coming after Aurora. Stupid mistake. Now they were hoping Charles' men would make another mistake.

"You can go back to bed, now." Aurora told her. "We'll wake you if we find what we are looking for."

"Oh, no. You woke me up and now you've got to put up with me. Is there any coffee?"

"No, but I'll go and make some. You know I think you may be less of a morning person than I am, and that's saying a lot."

Kami made a face at her and followed her into the kitchen where Aurora started a fresh pot of coffee. It was strange that she felt so comfortable with Jordan's partner, but the silence they shared while waiting on Jordan was companionable. Not tense, as she'd feared.

"Here are your files." Jordan said as he sat down two boxes on the table. The kitchen wasn't nearly as formal as the dining room. Aurora felt comfortable in this room, but the dining room, even though beautiful, was more than slightly intimidating. "By the way how did you get these, Kam? I know all of them weren't at Aurora's apartment and you would have had to bulldoze your way through people to get anything from the cops."

Kami's eyes lit with mischief, and Jordan was somewhat afraid of her answer. But Kami didn't hesitate. "Well, there's this really hot

LAPD officer I think his name is Daniel Jenkins. Anyway, I went over to LAPD headquarters and talked with him a little..."

"Talked? Yeah, right. More like flirted!" Jordan interjected.

Kami smiled and continued as if Jordan hadn't interrupted her. "And I asked him for some help. He asked me if you were the one needing them and if we were keeping you safe. I told him you were and we were. Then he got me the files that were in Aurora's office and said that if I saw her to tell his 'big sis' hello and to stay out of trouble, but he knew that she wouldn't listen to him. He sounded genuinely concerned for you, Roar. He sent you a message to partner," she looked at Jordan with amusement written all over her face. "He said, tell agent Reiley to take care of her because she has a tendency to depend only on herself and that gets her into trouble sometimes. He didn't think anyone could keep her out of trouble but thought you might have the best chance out of everyone he knows."

Aurora smiled. Daniel sounded just like a protective brother. Even though they had been at the LAPD before her, Aurora had always thought of Daniel and J.D. as 'little brothers' and they referred to her as their 'big sis.' Even though both of them were a lot bigger than she was, and were actually a few years older. But it seemed like she was always getting them out of some sort of trouble. It was the kind of thing a big sister would do for her younger, troublesome brothers. The trouble they got into ranged anywhere from girls to problems at work. She had done everything for them from posing as their girlfriend in front of an old flame to make the girl jealous, to getting them out of shootouts unharmed. Those two men definitely made her life interesting, and one of them might be trying to have her killed. The thought ran unwanted through her mind, and she tried to shake off the feeling of trepidation that almost overwhelmed her.

Aurora hid her feelings and groaned good-naturedly at Kami. "You and Daniel? That would be an interesting match. Actually the two of you would probably do pretty well together; you seem to have quite a bit in common, now that I think about it. He has terrible taste in women and you have terrible taste in men, so maybe you've found your perfect match, Kami." Aurora teased to cover up her reluctance. She wasn't sure she wanted one of her 'little brothers' getting into a serious relationship with Jordan's partner. If something went wrong then there would always be tension when they were around each other and they were going to meet since she and Jordan were going to be married.

Kami smiled triumphantly at Jordan. "I thought so too, but anyways I knew he was one of the suspects so I told him that this was an FBI investigation and we thought there was some information in those files that might be helpful in putting Charles away for a long time. He was very willing to help. My gut tells me that he isn't the man we are looking for." Jordan shot her an amused look.

"Then again, we all know about how good I am at reading men." She admitted reluctantly.

"Well, maybe you're not the best judge of character, but I think I agree with you on this one. At least I hope you're right." Aurora told her as she opened the first of two boxes and started flipping through her files. She hoped there was someone else, anyone else, who could be the traitor but felt as if a huge weight were being put on her heart. One of her friends was dirty and there wasn't a thing she could do about it except find the evidence to prove it and have them put in jail where they couldn't hurt anyone else.

"What are you looking for? Maybe if you tell us we can find it." Jordan offered when he noticed she wasn't reading most of the files only scanning them and then moving on to the next one.

"I'm not sure exactly, but I'll know it when I see it." Aurora answered distractedly.

"Is there anything we can do to help?" Kami offered with a small yawn she tried to hide.

"No, it will just be some little something that didn't seem significant before, but I think when I see it now I'll know who the traitor is. The bad part is that it has been staring me in the face for the past five years, if I'm right." She admitted disgusted with herself for not realizing sooner all the inconsistencies in her search for Lance's murderer. Jordan lightly squeezed her shoulder and she smiled sleepily up at him. It had been a long night for all of them.

"The two of you really should go get some sleep. I won't be able to sleep until I find what I'm looking for and I'll come and wake you up as soon as I've found it."

"No." Jordan answered automatically.

Right now she needed to be alone to concentrate; it irked her that Jordan hadn't even considered her suggestion before he rejected it. She controlled her temper. She knew he was just worried about her.

She tried to keep her voice soft and patient even though that was the exact opposite of the way she felt. "Jordan, I'm a big girl. I can stay up all night by myself and besides when I find out who we're after you're gonna have to be well rested so you can arrest him and put him into jail without much of a fight." When Jordan started to protest again she put her hand on his arm and said, "I promise I'll wake you as soon as I've found something."

Kami nodded and turned to walk back to her room, leaving them alone to decide. She didn't want to be there if an argument occurred, but she thought maybe Jordan had met his match. Aurora seemed almost as stubborn as Kami's mule-headed partner. She smiled to herself, on second thought it could be very interesting to watch them battle this out, but she was too tired to eavesdrop tonight.

Jordan waited until Kami was out of earshot. "I still don't like it, Roar. You've just had a nightmare about your brother and now you want to look for the killer by yourself? I don't think it's a good idea."

"Jordan, I'm not really looking for the killer, I'm looking for evidence of who the killer is. The two are completely different. I'm not in any real danger. I'm just sitting here looking through files, the same thing I've done for the past week at your house. You need sleep, so go to bed. I'll be ok. I promise if I need you I know where you are sleeping and I'll come wake you up. Besides your eye is starting to turn black and it's making me feel guilty."

"Are you sure you're all right?" Jordan asked concerned completely ignoring her comment about his eye even though it did hurt.

"Positive, now stop worrying and go to bed."

"Ok, just be sure to wake me up when you solve this case." He warned.

"Will do, sir." She gave him a mock salute. He grimaced at her and then turned and walked towards his room.

Aurora sat alone for a moment in the silence before getting up and fixing herself a cup of the coffee she had put on for Kami. By the time the other three woke up Aurora was pretty sure that she would be working on her second pot of coffee.

She glared at the papers in front of her. There was evidence in here that one of her close friends was a traitor, and possibly a murderer. He had at the least set up an attempted murder. She needed some objective advice at the moment. She glanced at the clock; it was four-thirty in the morning. Oh well, she hadn't gotten any sleep tonight, so why should her partner? Besides Joe was use to her calling at all times of the night to talk to either him or Alex. She was a night owl and it used to drive him crazy but he'd gotten used to it over the years. She needed to hear his voice for reassurance anyway.

CHAPTER 16

Joe couldn't shake the nagging feeling that he needed to talk to Aurora but he had been trying to reach them at Jordan's house since about ten o'clock but all he got was the answering machine. It wasn't like Jordan to just disappear with Aurora without letting him know. Unless something had happened.

He fidgeted worriedly on his hospital bed. Where could they be? He'd try them one more time. Besides, what else was he going to do at night in a hospital? There was too much noise to sleep and he'd sent Alex home hours ago to get some much-needed sleep. There was no use in both of them being stuck here and neither of them getting any sleep all night. It had taken him over an hour to convince Alex of that, and now she was safe at home asleep. Now if only he could only talk to Aurora and make sure that she was ok. Joe reached for the phone but it rang as soon as he touched it.

He immediately picked it up, "Aurora?"

"Hi, Joe."

"Hey beautiful. What's wrong? You sound more tired than I feel. Did you have another nightmare? Where are you?" He relaxed knowing that if she was in immediate danger she would have already said or asked for whatever she needed.

"It's nice to hear you're voice too, partner." Aurora teased.

"What's wrong?" He insisted, the uneasy feeling he'd had all night was still with him and he wouldn't be able to shake it until he knew for sure that she was all right.

"I just missed the sound of your voice." She was stalling for time and knew it would be obvious to her partner. She knew Joe wouldn't be happy when he learned that Garland, a professional assassin, had been sent to kill her and she wanted to stall as long as possible before she told him. Her partner had a tendency to be a bit overprotective of her and right now there was nothing he could do for her besides listen to her problems and give advice. Joe was a hands-on person and it would drive him crazy to not be in the middle of this when he found out all of the details.

Joe wasn't fooled for a minute. "Come on Aurora, spill. Why are you calling me at four-thirty in the morning, and why aren't you at Jordan's?"

"You're awfully persistent, has anyone ever told you that?" Aurora couldn't resist trying to shock him so she said, "besides, my fiancé went to bed and left me awake, alone in a strange house." She'd compromised. There was good news and bad news tonight. Actually more bad news than good, but her good news was the best news in the world, in her opinion of course. Besides, bad news was always better when told after really, really good news.

"Your fiancé?" Joe asked in disbelief. He sounded happy but unsure if he had heard her right at the same time.

Aurora laughed at her partner's obvious skepticism and couldn't resist giving him a hard time about it. "Yes, you know the hunk that is now my bodyguard, FBI agent, my former fiancé? Any of that ring a bell?"

"Yes, but when? How? Why so sudden? I figured it would take him at least a week or two." Joe answered, only half kidding he knew how eager Jordan was to have Aurora back in his life but this was so sudden.

"Well, it didn't help that last night someone tried to kill us. Again. Have you ever heard of the assassin Garland?" Aurora quizzed.

"I vaguely remember hearing about him. He has evaded law

enforcement agencies for years. He's supposed to be the best gun that money can buy. Why?"

"He has now been taken off of the most wanted list."

"What do you mean?" He asked confused by her answers but immediately on guard.

She released a long breath and launched right into her story. "I mean that Garland was hired to kill me, and when Jordan started protecting me, apparently he was added to the hit list. Tonight we were run off the road and Garland would have killed us except that Jordan's friend and coworker Cassie Williams shot him before he could shoot us and he is now in a morgue."

"Are you all right?" Joe asked alarmed. He was aggravated and frustrated that he couldn't be out there helping his partner when she needed him most. Maybe he could talk the doctor into releasing him early.

"Don't even think about it." Aurora warned.

"What?" Joe asked innocently.

"I can almost hear the wheels turning in your head. There is no way you are getting out of the hospital to protect me." She said forcefully.

"Why are you so sure that I was even thinking about it?" He was relieved that she was still 'in tune' with him. They were as good of friends as they were partners, and she knew right now he was worried about her and would do everything in his power to keep her safe.

"I've known you long enough to know that you are an overly protective friend. Besides, I would feel the same way if it were me in that hospital bed and someone was trying to kill you. Besides you've already got an overprotective bodyguard watching me. I love you for being so protective, but I've not told you the worst of my news yet."

"You mean there's more?"

"Yes, and it involves LAPD." She answered slowly unsure of his reaction to what she was about to tell him.

"Tell me, and don't leave any detail out." He demanded. For a man lying in a hospital bed with a bullet wound, he was still someone she wouldn't want to cross. Aurora told him the whole story, from the FBI suspecting a LAPD officer to the names of the men now suspected and then she told him her theory of who it was because of what she'd seen in her dream.

Joe let out a low whistle that hurt so bad he winced. He was going to have to remember not to do things like that for a while. They had his chest taped and the tape pulled when he breathed deep. "Do you have any evidence to back up your theory?"

"Not at the moment. I think it is here in my files, if only I can find it. Other than that all I have is my dream and I really don't think that will hold up in a trial." She sounded frustrated, and Joe couldn't blame her. He felt frustrated.

At first he hadn't wanted to believe that anyone on the force was capable of that kind of deception, but Aurora's argument made sense. He had a terrible feeling that she was right about the culprit too, and that scared him worse than anything. If she knew who he was and could identify him, she'd just put herself at higher risk, and there was nothing he could do from the hospital bed that he was told he had to stay in for at least two more days. He had to trust in Jordan and his team to keep her safe something he didn't doubt they could do he just wanted to be there to make sure they did it right.

"If the evidence is there, you'll find it Roar. You're the best cop on the force at finding things that no one else even notices." He encouraged her.

"Thanks, Joe. I needed that. By the way, when Alex gets back, go ahead and tell her about my decision about God and about my engagement to Jordan." Joe knew by the sound of her voice that Aurora knew the consequences of the position she was putting herself in and he was thankful that since she was putting herself in that position, at least now she was right with God. He silently thanked God for his many blessings. "By the way, Jordan said that he wishes you would have passed on the information of how to wake me up from one of those dreams." Aurora informed him with a smile in her voice.

"The poor guy. What did you do to him?" Joe felt sympathy for his friend. Aurora was a bear no matter when she was awakened, and that was one of the reasons she had the nickname Roar, but he'd seen first hand what she was like when she'd been having a nightmare about the night Lance was murdered. He winced as he thought about the pain she'd probably inflicted on Jordan.

"Well, after I knocked him onto the floor, I scratched and punched him. Other than that I was as nice as I could be to him. I told him you'd had enough common sense to pin me before you tried to wake me up."

"So, is he going to have a black eye the next time I see him?"

"It's a good possibility." Aurora admitted sheepishly and Joe laughed so loud that one of the nurses on duty stepped in to check on him. He waved her out of the room with a smile and she looked at him like he was crazy before she left.

"Remind me to give Jordan a few pointers the next time I see him on how to handle you." Aurora snorted at his suggestion. "Oh, I just remembered!" He sat up bolt right in his bed. Chastening himself for forgetting to tell Aurora the best news in the world. He grinned from ear to ear, just thinking about it.

"What?"

"You're going to be an aunt." Joe said proudly.

He couldn't contain his excitement. He and Alex had agreed that whoever talked to Aurora next would tell her as soon as possible. They knew she was in a dangerous situation and neither of them wanted something to happen to her and she not know about the baby.

"Huh?" She was now completely confused. How could she be an aunt?

Joe chuckled at her denseness and then explained slowly. "Alex is pregnant. We're going to have a baby. You're going to be an aunt."

There was a deafening silence on the other end of the line for a few moments while the news sunk in and then Joe heard a loud *whoop* of joy. "You're serious, Joe? You aren't kidding me are you?" She looked around quickly to make sure she hadn't woke anyone up with her happiness.

"I'm completely serious." Joe answered his joy matching Aurora's.

"Congratulations! When did you find out?"

"Just this morning. You're the first person I've told."

"Thank you." Aurora said softly, overwhelmed by the sweetness of the moment. It hit her full force what she had been missing for the past few years. She'd been there for her friends, but she hadn't let them be there for her. There was no telling how many moments like this she had missed over the years. "Tell Alex I said congratulations too, ok?"

"Absolutely." Joe sensed her mood change but said nothing. He knew that she would feel guilty about the last five years and knew there was nothing he could say to change that. He would just be here for her when she needed him. The best he could do right now was to put her mind back to a happier subject. "So is the wedding going to be before or after the baby is born?"

"That depends. When is the due date?"

"June first."

"Before." Aurora replied promptly and Joe laughed. "Does Jordan know this?"

"Not yet, but I don't think he'll object. Do you?"

"Nope. You tell him when and where and that man will show up to marry you no matter what he has to do to get there. I think he would break every law in the book if necessary." Joe teased, and Aurora felt herself blush.

She knew Jordan loved her, but she didn't realize that it was that obvious to everyone else. She wondered if it had been that obvious that she was still in love with him but didn't want to ask her partner because she was afraid she'd been as transparent as Jordan seemed to be.

"I guess as soon as this investigation is over we need to set a date and send out invitations. Alex will kill me if I wait too long and she has to have her maid of honor dress adjusted ten times because of her growing belly." Aurora laughed.

"Definitely finish the case soon so you can come home." Joe told her quietly.

"I'll be home as soon as I can. Oh, and by the way *dad*... can I bring a boy home for dinner?" She teased. "You do know that you'll have to get used to that before too long don't you?"

"Not if the baby's a boy." Joe pointed out.

Aurora scoffed at the idea. "Not possible. Alex wouldn't do something like that, it's gonna be a girl."

Joe laughed, "And what makes you so sure about that?"

"Woman's intuition." Aurora answered with a laugh of her own. It had been too long since she and Joe had talked like this and it felt good to be able to laugh and joke with her friend.

"I'll tell Alex you said that."

"You do that Joe. And, Joe?"

"Hmm?" He was starting to sound tired and Aurora wondered if the doctor had given him some pain medicine.

"Get some rest. I'm as safe as I can be at the moment, and I'm gonna solve this case as quickly as possible. You concentrate on getting well. Jordan won't want one of his groomsmen to look like he just got out of the hospital or something."

"Ok, Aurora. Go to work and solve this case. I'm ready for you to come home. Besides, Alex is worrying about you." Aurora knew Alex wasn't the only one worrying about her. It was obvious from her partner's voice he was worried too.

"Tell her I'm fine and I'll try to be home in time for dinner Friday."

"That's only two days away." Joe pointed out.

"Then I guess I'll have to work fast, huh? Now get some sleep."

"Stay safe, Roar."

"Always. Good night Joe."

"Night."

Aurora hung up the phone more determined than ever to solve this case. She had a *niece* that she had to get ready for and a wedding to plan before her friend got the size of a whale. Aurora giggled at the mental picture she had of petite, little Alex pregnant. She would be beautiful, there was no doubt in Aurora's mind, but this would definitely be something she didn't want to miss. For once in her lifetime, Aurora would be smaller than Alex. That was one thing she wouldn't miss for the world, and she would take pictures so she would have proof! Otherwise Alex would never admit it.

She glanced at the clock amazed to find that she'd been on the phone with Joe for almost an hour, but talking to him had helped her. He was someone not directly involved with the investigation of this case that she knew she could talk to and he would give her his honest opinion. He hadn't been overly surprised about a LAPD officer suspected to be dirty, but he had seemed to be surprised at the suspects. There was a bitter sweetness to knowing that her partner had agreed with her on who she believed the traitor was. There was only one question running through her head now, *why?*

Aurora took a sip of her coffee and grimaced, it was cold. She got up and refilled her cup with hot coffee and then dove into the files. The evidence she needed was somewhere in this pile just waiting to be found, and she wouldn't rest until she found it.

CHAPTER 17

She'd found it! It had taken a little over three and a half hours, but she'd found it! It had been like piecing a jigsaw puzzle together all night, but the end result was amazing. And terrifying! She never would have imagined such an elaborate set up. She would have never known her report of that night had been doctored if she hadn't seen this original. Every other time she'd only seen a copy of what she'd written, but this was her actual report. Someone, someone she'd trusted with her and her friend's lives had done this to her.

She felt like dancing and crying at the same time. For the most part, she was happy that this whole ordeal would soon be behind her and she could move on with her life, but there was a part of her that died inside knowing that her friend was capable of conspiring with a criminal mastermind like Charles. He not only conspired but set up his own people, his fellow LAPD officers to be killed or captured.

"Jordan, wake up." Aurora hollered excitedly as she raced into his room.

"No." Jordan answered without opening his eyes. If she hadn't been so excited Aurora might have felt bad about waking him after the long night they'd had, but as it was she had to show someone her evidence or she would burst.

She shook his shoulder and grinned when he finally, even if somewhat reluctantly, opened his eyes. She waved a piece of paper in front of his nose and he squinted, trying to read as she waved it back and forth. He finally grabbed it and held it still so he could read it. When he looked up at her there was sympathy as well as triumph in his gaze. They now had the evidence to convict the man, but he was one of Aurora's friends and her dream had been right. He knew this was hurting her inside, but the end to all of this was now in sight.

She loved this man like family and he'd betrayed her. Not only her, but also he'd betrayed the rest of the people she considered family, people she'd thought he considered his family too.

"That's not all of it either." Aurora informed him triumphantly hiding her true feelings of hurt and confusion over her friend's actions. She was happy about finding the information. Really. It just hurt more than she could say that her friend had betrayed her. "There is more that shows he tipped Charles off on a lot of drug raids. That's how Charles has kept from being caught all these years. It wasn't because of 'luck' or bad timing on our part, it was because he's had a cop in his back pocket this whole time."

"You know this proves he set you and Lance up five years ago, don't you?" Jordan asked her gently. He wasn't sure if she had realized this man had set her brother up to be killed yet or not, and he had to ask. He didn't want there to be anymore horrible surprises waiting for her to discover. He watched as sadness filled her eyes and all the joy of finding the confirmation of a traitor faded from her face.

Aurora nodded, unable to speak and tears prickled the backs of her eyelids. Jordan got up and folded her into his arms.

"He couldn't have known that man would kill Lance. Could he? He wouldn't have been that cruel to me." She had to ask, but wasn't sure that she wanted to know the answer. She'd been searching for Lance's killer for five years and now she still hadn't found the man who pulled the trigger, but she'd found the man who'd given him the information to do it. She knew there would be more investigating into Lance's murder, but she was still having trouble understanding the fact that someone she'd trusted had sent someone to kill not only her but also, Lance, Joe, and Jordan. She felt free of a burden but had a heavy heart at the same time.

"I don't know, honey." Jordan answered honestly and kissed the top of her head. "Why don't we get Cassie and Kami and go ask him?"

Aurora stepped back and nodded, then turned to go wake Kami and Cassie. She stopped at the door and turned back to Jordan, and he was surprised to see the joy back in her eyes.

"I almost forgot. I'm gonna be an aunt." She announced happily.

Jordan grinned, his first real smile of the day. "Does that mean that I'm gonna be an uncle too?"

She tilted her head to the side pretending to think about his question. "Maybe after we get married. Until then you're just an *almost* uncle." Aurora teased.

"Then we'll have to get married before the baby comes. I don't want to be known as the 'almost uncle.'" She grinned at his suggestion. She would have to tell Joe that it was Jordan's idea, not hers, that they get married before the baby came. "I'll have to call Alex and Joe later and congratulate them."

"I'm sure they'd be happy to hear from you. Now hurry and get ready because I want to have a meeting in the living room in five minutes." Aurora ordered, and then turned to go wake the others.

Jordan looked down at the paper he still held in his hand. It was written in Aurora's handwriting and plainly told who had set her brother up to be murdered. There was only one person besides Joe that she'd told she was going to meet Lance that night. It was still unreal that the evidence had been in Aurora's personal files the whole time. She'd kept a journal of everything police related ever since she'd joined the force. One of the worst things about it was that this man had comforted Aurora after Lance's death and vowed to help her find the murderer.

Jordan remembered the day Lance was murdered as if it was yesterday, and it still brought bittersweet memories. His best friend had found out something he couldn't wait to tell Aurora and had raced off before Jordan had a chance to go with him. Jordan had always wondered if he'd not been tied up in paper work and gone with Lance if he could have done anything to help him. That thought had really bothered him for the first few months until Joe had found him brooding over it one day and had forced him to talk about it. When Jordan had finally admitted the truth Joe had looked him in the eye and asked a simple question that had cleared everything up for him.

It was actually a very simple question. He'd asked, *'Do you believe that God is sovereign and knows what is best for his children?'* Jordan had been quick to answer yes and Joe had in his quiet way asked *'Then why do you wonder if you could have changed what was already God's will? If God hadn't wanted Lance to come home to be with Him then Lance would still be here with us, but you've just admitted to me that God knows what is best so don't blame yourself, understand that your best friend is in a much better place. Remember the good times you two had and never forget them.'*

Jordan had sat there for a long time after Joe left, thinking about what he had said and then had a long talk to God about it, and realized that there was nothing he could have done to change what had happened and no reason to worry about him because Lance was in a better place. He was with God and that is the best place to be. Everything is in God's hands no matter what happens; He is in control. When he'd gotten home that night there had been a message on his answering machine from Joe. All he said was John 10:27–30 (NKJV). Jordan had immediately gotten his Bible and read the verses:

> [27]My sheep hear my voice and I know them and they follow me. [28]And I give unto them eternal life; and they shall never perish, neither shall any man pluck them out of my hand. [29] My Father, which gave them me, is greater than all; and no man is able to pluck them out of my Father's hand. [30] I and my Father are one.'

When Jordan had read those words, he felt ashamed of himself. He knew it was human to wonder what he could have done, but it shouldn't have taken someone else pointing out the divinity of God to make him see how unreasonable he was being. He asked God's forgiveness for being so stubborn and had thanked Him for giving Jordan friends like Joe. Friends that weren't afraid to tell you when you were wrong. Later, he'd told Joe how much those verses had meant to him, and they had become even closer friends. He was the one that Jordan talked to when he had problems dealing with Lance's death. Jordan still felt the ache in his heart from missing his friend. It was like a part of him was missing too.

Jordan remembered everything he and Lance had done and every detail of that last day. He and Lance had played racquetball earlier that morning. It was their favorite sport because they were both good at it, and it was a running tradition that the loser had to buy lunch, and that lunch had to be whatever the winner chose. That morning Lance had won and Jordan had wound up buying steaks for lunch.

After that the day had passed quickly. Both men were swamped in the office but as usual they'd given each other a hard time when given the opportunity. Then while they were in a meeting, Lance had gotten an urgent phone call, and immediately after he finished with that call, he'd called Aurora to set up a meeting. Jordan had wondered at the time what was so important but had to go get some paperwork done. He had gotten sidetracked and didn't think again until later to ask, but Lance had been on his way out the door. Lance was supposed to have left immediately but had gotten tied up for a while and was late leaving. Jordan had hollered at him to be careful as Lance raced out the door. He hadn't seen his partner in such a hurry in a long time but Jordan had assumed he was in a rush because he was so late. Jordan had immediately turned his attention back to work. He didn't worry about Lance and Aurora, he knew that Lance would keep his fiancé safe and as for Lance, that man knew how to take care of himself, and besides he expected to see Lance again in a few hours.

There would always be things he wished he'd said to his best friend before he died, things he'd never really told him. But he had a feeling that Lance already knew everything he would have said anyway. That gave him comfort. He knew that if the situation had been reversed he would know how Lance felt about him even if they'd never told each other. He was glad their last day together had been full of happy memories and not bad ones that would have haunted him for the rest of his life.

Looking down at the paper, Jordan now had a different idea of what had happened that day. He figured Lance had gotten a tip on a dirty LAPD officer and was going to warn Aurora, but had been killed before he got the opportunity. He'd been a big brother protecting his sister from danger the only way that he knew how and it had gotten him killed. Now it was Jordan's job to keep Aurora safe and he had more information than his partner had five years ago. Now he knew the name and the face of the traitor, the man responsible for his partner's death. Anger coursed though his veins at the man, but at the same time he felt pity for the man. There was no hiding for him now, his whole life had been a sham, and everything he supposedly believed had been a lie, and now everyone would soon know the truth. Jordan would make sure of that!

***

"Well, the evidence is all here. It's just as plain as the nose on your face." Cassie muttered as she finished looking at the papers Aurora had spread out for them. It hadn't been obvious in the beginning what the inconsistencies in the documents meant, but when they were all put together there was no doubting who the traitor at LAPD was. The documents Aurora had been working with for the past five years had been copies she'd made from what she'd thought were the original notes, but someone had left the copies along with the originals in the boxes Kami had picked up from Aurora's office. Someone had gone to great lengths to cover this up and now Aurora knew who and why. It seemed almost all of the documents had been doctored in a way to make sure she never saw the connection. It hurt her to know someone she'd considered a friend had done this to her.

Kami nodded at Cassie's comment but didn't take her eyes off of the sheet she was reading. The look on her face told the whole story.

"This man is sick!" She said after a few minutes of reading, and everyone stopped what they were doing and looked at her. She shook the paper in anger. "He's been working for LAPD for years supposedly trying to find a way to link Charles to drug trafficking or anything to get him behind bars. He's the one who lead the investigations for heaven's sake! And the whole time he's been telling Charles every move and putting good men in danger. From the looks of it he's even had some of them killed." Kami gasped as she realized what she'd just said, and her gaze darted to Jordan and he grimaced and nodded, confirming her suspicion. "You mean he really...?"

Aurora laid her hand on Kami's arm and held back her tears with great effort. Jordan felt his heart squeeze at the obvious hurt in her eyes and wanted to reach out to her but was afraid if he did she wouldn't be able to hold back the tears. So he sat back and listened to her. "He was the only one that knew besides Joe and Jordan that I was meeting Lance that night. I know for a fact the other two didn't have anything to do with Lance's murder. There is no way that it was an accident because the man was there waiting for us and even though I was undercover and had been since coming out of the academy, he'd known I was a cop. This man," she said pointing to the paper unable to say his name for fear of breaking down in tears. "He was really the only suspect left. The whole time I was looking for some evil man in black that I didn't know and he was sitting right under my nose the whole time. Except I'd never thought of him that way and had missed the link."

A fierce fire burned in Kami's eyes, and Aurora knew she never wanted Kami to be mad at her. "I say we go and pay this man a little visit."

"I agree, but we will need a warrant and some backup. Kami get on the phone with Judge Malden and get us a warrant ASAP." Cassie then turned to look at Aurora. "You have anyone in mind you think should go with us?"

Aurora nodded immediately. She knew exactly who she wanted

to be there with her. It was great having Jordan, Kami, and Cassie with her she trusted them, but she was LAPD and they were FBI. Two different worlds even though they were both law enforcement. She needed her 'family' to be with her when she took this man down. If for no other reason than they needed to know the whole truth and because this man had been a special part of the strange family they made up and he'd betrayed them all. She had been close to this man and so had these two men. They were a family of their own making and they needed to be there with her. "I'll go call them and tell them we'll get a warrant and to meet us here. I'm also gonna call Joe and tell him that I have the proof I've been looking for." Aurora chewed on her bottom lip for a moment studying the picture of her former friend.

How could she have been so wrong about this man? Fear was running rampant through her veins. She was really going to arrest a fellow LAPD officer. It seemed unreal. She shivered knowing that soon all of this would be over and she didn't know what she was going to do. This man had tried to have her, her partner, and her fiancé all killed and probably set her brother up to be murdered. She hated him in a way, but then again she didn't. She still loved this man, and he would always be in her heart because he had been like family to her for years. She had cried on his shoulder more than once and he had always encouraged her to go after her dreams. She was hurt at his betrayal and knew that everyone else would be too. In reality, she hated his actions, not the man.

Jordan reached over and laid a hand on her shoulder. "I know this is hard, honey, but we really need to hurry."

"What's the rush?" Kami asked, her eyes still burning with unleashed fury. "I mean, besides the fact that he needs thrown in jail and locked up for a few hundred years as soon as humanly possible."

Jordan answered Kami, but his eyes never left Aurora's face. "Well, there is a chance that Charles will go after him because we are still alive. Garland didn't succeed and now Charles may think that he turned on him and can't be trusted. Or maybe Charles will think that he is a liability, one that he can't afford to leave alive.

Either way we need to get to him as soon as possible. He will be a witness if we can get him to turn against Charles, we'll have to protect him because Charles will come after him."

Aurora hadn't thought about that. She didn't want Charles to kill him! She wanted to see justice served, but not by that criminal. It would have to come from a trial and jury. Whatever sentence he received from it. She nodded to Jordan, letting him know that she was all right and went into the kitchen to make her phone calls.

The first two took no more than two minutes. She had known that if she called these men and told them that she needed them that they would come without question. Tears stung her eyes. She would not cry! She never cried! She'd just had an emotional week. Soon, she would be back to her old self.

Her friends had dropped everything and were on their way. She just couldn't believe that she'd never realized before how good and full her life really was. She had friends that she could count on for anything, and she didn't think she could still surprise those two men. But she had. They hadn't been surprised by her call, in fact, they'd been expecting her to check in sometime soon, what had surprised them was her request for help. She'd never actually asked them for help and they were more than happy to try to repay her for all the times she'd helped them. The next call was a little harder, but still short.

Joe answered on the first ring. "You got it?"

"Yes." She didn't ask how he'd known it was her, but Aurora was glad he'd known. She didn't think that she could explain everything even one more time.

"Then go get him, bring him in, and then come home, Roar." Joe told her compassionately. She knew that he was hurting as much as she was with the sting of this man's betrayal, but he was worrying about her.

"Don't worry, Joe, I've got good back up on this one." Aurora told him who was going with her and he agreed she'd made a good choice.

"Just do me one favor?" He requested quietly.

"Anything."

"Now you're the one that's being brave." He teased her and she couldn't help but smile. She would do anything within her power for Joe. "I want you to be careful. You don't know what's going to be there waiting on you when you get there and I want you to still be alive when all this is over. You have a niece or nephew on the way that needs you there to spoil them."

"You're just worried because you aren't gonna be there to cover my back." Aurora teased him back, but then said seriously. "I'll be careful Joe, promise. Besides, my overprotective fiancé will probably never leave my side for me to get into any trouble."

"Good. I always knew that man would be good for something. Besides, you need someone to take care of you for a change. You're always taking care of everyone else, and someone needs to take care of you, and Jordan's a good man... even if he did choose the most stubborn woman on the face of the earth."

"I'll call you when everything's over."

"Stay safe."

"Always." She hung up and turned around to find Jordan standing right behind her staring at her.

"Hasn't anyone ever told you that it isn't polite to listen in on other people's conversations?" She told him with a mock frown.

"Has anyone ever told you that you're the most beautiful woman in the world?" He countered staring into her eyes.

She stood there for a minute staring up at him, surprised by his comeback. She saw his eyes dancing in merriment at her shocked silence. "Well?" He prompted.

She finally found her voice. "Only this one guy, but I think he's a little crazy. Maybe got kicked in the head by a cow on his parent's farm or something."

The teasing light left Jordan's eyes and he reached out a hand and cupped her cheek and she leaned into its warm comfort. "Actually, I'd have to say that he is one of the smartest men in the world. Not to mention the luckiest because if I heard correctly, she's gonna marry that man."

"Well, you heard right." She smiled up at him. "I guess that even if he's not smart enough to see that I'm not the most beautiful woman in the world that I'll marry him just so I can get compliments like that all the time."

"I'll make sure to tell him that."

"You do that." She stood up on her tiptoes and kissed him lightly on the mouth. "By the way, thank you, that was a sweet compliment."

"The truth." He argued. She rolled her eyes at him but didn't argue farther. She knew it would be pointless anyway. He wouldn't give up on this one until he won the argument. "Whatever you say."

"Now that's what I like to hear from my woman." He growled in her ear.

CHAPTER 18

Less than thirty minutes later they were all there and ready to go. Her two friends had greeted her warmly and they'd even congratulated her on her engagement. They'd given her hugs and a hard time about running off just so she didn't have to do all the paper work. She hadn't realized how worried they'd be about her and it made her smile to know that she'd been missed. All three of them had acted happier than usual so they didn't have to admit that they were fixing to do something that would hurt them all terribly. Both men had looked at Jordan's black eye with interest but neither had asked any questions. She knew after the story was out, Jordan would never live it down.

She had chosen to ride in the LAPD patrol car with her friends. Even though Jordan hadn't objected, or said anything for that matter, she knew he wasn't happy about it. He wanted her within arms reach at all times. He was worried about her and she loved him for it, but she needed to be with these men right now. She wasn't pushing him away or even trying to, it was just that these men shared something with her that he never would... they'd all been betrayed by the one man they'd all looked up to and trusted like a father.

"I still can't believe he did this to us." J.D. said in a hushed whisper even though they were all in the car alone. "Why would he?"

"I don't know, little brother, but I think we need to find out."

Daniel was a little more vocal about his anger. "Yeah. I think we should beat it out of him." Aurora knew that Daniel didn't mean it, but she also knew that he was hurting more than both she and J.D. right now. Daniel had never had a father and said he never wanted one, but in a way he had always looked to Corey as a father figure, even more so than the rest of them.

Aurora laid a hand on his shoulder and felt his muscles tense beneath her hand as if he was ready to spring into action. "I know how you feel, but we can't let our emotions rule on this bust guys. We have to stay somewhat objective or we lose everything." She reminded them.

Neither man had wanted to believe her when she'd told them about what they were going to do. Both had said she had to be mistaken... until they looked at the evidence. J.D. had hung his head in defeat. Daniel had the exact opposite reaction. He'd looked up at Aurora with fire burning bright in his gray-blue eyes and said, "let's take him down. Hard."

She now focused on where they were going. Only two more blocks until they reached Sergeant Corey's house, she held her breath. They parked half a block away on what looked like a curve. Here they were out of the direct line of sight of his house, but could still see it. No one could get in or leave without them seeing.

There were only six of them, not nearly as many as should have been there for such an important bust, but they had all agreed they didn't want a whole squad there. If they'd done that, the news coverage would have been unbearable. That left them with few options.

"I think we should break down the door first and ask questions later." Daniel grumbled.

Aurora hugged her little brother and was surprised that he allowed her to and even hugged her back. "I think we will take the front door and you three should come in the back." Aurora informed them, taking charge before Jordan could. She knew he would want to do it differently but she knew this way would be the best for everyone involved.

Kami and Cassie nodded, obviously willing to let them handle it any way they needed to. Jordan was another matter. His glare practically scorched her. She was sure that he would argue or try to talk her out of it. He stared at her for what seemed an hour, but in reality was only a few seconds and then brusquely nodded. It was not at all what she'd expected.

"Fine, but I want to talk to you for a minute."

Aurora nodded mutely and followed him to the rear of the car, as far away from the others as they could get without being seen from Corey's house.

"You're sure about this?" Jordan's question surprised her and she looked up at him. His mood had changed dramatically. There wasn't a trace of the anger she'd seen only a moment ago only worry.

"Yes."

"Ok then that's how we'll do it. I just wanted to be sure this is what you really want."

Aurora had expected, well... something entirely different. Maybe anger. She didn't know exactly, but when she looked up into his eyes she saw concern—concern for her. She squeezed his hand in silent thank you. He smiled down at her.

"Be careful." He warned and pulled her into his arms for a quick hug.

"I will." She promised.

Jordan had been angry at Aurora for wanting to go with J.D. and Daniel instead of with him, but had realized, even if a little late, that they were the ones whom she worked best with. She was used to them and they had a routine. Most importantly, this was all extremely personal to all of them. He still wanted to be close enough to protect her, but in reality, she was a cop. This was her job and he wouldn't change who she was for anything.

He only wanted her safe.

***

"Knock, J.D., and announce us." Aurora said quietly as they stood outside Sergeant Corey's home with their guns drawn. They were ready for anything. At least they told themselves they were. J.D. took a deep breath and nodded.

"Corey Nickels this is the Los Angeles Police Department," J.D. yelled as he knocked loudly on the door. "We have a warrant for your arrest and to search your house."

They waited in a torturing silence and Aurora nodded to J.D. to try again. Still there was nothing. His car was in the driveway and he had a day off of work. Where was he if not here? Most importantly how did he get there?

Daniel looked over at her and she knew what he was thinking. Nickels had skipped town to keep from being caught, and right now she had to agree with his assumption, but they wouldn't know for sure until they checked the house. "I guess we could try the knob before we break the door down." She suggested and Daniel gave her a disgusted look that in any other circumstances would have made her laugh. But right now her stomach was churning too much to laugh. He wanted to take some of his anger out on the door and she didn't blame him. Hitting something sounded pretty good about now.

J.D. reached out and slowly tried the knob and it turned easily under his hand. Everyone stared into the house.

"What the..."

"Don't you dare swear, Daniel!" Aurora warned. He was usually too much of a gentleman to swear in front of her, but right now Aurora knew he wasn't thinking that way. They all stared at the door as if it would give them all the answers if they only looked long enough.

"What's taking so long?" Jordan's voice crackled over the radio and startled Aurora so much that she jumped and the two men with her jerked to attention.

Jordan, Cassie, and Kami had decided to let them handle Corey before they came in, and for that Aurora was thankful. Her team was to make sure Nickels was inside, radio them and tell them what needed done. They were surprisingly quick to agree to the arrangement.

Aurora looked at the open door, confused. It didn't make sense for Sergeant Nickels to have left his door open. He was always nagging everyone at the station about good safety habits and this was definitely not a good one.

"No answer." Aurora responded. "But the door was unlocked so we're going in."

"Be careful guys."

"We will."

She looked at the two men with her for a moment before she pushed the door open further. Daniel silently slipped in to the right and Aurora to the left and finally J.D. came in the middle. Silently they searched through the house looking for anything unusual. The last room on Aurora's side was Corey's study. She slowly slipped in searching for anything unusual. All the books were on his shelf as usual. He'd left his computer running. That was a strange thing for a man who'd skipped town to do, unless he'd been in too much of a hurry to turn it off. Aurora circled the desk and stopped short.

"Jordan!" Aurora didn't even recognize her own voice. She didn't know how she could sound so calm when she was absolutely terrified. At least she hadn't broken into hysterics. She concentrated on her breathing as she heard J.D. and Daniel join her. Over the radio she heard Jordan's hard breathing as he hurried to get to her.

Aurora's hoarse whisper of his name spoke volumes. It got more of a reaction than if she'd yelled and Jordan's heart was beating double time. There was something wrong. He bolted into immediate action. He was up the back step and through the back door before either Kami or Cassie moved.

"Which room?" He demanded as he rushed into the house.

"Last door at the end of the hall." Their voices sounded so strange Jordan thought as he hurried to get to Aurora. He was only vaguely aware of Cassie and Kami following him. When he reached the room the sight made him stop in his tracks.

Aurora, J.D, and Daniel were all three standing behind the desk, staring at the dead body of Sergeant Corey Nickels.

Aurora knew she should look away but it was impossible. She couldn't avert her gaze from the horrible sight in front of her. Jordan went over to them, wanting to shield them to where they couldn't see the body. He knew it was useless. They had already seen him, but he wished he could save them from the pain he knew they were feeling. Jordan took her chin and lifted her gaze to his. His eyes held sympathy, love, and strength. His gaze gave her the reassurance and strength to focus on something besides the horrific sight.

"It's ok, Jordan." Aurora told him quietly. Her voice still sounded strained and Jordan's other hand reached out enveloped both her hands. They were freezing! He prayed she wouldn't go into shock.

"I'm fine, really. Just shocked. I really expected him to be somewhere he couldn't hear us, maybe in the shower or something, and we would surprise him. I never expected this." She told him. She knew she was rambling so she closed her mouth. She gave Jordan's hand a reassuring squeeze and then turned to her two 'little brothers,' and as if it were the most natural thing in the world they all three hugged. They were shocked, needing each other's support. Jordan wanted to be the one she leaned on, but knew right now she needed her friends to share their mutual loss.

"Who found him?" Cassie asked in her quiet voice.

"I did." Aurora turned from the two men and spoke to Cassie. "I was checking out the room and noticed his computer on. I was wondering why he'd leave his computer on and came around to see if there was anything else strange in the room when I saw him." She swallowed hard as she finished her sentence.

Jordan saw the compassion in the looks on Kami and Cassie's faces but neither of them dared express their sympathy verbally at the moment for fear of upsetting the LAPD officers further.

"I'll go call this in." Daniel said, turning away from the body, his voice was a mixture of shock and grief, but his face was a stony mask.

"I think I'll go with you." J.D. followed his partner out with a hand on his shoulder. They needed each other's support. Aurora knew they would both take Corey's death hard. She just hoped that Daniel let J.D. be there for him and would talk to his partner, not shove him out of his life like Aurora had done to Joe. She silently prayed for both men.

"While we're in here I think we might as well see what's on his computer. I mean when the cops get here they'll want to confiscate it... even though, because of the circumstances, we'll have jurisdiction over the case. It would be good to get a jump-start on things. You know, make sure there aren't any nasty surprises on here." Kami said, as she turned to the computer, careful not to step in any of the blood or touch anything except the computer. Jordan, Cassie, and Aurora watched as her fingers flew over the keyboard and she searched the computer files.

"I think this one might be interesting." Kami mumbled as she clicked on a file.

"What is it?" Jordan asked uncertainly. He could tell by Kami's face that it was something important, but wasn't sure that he wanted Aurora in here when they found any evidence in case it had to do with Lance's murder.

"A file that is titled, Aurora Kavvan... dang! You have to have a password to get into it." She turned to Aurora, "Any ideas?"

Aurora thought for a moment. "Try Lance's name."

Kami quickly typed his name in several different ways but the screen flashed, Access denied.

"How about the date I joined the force?"

"Worth a try." Aurora recited the date and Kami tried it forwards and backwards.

Access denied.

"What about the date of Lance's murder?" Jordan suggested and Aurora paled.

"Why would he use that day?" She asked in a quiet, fearful voice. And Jordan wished for a moment he hadn't suggested it, but knew that they needed to know whatever was in that file. He knew Aurora was strong enough to handle any surprises that lay in the file. He only wanted to save her from the pain of finding any more evidence against her friend. He gently squeezed her hand.

"Because he knew it would be something you would never forget." Cassie told her in a quiet voice, but Aurora could tell that all three FBI agents thought there was more to it than that. She listened as Kami typed in the date that Jordan told her and saw the words, "Hello, Aurora Kavvan" flash across the screen. Aurora felt sick to her stomach, but maybe this didn't mean what she was afraid it meant. She had prayed that she was wrong about Corey setting Lance and her up at the park that night, but now she would know the truth. She wasn't sure she wanted to know.

They watched as Kami read a few paragraphs before turning the screen towards Aurora. "I think you should read this. It's personal." Kami's voice was softer than Aurora had ever heard and that scared her. What was waiting for her on that screen? She wasn't sure she wanted to know the answer to that question.

Aurora nodded but stood there afraid to move, much less read what her former Sergeant had written to her. She still couldn't believe he was gone. She heard J.D. and Daniel come back in and didn't want them to be in the room when she read this. She silently motioned Kami to take them out. Kami and Cassie took the two men outside to wait for the other officers that were on their way, but Jordan stayed behind with Aurora.

"Would you rather me read it to you?" He asked her gently.

She shook her head and stared determinedly at the screen. She still didn't move any closer to the screen. I have to read this! she told herself and forced her legs to move. Jordan stayed right behind her, afraid of her reaction to Sergeant Nickels's message. They silently read together the letter that was dated the day before:

Dearest Aurora,

When you read this you will already know the truth about me. Of my betrayal and deceit. For all of this I am truly sorry, I know that it has caused much hurt and grief to many people that I care about. I'm writing to you because I've betrayed you even more than I have the others. I vowed to you on the day that Lance was murdered I would find the man who killed him and put him away for life. I meant that promise, I'm just sorry that it has taken me this long, and knowing I'll soon die, to tell you the truth. I left the original documents in your files, hoping you would find out the truth before Charles got to you, but this letter is to ensure you know what happened and to explain my deceit. In this letter I will tell you everything that happened to set up Lance's death.

I had already been working for Charles a few months when you and Joe went undercover. It seems like an eternity ago. I never dreamed he would find out about the two of you. In all honesty I still don't know how he found out about you because I never told him. I secretly wanted you two to find something to put him in jail for life. It would get me out of my association with him, but at the same time I was scared that you would find something and I would be out of a job. But I honestly never told him about your undercover operation.

When he first came to me, I tried to refuse to work for him, I knew that I'd eventually be found out and I didn't want to be known as the cop who was owned by a known drug dealer. Even if by some strange twist of fate no one found out, I would know that I had broken all laws in working for him... laws that I was supposed to be upholding. I honestly didn't want to work for him but he had some evidence against me. I had taken some drug money and somehow he had pictures of it. I know that isn't a reason, just an excuse, but I was afraid to lose my job at the time. What a laugh! I wasn't doing my job anyway. I'd sold out my fellow officers because I was afraid. I'm such a coward. After the first job it just got easier and easier to give him whatever he needed, especially because he paid me much more than I would ever earn as a cop. It was also somewhat thrilling. Now I know why some people break the law and say they did it just because they could. I cannot tell you how many times I wanted to tell someone, but couldn't. Everyone looked up to me. It was my unit! But I was the traitor. I failed so many people that I truly thought of as family, and now I know they can never forgive me.

Charles called me the day before Lance was murdered and told me that you and Joe were getting too close and he wanted to warn you to stay away. I was surprised that he knew about the job and he didn't even ask why I hadn't told him. That right there scared me to death because I knew he knew that I wanted him caught. I knew that I would have to give him something to make up for what he saw as betrayal. He told me that if I knew of any way he could send a message, to tell him and it would earn me a huge bonus. At the time I needed money badly. I had some huge gambling debts and no way to pay them off. So I told him that as long as no one got hurt I would tell him as soon as I knew something. He promised that he would only warn you, that no physical harm would come to you. Then the next day you called me and told me that you were going to meet Lance at the park because he had something big to tell you. I thought, this is my lucky break and as soon as I got off the phone with you I called Charles and told him about it. Believe me when I tell you that I didn't know he was going to kill Lance. He had promised no physical harm would come to you. It was a selfish act that I wish I could take back. I should never have called him, but I was terrified for myself. I'm a self-serving man, and I'm sorry. I never thought that he would hurt Lance because it was you he wanted to teach a lesson, but I should have known.

After Lance's funeral, I told him I wasn't going to let him get away with it. That it didn't matter what happened to my career or me, he was going to pay for what he'd done. He laughed and told me that if I did something that stupid, he would make it look like I had killed Lance. I couldn't believe it possible, but he described in great detail what he would do and I didn't want you thinking that I'd killed your brother nor did I want everyone else to think I'd killed a fellow lawman. I was afraid and did nothing. I'm a coward, Aurora and I'm sorry for that.

    I admit that I also told him about the stakeout you and Joe were on last week. I thought as long as he knew you were there he wouldn't do anything to you. I thought he would just forego his business while we were watching. Tell Joe I'm sorry, I never meant him harm. I know this will be impossible to keep quiet, but tell the people at the station that I'm truly sorry. I know Daniel will never forgive me and tell him that I'll never be able to forgive myself for betraying him. He was like the son I never had. Tell J.D. to stay with him and not let him do anything stupid. Please. He has a tendency to act before he thinks and he needs someone to keep him grounded.

    I know I can never do anything to bring back your brother or even make up for any of my betrayal, but I do have one good thing to give you. In my locker at the station, there is a false bottom. In there you will find several tapes of Charles talking about his drug rings and there is even one where he admits to killing your brother and hiring an assassin to kill you. I know this isn't much but it is all I can do. I know I don't deserve it, but please, Aurora, find it in your heart to forgive me.

    I'm sorry,

    Corey.

Jordan stared at the screen in astonishment. In one breath this man had told Aurora that he'd had her brother set up for murder and asked her for forgiveness. He'd been the one to leave the files for Aurora to find the truth. Jordan couldn't believe the man's audacity! He could understand the man needing Aurora's forgiveness, but he couldn't believe Corey had actually followed up that story about setting Lance up with a plea for her forgiveness. He felt his anger rising at Sergeant Nickels. Jordan took a deep breath and tried to calm himself. He would be no good to Aurora if he let his anger rule his head.

The man had known he was going to die, Jordan reasoned to himself, and had written this to Aurora as one of his final acts, that should count for something. If it was real then they finally had enough evidence to put Charles away for life. He grudgingly admitted that Corey's asking for forgiveness wasn't that bad, but the evidence he'd given could never bring back Lance. Nickels should have spent his life in prison, in reality he'd gotten off easy because cops aren't the best-loved people in prisons.

"Let's go tell the others what we've found." Aurora sounded small and tired. He felt his heart squeeze at the pain in her voice. He really wanted to shield her from all of the pain but knew he couldn't. When she turned around and he saw silent tears running down her cheeks that she wasn't even trying to hide, all his anger fled. This was a man that Aurora had cared about and she needed Jordan to be there for her, not going off the deep end.

He silently reached out and pulled her against his chest. He said nothing, only stroked her hair and held her. He could feel her tears soaking through his shirt and felt helpless because he could do nothing to fix what was hurting her.

"Are you okay?" He asked, knowing the answer was no, but needing her to say something. If it was possible her face had gone paler while she read the letter and he was afraid she would pass out on him.

"I'm fine." She answered. Jordan looked into her eyes and it was obvious she was in a daze and she didn't have a clue what she was doing or saying. She was anything but fine.

"I think you need to sit down for a few minutes." He guided her to a chair on the opposite side of the room. As far away from Corey's body as he could possibly get her and she willingly went along with him but when he tried to ease her down in the chair she looked up at him startled.

"Huh? Oh, no... I—I'm fine, really." She tried to push herself up but he stood firm, easily blocking her path and not allowing her to move. To his amazement she didn't try to push him out of the way, instead she settled back in the chair and chewed her bottom lip, lost in thought.

After a few moments of silence, Aurora sighed and closed her eyes. She leaned her head back against the back of the chair and sat there saying absolutely nothing but there was emotion after emotion crossing her face.

"What's going on inside that pretty head of yours?" Jordan asked quietly trying to distract her from her thoughts that were obviously less than happy, and she gave him a weak smile for his effort.

"I was just thinking about Corey." She sniffled and for the second time in a matter of minutes he wished he hadn't asked the question that was on his mind.

That wish only lasted until she looked up at him with clear eyes and said, "I thought he was a good friend. Someone I could count on and he betrayed me. It hurts but I know he was hurting when he wrote that note to me. I really want to forgive him, and I think that I'm ready to."

Forgiving the man had been the last thing on Jordan's mind. He felt terrible. About two inches tall to be exact. Not only had he been wishing bad things on a dead man, but also the person who was supposed to be the maddest at the man and never wanting to forgive him had just told Jordan that she really wanted to forgive him. It was a very humbling experience. He sighed and silently prayed for forgiveness and guidance.

"I really don't know what to say." He told her after a moment of silence. "I'm not sure that I could even want to forgive him if I was in your position. You're way ahead of me in that respect. I'm not only unsure of that but I'm also unsure that I can forgive him now and he didn't even ask that of me." He silently rubbed his chin and ducked his head in an obvious sign that he was embarrassed.

Aurora shook her head and looked him in the eye. "After you think about it for a while and really pray about it you will want to forgive him and in all honesty you need to forgive him as much as I do. You lost your best friend that day Jordan, I lost my brother. It's not something you immediately forgive. It takes time and healing. You need to forgive him so you can still have a close walk with God and so that there is nothing standing between you and Him." The wisdom in her words rocked him back on his heels. Jordan thought on her words for a moment and completely agreed.

"I think I've just been shown how human I am." He said somewhat disgusted with himself. "I know I need to forgive him for what he did. Not only five years ago, but what he's put you through and I really need to want to but it's all still such a shock. I always expected Lance's murderer to be a crook that had a rap sheet a mile long and that somehow I would be able to tell on sight that he was guilty. I never expected it to be someone that worked with you."

"I know. It was a shock to me to. A week ago I would have hated, or at least wanted to hate Corey for the rest of my life for what he did, but it's taken me five years to get my life back on track and Corey asked me for my forgiveness. God forgave me for turning my back on him for five years, how could I not do the same for Corey?"

"You humble me, honey. I'm supposed to be the stronger Christian here. You've just come back to God and you are acting more like Him than I am. I should have forgiven Corey the moment I read his letter. He has my forgiveness." Jordan felt as if a weight was being lifted off his chest as he said those words. He really did forgive Corey Nickels.

Now it would be God who judged him for what he had done here on earth.

Aurora wrapped her arms around his waist and gave a surprisingly strong squeeze. "I knew he would." She whispered.

CHAPTER 19

Aurora paced the tiny space outside Jordan's office. She hated waiting. This was a lot like getting sent to the principal's office in school. The LAPD had officially been taken off of Charles's case, which included Corey's murder. She was glad in a way that the department wouldn't have to uncover all of the horrible betrayal that had really come from their Sergeant. A few already knew most of the story, but most didn't have a clue. The FBI were trying to keep things quiet until they found all the evidence and someone was arrested, then they would have something substantial to tell the LAPD officers.

Jordan had called in an FBI team to Corey's house and Cassie hadn't allowed any of the LAPD officers to step inside the house until the FBI unit had gotten there. Aurora knew part of that was to protect the crime scene but she also knew that part of that was to help the LAPD officers. At least they hadn't had to see Corey lying in a pool of blood behind his desk. Aurora knew that would be another of the terrible scenes in one of her nightmares. She quietly shivered. She had to concentrate on something else. Anything else. She stared down at the floor. Apparently she hadn't been as careful at the crime scene as she thought. On the tip of her left shoe was blood. She felt the tears she'd thought long dry prick the backs of her eyelids.

She felt betrayed by Corey's actions, but she'd been able to forgive him through God's grace. The person that she hurt the worst for was Daniel. He'd been so close to Corey. Looked up to him and almost idolized him. For years Corey had asked Daniel to come to church with him and Daniel had refused saying that all churchgoers were hypocrites, but he'd finally gone a few months ago. Aurora knew now that part of Daniel's problem was she'd turned her back on God after Lance's murder. At the time, Daniel said he didn't want that kind of relationship with God. According to Daniel, apparently God wasn't that good of a friend or he wouldn't let bad things happen to the people he called his children. At the time Aurora agreed with him but now it pained her to realize just how far away from God she'd really gotten and she silently thanked Him for bringing her back to His side.

She prayed that Corey's profession of faith was real, for his sake. Even through all of the terrible things he'd done, Corey had still been worried about Daniels life after death more than anything. When Daniel had finally agreed a few months ago to go to church with Corey he said that if it was the only way to get the old man off his back then he'd do it once. The once had turned into twice... and he was still going. Aurora prayed that Corey's betrayal wouldn't affect the decision she'd thought Daniel was so close to making but she was almost positive it would. Aurora would always feel guilty for being a stumbling block to one of her closest friends and prayed that God would help him overcome it. Corey's betrayal will have brought back all the painful memories that Daniel kept of his real father leaving him. He had always felt abandoned and unwanted. His father had left his mother when he'd found out she was pregnant and Daniel had never seen or heard from the man. Aurora knew he always wished he could have at least known what a father was like while he was growing up, but there was nothing she could do to change the past for him. Now she would pray for him as she had never prayed before. She couldn't even imagine the pain her friend was feeling and prayed that God would give him the strength to get through this trial.

The FBI had offered all three of them, J.D., Daniel, and her, a position on the investigative team. They'd said that it was because of their first hand knowledge of the case information, but Aurora knew that Jordan had pulled strings to initiate the offer. She'd even heard Cassie and Kami going out on a limb for her and her friends. Daniel had immediately turned down the offer and walked out. J.D. had been torn between wanting to solve the case and needing to be there for his friend. Aurora had known the whole time, which he would choose. He was a friend first and a cop second. If it was a choice between the job and Daniel's happiness, Daniel would win hands down every time. J.D. would never let his friend suffer alone. He would be there with him every step of the way helping in any way he could. Aurora would be there too, as would many friends, but partners knew each other on a completely different level than anyone else knew them.

Now Aurora was the only LAPD officer left on a case full of FBI. It should be interesting to say the least.

The door behind her opened and she spun towards Jordan as he emerged from his office. "Sorry it took so long. You ready to go?"

Aurora's hesitation was only for a second, but Jordan immediately picked up on it. "You don't have to go, you know."

"I know, but I need to be there when the evidence is found." Jordan had sent a team over to keep watch over the lockers at LAPD headquarters saying they couldn't be too careful. You never know if Charles had another officer on his payroll. Aurora hoped it was just a precaution and wouldn't turn out to be anything more. She hoped this ordeal would soon be over. Jordan eyed her speculatively for a moment and then nodded and led the way out to his truck.

***

"I can't believe it's all here." Aurora said in wonder as they sorted through a box of tapes later that night in Cassie's house. The false bottom of the locker had proven to be a treasure trove of information. The tapes dated back at least three years, some maybe longer. Aurora was still in shock over hearing Corey talking to the top drug supplier in Los Angeles about all of the terrible things he'd been paid to do. She really had never known this man. The man she'd thought she had known and loved could never have done something like this.

"I do have one good thing to say about Corey Nickels, he did a good job of documenting everything. It's a shame that he didn't use this information and come forward publicly a long time ago." Kami said as she chewed on a carrot and pulled the last tape out of the cassette player. "There's definitely enough here for an arrest warrant, Cassie you think you can get Judge Brown to issue a warrant at this time of night?"

"No problem; with all of this evidence he won't mind waking up. Besides he's wanted to get Charles off the streets for years, but no one could ever get the evidence to stick. I'll go call him."

"We need to get everything ready, in order. I want to get him tonight before he has a chance to skip town. I also don't want him to get off on a technicality. After all of these years, that would be the worst thing that could happen." Jordan said. "We need to be ready to go in and take him down as soon as the warrants come through. But we also have to have every i dotted and every t crossed."

"We will." Kami promised.

***

"LAPD! Charles Deveraux you're under arrest." Aurora said as she handcuffed Charles in his own office. "It's over."

Their appearance seemed to catch Charles completely off guard and he was left speechless. A deep feeling of satisfaction wound its way through her and she couldn't have been happier. *I got him, Lance.*

There was a smile on Charles's face that Aurora hated. "Oh, no Miss Kavvan. It's just starting." He promised her. The voice she heard sent her back five years to the lakeside. He was most definitely the man who had killed Lance and no matter what he said, it was over for him. He would never be able to hurt anyone ever again. He would go to jail and they would ask for the death penalty.

Aurora handed Charles over to an FBI agent standing at a

waiting car outside. The agent took him with seeming pleasure and read him his rights as he put him in the back seat of the car. She'd been ready for this operation to take weeks or at least days to complete, but the time had flown and the whole drug operation had been taken down in a matter of hours. Corey's tapes had provided locations for all of the local operations as well as information on future shipments and the waiting dealers. This bust may have just saved lives.

Everything had seemed to just fall into place tonight. The warrants had come through in record time and they'd been able to walk up to Charles' door and issue them personally. It looked like the whole FBI had shown up for the occasion too. Everywhere she turned there were FBI agents and most had someone in handcuffs.

"I told you that God answers prayers." Kami said as she walked up and put her arm around Aurora's shoulder.

"He most certainly does." Aurora agreed whole-heartedly as she watched the car pull away with Charles in the back seat. "Charles will be put away for a long time. I just wish we could have found his son and something to charge him with, but Charles was very careful to keep Chris' name out of everything. Wasn't he?"

"Yes, but the system works. We'll be able to find Chris and watch him. From what I hear this apple didn't fall far from the tree. He is supposed to be as bad as his father so we shouldn't have too much trouble finding evidence against him since his father is now in custody. I figure he will assume responsibility of the whole organization and we'll nail him the first chance we get."

***

"Your father's been arrested." Jim informed Chris as they were flying somewhere over eastern Texas. There were also very few men left in their operation that weren't now in police custody.

No matter what his father had told him to do, Chris was a grown man capable of making his own decisions. His father wanted him to go to Florida but Chris had a different destination in mind.

A destination where he was sure a brilliant idea would hit him and send him on another mission.

"He knew he would be." Chris said with no sympathy for his father. On the outside Chris seemed to be a complete idiot. Not capable of running a VCR much less a major drug operation, but Jim knew better. The kid had brains and could use them. Not only that, but the kid seemed even more ruthless than his father.

"Looks like you're the new boss. What's the plan?"

"We go to the ranch and discuss different scenarios. See what strikes our fancy. I believe revenge is in order."

CHAPTER 20

"I recall you saying something about a knight in shining armor before everything broke loose and you promised to tell me what you meant. Would you care to enlighten me now?" Jordan asked in a teasing voice as they sat on a blanket on the floor of her apartment. They both loved picnics and this was their version of a winter picnic since they would have frozen at the park.

It had been almost a week since they'd taken down Charles' drug operation and life couldn't get any better. He and Aurora had spent all their free time together talking. Sunday they had gone to church together and everyone had been surprised. Apparently their friends hadn't had the opportunity to tell everyone about the engagement... yet. Going to church together was like their announcement to the world that they were back together. Forever.

It had been a wonderful feeling to walk through the church doors with Aurora on his arm and know that she belonged there. She would be there for years to come. The service had been great. Pastor C.E. Madison had read the scripture Romans 8:28 (NKJV).

"And we know that all things work together for good to them that love God, to them who are the called according to his purpose."

From there he told the story of Job and how God had allowed Satan to torment Job and still Job never once cursed God. Because of that, God had blessed Job with even more than he'd had before. Pastor Madison had said that no matter what we are going through in life, we should trust in God. He always knows what is best for us and He tells us that everything will work out for the good.

The sermon seemed to fit perfectly into Jordan and Aurora's lives. Before the terrible events of the past week, it had seemed that any relationship between them was doomed, but God had brought them together through those events. It showed that God does answer prayers and that things have to be done in His time, not man's time.

Jordan and Aurora had already had several discussions about the sermon and agreed that it was the perfect way to end the week they'd had. It was a positive end to a terrible ordeal. In fact, their discussions had covered pretty much everything they could think of. Well, almost everything. The only discussion they hadn't had yet was about the wedding date, and he was ready to set it. First he had to hear this story though. It sounded amusing... he'd never thought of himself as a knight in shining armor.

Aurora's face turned slightly pink as she stared up at the ceiling fan. "Well, it's about the night Garland came to my apartment." She glanced over at Jordan and noticed his eyes darkened at the memory.

"I wanted to kill him. I thought he had done something awful to you. And it made me crazy." Jordan's confession touched her and made her smile.

"Anyway," she continued but kept her eyes on Jordan. "I remember thinking there was no way out of this, it wasn't like the fairy tales. No knight in shining armor would come charging in and rescue me. Then he knocked me out and when I woke up there you were to rescue me. So you're my knight in shining armor charging to the rescue."

"I'm so glad I got there in time." His voice shook as if he were thinking of what life would be like without her. Aurora reached over and squeezed his hand. He looked at her and all the darkness left his eyes and they were filled with love. She was one lucky woman to have a man like him.

"So Miss Kavvan, what do you see happening in your life in the near future?" It was good to see that mischievous glint back in his eyes.

"A nap." Aurora replied as she laid back and closed her eyes. "All that food made me sleepy."

Jordan couldn't believe it! She was completely serious. There was no way she could get out of this discussion. Not today anyway. He'd been patient enough. He'd given her a week to get her life back in order before he tried to turn it completely upside-down again. And he definitely planned to. "You shouldn't have eaten so much, I want to talk." He nudged her arm but she didn't open her eyes when she answered.

"Talk away, but don't expect me to join in. If you'd wanted to have a conversation with me, you shouldn't have bought El Mexicano for our picnic."

"You're the one who was complaining about never eating there any more." He pointed out.

"Technically I've still not eaten there."

"A minor technicality. Are you really planning on taking a nap?" He asked as he picked up a piece of a napkin and began tickling her nose with it.

"If you'll leave me alone, I have every intention of taking at least an hour nap. After that we can talk about whatever is on your mind."

"Okay have it your way. I just thought we'd discuss the wedding." Jordan said baiting her. He knew she wouldn't be able to resist. She cracked one eye and looked at him speculatively.

"What did you have in mind?" She finally asked giving up on her nap.

"Never mind. Go ahead and take your nap." He said as he pulled a book out of the bag he'd brought and started reading it.

"Not fair, Reiley."

"What?" He asked innocently.

She rolled over on her side to face him. "You can't start a conversation like that and then just leave it."

"You said you wanted to take a nap."

"You deliberately made it to where I couldn't sleep."

"No, I simply mentioned the wedding." He replied stubbornly, but a smile twitched the corners of his mouth. He was having trouble keeping a straight face. Especially since outrage was written all over hers. He was really enjoying this way too much.

"Same difference. So what did you have in mind to discuss today?"

"A wedding date." He said simply and watched her eyes go wide with shock. "What? You didn't think I'd forgotten did you?"

"No, it's just that we've not talked about it and I wasn't sure if you were still wanting it to be soon or wait or what."

"Soon." He answered simply.

"How soon is soon?" She asked cautiously.

"Well, I originally thought Christmas." He watched her eyes and saw the shock. Christmas was only a little over a month away. Smiling at her expression he continued. "But I don't think we can put together that big of a wedding by then."

"Big?" She asked with a note of fear in her voice. Jordan was amused. Give her a gun and a bad man and she was fine, a wedding on the other hand... Still he knew she would be a beautiful bride, with a white lace wedding gown and her hair up on the top of her head. He could see it all and couldn't wait for his daydream to come true. He had a pretty good idea that anything he imagined wouldn't even come close to matching how beautiful she would really be on their wedding day.

"Yes, it will have to be big since my family will be involved. They don't know how to do anything small. Even birthday parties are huge events with my family. You know that." He told her earnestly and she smiled at his exaggeration.

"I was thinking just a quiet little ceremony or eloping." She told him with a twinkle in her eyes that she tried in vain to hide.

"My family would never forgive me if we eloped and there is no such thing as a quiet little ceremony. My family members have connections and there is no way we could keep them from knowing, so we'll just have to throw the biggest wedding this town has ever seen. Besides it will be the first Reiley family wedding. We'll be setting the standard for all the others. We want them to have to get creative to out do us."

"Well, it will either have to be before Alex gets huge with the baby or after she has it because she will never forgive me if she looks like the Goodyear Blimp in my wedding pictures."

"Before." Jordan answered quickly. "In fact, I was thinking about New Years. Midnight. As the ball drops we say our vows. What do you think?"

"I think it would be a great way to start the New Year. Very romantic too. I'm glad you thought of it."

"Good, because I already told Kerry my idea and she thought it was great and she's flying in as soon as school is out to help with the planning."

"Jordan, New Years is only two months away! There's no way that everything will be planned in time."

"Yes it will, don't worry. My family has already agreed it will be the social event of the year. They are thinking of it as the standard for all the Reiley weddings to come. So who do you think we should call first and tell the date to?"

"Let's see you've already told your family before you told me, so I guess now I should call my family. Joe is out of the hospital, but according to Alex he's not being a very good patient. He's too eager to get back to work and she's afraid he'll hurt himself further. Maybe this will give him something to look forward to and think about because he's gonna have to get well if he's gonna walk me down the isle."

Jordan squirmed and looked a little sheepish as he admitted, "I would agree, but I kinda forgot to ask permission to marry you, so I had to ask permission to set a wedding date. He and Alex are waiting outside the door as we speak." Jordan nodded at her shocked expression and Aurora jumped up and opened the door. Sure enough, there right in front of her stood Alex with Joe right behind. She couldn't believe they'd stood out there in the cold waiting. Oh well, time to start planning for the wedding of the century.

"Congratulations." Alex said as she stepped through the door and gave Aurora a huge hug.

"Thank you. So, are you ready to walk me down the aisle on New Years?" She asked turning towards her partner who was walking much slower than usual and still using a sling for his left arm. She looked him over from head to toe and raised a questioning eyebrow and he nodded. Joe would be fine. A little more cautious probably but other than that he would be the same old Joe.

"Are you sure this man is good enough for you?" Joe teased.

"Probably too good."

"Not possible, Roar." He responded quickly and he meant every word. "But yes I would be honored to walk you down the aisle, just tell me when and where and I'll be there. I'll even wear any tux you pick out."

"Brave man. Agreeing to get dressed up in a tux and walk in front of all those people. Are you sure you can handle it?"

"I wouldn't be doing it if it wasn't for that sparkle in your eyes being back. It looks to me like you've found happiness, Roar."

She glanced up at Jordan to find him staring down at her with such love in his eyes that she thought she was dreaming. Only in this dream she'd found her knight in shining armor and he wouldn't leave her. "Yes, I've definitely found my happiness."

Jordan leaned down and kissed her softly. "So have I, honey. So have I."